SEE ALSO DECEPTION

ALSO BY LARRY D. SWEAZY

See Also Murder

A Thousand Falling Crows

SEE ALSO DECEPTION

A MARJORIE TRUMAINE MYSTERY

LARRY D. SWEAZY

SEVENTH STREET BOOKS®
AN IMPRINT OF PROMETHEUS BOOKS
59 JOHN GLENN DRIVE • AMHERST, NY 14228
www.seventhstreetbooks.com

Published 2016 by Seventh Street Books®, an imprint of Prometheus Books

See Also Deception. Copyright © 2016 by Larry D. Sweazy. All rights reserved. No part
of this publication may be reproduced, stored in a retrieval system, or transmitted in
any form or by any means, digital, electronic, mechanical, photocopying, recording, or
otherwise, or conveyed via the Internet or a website without prior written permission
of the publisher, except in the case of brief quotations embodied in critical articles and
reviews.

This is a work of fiction. Characters, organizations, products, locales, and events
portrayed in this novel either are products of the author's imagination or are used
fictitiously.

Cover design by Jacqueline Nasso Cooke
Cover images © Corbis

Inquiries should be addressed to
Seventh Street Books
59 John Glenn Drive
Amherst, New York 14228
VOICE: 716–691–0133 • FAX: 716–691–0137
WWW.SEVENTHSTREETBOOKS.COM

20 19 18 17 16 • 5 4 3 2 1

Library of Congress Cataloging-in-Publication Data Pending

ISBN 978-1-63388-126-6 (pbk)
ISBN 978-1-63388-127-3 (ebk)

Printed in the United States of America

To Rose

"Absence and death are the same—only that in death there is no suffering."

—Theodore Roosevelt

"Indexing work is not recommended to those who lack an orderly mind and a capacity for taking pains. A good index is a minor work of art but it is also the product of clear thought and meticulous care."

—Peter Farrell

CHAPTER 1

October 1964

By the fourth ring, concern started to creep into my heart and mind. Calla Eltmore had always been one of the most consistently reliable people that I'd ever known. Her enduring presence at the other end of the telephone line was a matter of expectation on my part, and Calla's, too, as far as that went. She'd been the librarian at the public library in Dickinson for as long as I could remember, and she'd always held a strict policy of answering the phone promptly. More than once, Calla had said that she could get to the phone in three rings or less from anywhere in the library, then proven that statement to be true time and time again. My growing concern was not unfounded.

With each ring I gripped the receiver and tapped my red ink pen against the wall more emphatically. If I'd had another hand I would have chewed at the tip of my reading glasses, a bad habit I'd picked up recently. My nerves had yet to calm down from the unfortunate events that had occurred over the past summer.

I wasn't really pressed for time, though I was under a strict deadline—two in fact—with another indexing project waiting in the wings, a commitment made to my editor, Richard Rothstein, in New York, without much choice. But I had a question concerning the index that I was working on. A simple question that Calla could answer for me quickly, so I could move on to something else. So, like a thousand times before, I'd made my way from my desk to the phone in search of a resource that I did not possess, a book that needed to be added to my collection but never would be. At last count, the library in Dickinson held over twenty-one thousand volumes of text. The library had always been my salvation. The building, and Calla, had always been there for me in one way or another.

Was musk thistle a perennial plant or a biennial plant?

It was a basic question and one that I really should have known, since the noxious plant grew on our land. I could walk out my door and touch it, smell it, and feel it if I wanted to. But I'd never paid attention to its lifecycle, nor was the year of its growth mentioned anywhere in the text of the book that I was writing the index for, *Common Plants of the Western Plains: North Dakota*. It was a short book, more of a field guide than an in-depth study, and I was perplexed by the omission of such foundational information. *Perennial or a biennial plant?* How could the author, Leonard Adler, a native of Fargo, have missed such an important point about such a hated, invasive weed?

According to Mr. Adler, musk thistle had been introduced in the nineteenth century, most likely on a ship with livestock, and had spread from the eastern United States to North Dakota aggressively, replacing other native and more beneficial thistles in pastures and grasslands as it went. Farmers fought it when they had time to notice, but they mostly won the battle and lost the war.

I pulled the receiver from my ear and looked at the phone to make sure that it wasn't broken. The buzz of the unanswered rings sounded like a bee was trapped inside the black plastic earpiece. I knew better than that. Then I began to question whether I'd dialed the right number. *Of course I had.* I could have dialed the library in my sleep. But I still had to wonder. I'd been burning the candle at both ends for weeks, bouncing between the demands of the farm, my daily life tending to Hank, and writing indexes for an array of books, one right after the other. The variety of subject matter required my undue attention—common plants, travel by train in Europe, and a biography about George Armstrong Custer's wife, Elizabeth. Each new index I wrote became a journey into the unknown, an opportunity to learn, to better myself, to get paid for reading and writing, but I still had a life outside of books—whether I wanted to admit it or not.

It was obvious by the eleventh ring that Calla wasn't going to answer the phone, so I reluctantly hung up.

The tips of my fingers were cold to the bone. I had a deep urge to try and stop time, to walk out of my small house and grab at the wide blue sky that hung overhead and try to wrap it around my shoulders in a protective shawl against any bad thing that might be coming my way. I knew it was magical thinking, a childish wish, but I'd had enough tragedy to digest recently, and I could barely stand the prospect of dealing with anything else that came in the form of a dark cloud. Enough was enough.

Something is wrong. I know it.

I decided that I would just have to call back later, that the question about musk thistle would have to go unanswered for the moment. It wasn't the end of the world. I was on track to finish up the *Common Plants* index a few days early, leaving me a little extra time to dive full force into the second book that I had committed to indexing, *Zhanzheng: Five Hundred Years of Chinese War Strategy*.

Unlike the *Common Plants* book, the *Zhanzheng* title was a thick tome, four hundred pages, and I'd been given a month to complete the index. I was intimidated by the subject matter, since I didn't know a thing about China, much less its ways of war, but I was heartened by the structure of the book. At first glance at the first few page proofs I received in the mail, the book looked to have been edited well, which made all the difference in the world when it came to divining the most important terms and concepts out of such dense text and creating an index out of them.

But China would have to wait, too, just like my unanswered musk thistle question. I was almost sure that the thistle was a biennial plant once I thought about it, but *almost sure* wouldn't cut it. I had to know the *correct* answer. There was no guessing when it came to including an entry in an index. It had to be a solid fact. I needed verification of my assumption, otherwise I would risk the integrity of the index, of my livelihood, and that wasn't going to happen. I had to be just as reliable as Calla Eltmore had always been.

I pulled myself away from the phone and stopped at the bedroom door, just like I did every time I passed it. I had to make sure that Hank was all right, still breathing.

I would have preferred to be able to walk straight back to my desk and put a question mark by the biennial entry and move on to the next decision, the next question that needed to be answered for the reader, but that was not to be. The comfortably worn path of my life had been permanently altered a year ago and would never be the same again.

As I looked at Hank, I was silently relieved. *Today's not the day.* And silently sad for the same reason. Once again, death had not taken Hank gently in the night. The coming day would only bring more struggling—if only to breathe—than a good man like Hank Trumaine should ever have to endure.

I'd rested my hand on the same place on the door trim so many times that it was starting to show the wear of my presence. Smooth with hours of worry and dread, the white paint had started to fade, discolored by the labor of waiting and the acidic oils of my skin. The terrified grip of my fingers holding tight to the molding had left an unsavory mark.

I was not on a ship, but most days I needed steadying, fearful that the sway of everyday life, as it was now, would knock me off my feet and toss me overboard. I'd be lost in an endless sea of madness and fear from which there was no return. And no one to save me . . . but me.

I knew that I would never repair the door, dab fresh paint over the mar, for as long as I lived, for as long as I remained in the house. It was like the notches that marked the growth of a child as it sprang as eagerly as a weed toward adulthood. Only this was no march toward independence or a keepsake log of happy milestones. There was no hint of a child in our house; Hank and I had failed long ago at that effort. Instead, it was a march toward death, the result of a simple accident, one that had left my husband nearly unrecognizable; a withering, fragile man, blind, paralyzed from the neck down, instead of the hale and hearty one that I had married and fallen in love with so many years before.

The wear on the trim would forever remind me of Hank's struggle to live and the sad fact that there was nothing I could do to save him or relieve him of his suffering. The truth was, he wanted to die more than he wanted to live. But leaving me and leaving this earth was out of his hands, or harder than he would have ever acknowledged out loud. I was convinced that it was only his permanent stasis, his inability to move, that had saved him from the choice of suicide.

More than once Hank had begged me to put a pillow over his face and walk away. "No one would know," he'd whisper. He was mostly right. We were isolated, miles from town, our tiny house in the middle of seven hundred flat acres of durum wheat and silage. Our nearest neighbor's farm, Erik and Lida Knudsen's place, was three miles down the road; ten minutes as the crow flew but longer for my human legs. We were connected by a path carved out over the years by their sons, Peter and Jaeger, coming to help out when they could or were needed, and by the horrible tragedy that had befallen Erik and Lida three months ago.

But I'd know. I'd know and couldn't live with myself, couldn't live with the memory of the darkest sin a human being could commit. I wasn't capable of murder. I just wasn't. I could find no mercy in honoring Hank's request.

Hank would yell and curse at me—something he'd never done before the accident—when I'd disappear from the bedroom without saying a word. He would accuse me of being selfish, only to apologize later when it was time to eat or take a bath. Both of us were afraid. It was as simple as that. Lost and afraid, incapable of living the life we'd found ourselves in, but left with no other choice but to face every day the best we could.

CHAPTER 2

Shep, our ever-present border collie, appeared at my feet and watched my every move. He waited for me to flinch, to signal what was to come next. Sometimes, the dog's persistent attention drove me mad, but most of the time I found comfort in his intelligence and diligence. I'd said it more than once, but Shep would have made a great indexer if he'd been human.

We were both ready to get on with the work that needed to be done, but my feet were planted heavily on the wood plank floor, glued in place by hesitation and reticence, neither of which were familiar traits to me in the days before Hank's accident.

There *was* something in the way that Hank breathed that had changed since I'd last checked on him. It was a subtle sound, nothing visible, more like an echo in a far off canyon. A place that I didn't want to explore on my own, even though I knew I would have to.

"What's the matter?" Hank opened his pale, cloudy eyes at the same time as he spoke. He stared blankly up at the ceiling, his facial muscles still and unreadable.

I had to wonder how long he'd been awake, aware of my station at the door, his eyes closed, his ears open.

"Nothing. Nothing's the matter," I answered.

It was futile to expound on the lie any further. Even blind and in his motionless, incapable state, Hank knew the peaks and valleys of my voice, knew the truth when he heard it. Even Shep wasn't convinced. My tap-tap-tap of the pen against the wall had set the dog on edge, alarmed him. I was certain the dog could smell my frustration. Shep took his eyes off me and searched the floor for anything that moved. Nothing did.

"You want to try again?" Hank said.

I closed my eyes, strained to hear the strength and certainty in Hank's voice, imagine him healthy, upright, getting ready to leave the house and tend to his daily chores. But that was more of a fantasy than I could easily conjure at the moment. That man, that Hank, had been taken from me long before I was ready for it. Some days I could barely remember when he could actually fend for himself. Caring for him was the exercise of child rearing that I'd never experienced before.

"Calla's not answering the phone," I finally said.

"Maybe she's busy."

"She's never too busy to answer the phone."

"Personal business?"

"You don't understand."

"You're worried. Something's out of place. How could I not understand that?"

I didn't answer him right away. He was right. Hank had always been good about reading my moods. He knew the difference between my personal clouds as much as he did those that floated in the sky. "It was a year ago this week," I said. *All of the doctors said you wouldn't last a month, but here you are*, I wanted to say, but couldn't bring myself to.

"I know what time of the year it is," Hank said. "That wasn't it. The worry I heard."

I had to strain to hear Hank's words. His voice was weak and scratchy.

"I thought I heard a rattle in your chest is all," I said. "Doc Huddleston said we should always be wary of a cold, of something settling in your chest. The weather's changing." I cocked my head to the door, put an ear to the wind that rustled around the house looking for a way in. I could feel its cold fingers grabbing at my toes. "The box-elder bugs are gathering at the seams of the siding, trying to find their way in." I could already smell their frass mixed with the odor of human sickness and pity.

"Hibernation would be a nice option to have, wouldn't it?" Hank whispered. "Wake up in the spring when everything is normal, with no memory of the winter." The longing in his voice was painful to hear.

I turned my head and watched as one of the little black and red beetles scuttled across the window sill. I hated the bugs, globs of them pushing their way inside looking for a source of heat to keep them alive through the winter, but Hank was more forgiving. He admired their struggle and desire to survive, and I'd never seen him kill one. If only he'd felt the same way about killing ruffed grouse.

Hank had told me more than once that hunting grouse wasn't like hunting partridge or quail. The birds didn't congregate in coveys and flush in an explosive flock of feathers and fear. Grouse were mostly loners, except for the young males. They tended to hang loosely together, pecking at the gravel along the side of the roads to fill their gizzards. Those were the easy shots, like shooting fish in a barrel or a lame coyote unable to flee a human's presence. Hank liked to hunt the more elusive males, the mature ones that flittered in and out of the thin woods, filling up on the abundance of fall berries. It took skill to shoot grouse on the fly. "Evens up the game," Hank would say with a nod, as he polished the barrel of his grandfather's reliable shotgun in the same place, at the same time, in the same way year in and year out.

And it was that desire for fairness that had landed Hank flat on his back, unable to do anything but eat, sleep, shit, and hope to die.

To the best of everyone's figuring, Hank had stepped in a gopher hole as he went for a shot last season. He stumbled forward and somehow shot himself in the face. The worst of it came when he fell backward and broke his neck, paralyzing him instantly.

He couldn't remember a thing about the accident, and if there were any blessings in all of this it was that. He couldn't replay his actions in his head over and over again, belittling himself, trying to turn back time to employ the good sense he was born with. I was glad he didn't have the torture of that to face every day.

It had been a matter of luck that Hilo Jenkins, the former sheriff of Stark County, found Hank before he died. But Hank, of course, didn't see it that way at all. Luck had left us both that day and had yet to return.

"I'm not one for anniversaries or irony," Hank went on. "I feel fine. There's no worry for you on this day; I'm sure of it." The lilt in his voice was still detectible even in the whisper; a hint of ancient Norwegian and a lifetime spent on the North Dakota plains. His grandparents on his mother's side had come over on the boat as children from the old country, Norway, nearly a hundred years ago. My mother, Momma, had come over with her sister and parents when she was four. Our fathers' families, the Hoaglers and the Trumaines, had come from other parts of the world, Germany and England, at one time or another. Those family stories were lost in the dust of time. Most of what they had known about the old ways had been forgotten in their desire to be like everyone else—new and American. But I could still hear the snow and wind in Hank's voice, an old language trying to speak on a foreign, unforgiving land. He sang without singing, and I could listen to him talk all day, when he was in the mood, as we sat on the porch and watched the magpies, meadowlarks, and prairie dogs go about their business of living on their native land.

"All right," I said. "If you say so."

"I say so."

"I have work to do."

A slight nod shifted across Hank's face, and he blinked tiredly. "I'm glad of that. I'm sure Calla's fine. She's a hardy one. Been tested more than we know. She was helping someone, that's all. It's what she does." He hesitated, then arched his throat forward for emphasis. "Today's no different than any other day; you know that, Marjie. You know that."

CHAPTER 3

Outside the four walls of my little house, the country still grieved for the loss of a young president almost a year ago. Sadness and profound silence were palpable every time I went in to town, to the Red Owl grocery store, the Rexall drugstore, or Doc's office. Even the library was quieter, but I'd barely noticed, given my own circumstances of the last year. The strained gray mood of our nation seemed natural, expected, and certain beyond my own nose.

The Cold War was more visible in North Dakota than most anywhere else. Missile silos were being drilled into the flat-as-a-pancake ground less than an hour away from our farm, offering nuclear destruction to the world at the simple press of a button. Signs of human obliteration came in the form of rumbling B-52s flying overhead, giant airplanes capable of dropping bombs in case the missiles failed—a one-two-punch delivering extinction. We all feared the fireball in the sky, the mushroom cloud of our nightmares, becoming a reality. The closest thing we had to a bomb shelter was the root cellar. It would have to do, even though I had no desire to die in a nest of spiders and bugs who loved the darkness.

No one knew what the Russians would do in our moment of weakness, and I didn't care any more than normal. I just couldn't bring myself to be too concerned about the outside world going to hell in a handbasket. My world already had.

I'd been secretly grateful that Hank had resisted the temptation to bring a television into the house. His resistance to living in the future had saved me from seeing the images of an optimistic man and his wife in that pink pillbox hat arriving in Dallas before the tragedy, and a sad little boy saluting his father's coffin in the black and white aftermath. Maybe it would have been better if the morbid images *had* entered our house, if I had insisted that we keep up with our friends and neighbors and get one of those talking picture boxes, too. But I knew better. We had enough of everything to occupy our time, including grief, depression, and fear. There was no room for the chatter of the world's woes to be delivered by anything more than the radio that we already owned.

My connection to the outside world came into the house in the form of books. It always had, and there was no plan in my mind to change that anytime soon. It seemed like ages ago that Lloyd Gustaffson, our former extension agent, introduced me to the world of back-of-the-book indexing via a correspondence course offered by the United States Department of Agriculture. A series of droughts, hailstorms, and bad weather had dropped our yields to an all-time low, and with them went the surplus of our savings. Indexing, Lloyd had thought, knowing my love of books and reading, offered a way for me to make some extra income through the coming winter and beyond. And he'd been right. I took to indexing books like a grouse to sudden flight. It was books, and a good turn in the weather, that had saved us, put us back on an even plain.

I stared at the page of text from the *Common Plants* book lying on my desk one more time, trying to figure out what I was missing.

A prolific seed bearer, a single musk thistle (*Carduus nutans*) plant can produce up to twenty thousand seeds, though only about one-third prove to be viable. The tallest shoot, the terminal, flowers first, then shorter, lateral shoots develop in the leaf axils. An aggressive, healthy plant has the ability to produce over one hundred flowering heads over a seven-to-nine-week season. Seeds disseminate two weeks after the first bloom. The plant dies after it sets seed. Ninety percent of the lifecycle of musk thistle is spent as vegetative growth, thus making it difficult for the untrained eye to detect. Musk thistle is commonly confused with native or less productive invasive thistles such as bull thistle. Prevention of seed formation is the utmost action required in range management. Complete eradication is unlikely.

And that was that. There was nothing more than the description of the plant at various stages and the flowers. I flipped the page and there was nothing else there concerning musk thistle, either. The text moved on to another invasive thistle, plumeless thistle (*Carduus acanthoides*), and Leonard Adler went on writing and immediately identified this plant as a winter annual or biennial. Frustration continued to careen though my fingers as I tapped them against the marred walnut top of my desk, then flipped the page back and scanned the page on musk thistle once again to make sure my eyes hadn't glazed over, missing the information I was looking for—but nothing was there. The omission was maddening.

I turned my attention to the index card that I had inserted in my trusted, reliable, and prized Underwood typewriter. It said:

milk thistle. *See also* ??????

I was tempted to type in weeds after the blank *See also* reference, but the tone of the text dictated that I make the distinction between perennial and biennial plants, and also provide the reader another access point into the text. It was as simple as that. The section of the index I was working on was taking shape and nearly complete, and I was stumped.

B

biennial thistles
  bull thistle (*Cirsium vulgare*),
    256
  Flodman thistle (*Cirsium flodmanii*), 239
  musk thistle (*Carduus nutans*) ??????, 258
  tall thistle (*Cirsium altissimum*), 247

bull thistle (*Cirsium vulgare*), 256

I

invasive species
  thistles, 250
    bull thistle (*Cirsium vulgare*), 256
    Canada thistle (*Cirsium arvense*), 251

If Calla couldn't answer my question for me, I was going to have to call my editor and have him call Leonard Adler to find out.

You would think that as an indexer I would have a way to communicate with the author of all of the books that I worked on, but that was rarely the case. Sometimes, the author reached out to me once the index was assigned to me, but generally there was a locked door between us that only my editor had the key to.

Calling Richard Rothstein had never been on my list of favorite things to do, and today was no exception. Asking him to gather information for the index was an admittance of failure and put me in a line of fire that I didn't want to be in. His attitude had always been caustic and rude under the best of circumstances. Asking him to do a task that was distinctly my job would only make him less tolerable. He would be furious.

Failure was not an option, so I pushed away from my desk and trudged to the phone with Shep close behind. I'd call Calla one more time.

I tapped my red pen on the wall again and listened for Burlene Standish on the other end of the party line before I dialed. Thankfully, the line sounded quiet. Burlene's intrusiveness had lessened recently, but she still eavesdropped on the party line on occasion. Old habits were hard to break.

I dialed the library's number slowly, just to make certain that I didn't connect to the wrong number.

It was picked up on the second ring. "Hello?"

Only it wasn't Calla's voice on the other end. It was a man's voice. A man's voice that I recognized immediately. It was Guy Reinhardt, a Stark County sheriff's deputy. A policeman in the library.

My initial concern that something was wrong catapulted itself into a frightened reality. The sound of Guy's voice felt like an atom bomb had gone off inside my head.

CHAPTER 4

"**W**hat are you doing answering the phone at the library, Guy?"

Silence from Guy and static in the line answered me back. I could hear muffled voices in the background. It didn't sound like the library at all. I felt cold and tingly all over, and it wasn't from the weather.

"The library's closed, ma'am," Guy finally said.

"Guy it's me, Marjorie. Marjorie Trumaine. What's going on there? Why are you answering the phone at the library? It's a weekday; Calla should be there."

"Oh, hey there, Marjorie. I didn't recognize your voice. How are things out your way?"

There was no denying that he was doing his best to sound normal, but there was a nervous edge to his voice that instantly betrayed him.

I liked Guy, even though he was a bit troubled—going through his second divorce and rumored to like the taste of whiskey a little more than he should have. I suppose he had reason for that, even though I'd never seen any sign of it. In his youth, Guy had been a big time basketball hero in Stark County but had made some bad choices at the wrong time and ended up in a car wreck that had permanently injured his leg, ending any hope or dream of becoming a pro player. He still walked with a slight limp.

"What's going on there, Guy? Can I speak to Calla, please?"

More silence. I could hear Guy breathing, so he didn't have his hand cupped over the receiver like he was trying to hide something. Instead, it was like he was trying to decide what to say without telling me what was going on or lying to me.

I tapped the pen on the wall again. If I kept it up there'd be another mar to note my presence in the house. This old house was nicked and battered by the weather outside and my fingers on the inside. It was a wonder that it hadn't collapsed from such abuse.

"Library's closed, Marjorie," Guy said.

"I need to speak to Calla."

"That's not possible. Not possible at all."

I lowered my voice. "You tell me what's going on right now, Guy Reinhardt. You hear me. You tell me that Calla Eltmore is all right, that there's nothing the matter with her." The words jumped out of my mouth unfettered. I knew I was speaking with an officer of the law, but I couldn't help myself. That happened sometimes, a product of my bloodline and spending inordinate amounts of time alone. I had few filters to consider, especially when I was nervous.

"I can't tell you that, Marjorie. I can't tell you anything. I'm sorry, I really have to go. Goodbye, Marjorie." Then the phone clicked harshly in my ear and the line went dead.

I was stunned by Guy's action. He could've told me what was going on. It wasn't like I was Burlene Standish, apt to blab whatever he told me around half of Dickinson. I really needed to know that Calla was all right, but my gut feeling told me that wasn't the case. *Something was wrong.* Horribly wrong. I just didn't want to imagine what that something was.

For the second time in a day, I stood rigid, unbelieving, staring at the phone. I wanted to scream, *Tell me what's going on!* But I knew it wouldn't do me any good. Screams never changed anything.

I hung up the receiver, turned around, and slid down the wall on my back; gravity was stronger than my will. I suddenly found myself face-to-face with Shep, who, out of concern and brazen compassion, leaned in and licked off a nervous tear that had started to trail down my cheek.

Night fell and darkness wrapped itself around the house like it had a right to, even though I wished it wouldn't, covering everything in a thick blanket of petulant silence. The wind, almost ever-present in October, had whimpered away at last light and had not been heard from since. Such a thing could be disquieting and deeply unsettling. Sanity in the middle of nowhere had always been fragile, but it had felt even more so of late.

The world kept on changing, and there was nothing I could do to stop it. The days were growing shorter, and the time to prepare for the coming winter was long past the critical point. I barely had enough wood stacked outside to feed our two Franklin stoves through December. The reliable January deep-freeze was not something I was prepared for in any way.

Earlier in the day, I'd been tempted to grab up my purse, rush out the door, jump in the truck, and speed into town as quickly as I could after speaking with Guy, but I didn't have the freedom to come and go like I once did. I couldn't just leave Hank to himself. Not anymore. I was just as trapped by his condition as he was. There were times when that fact was beyond frustrating, but it just was what it was: Our lot to carry.

In the past, I could have called Lida Knudsen to come and sit with Hank while I tended to my town chores, but she was dead and buried, a fact that I still found to be unbelievable, especially in the moments when I needed her the most. All I'd had to do in the past was call, and she'd have been at my door in the blink of an eye, eager to help out. But with Lida and her husband gone, there was only their son, Jaeger Knudsen, to call on. His younger brother, Peter, was off in the Air Force.

I hadn't wanted to bother Jaeger earlier, and now it was too late to go into town. I had already put up the chickens, fed the winter hog, closed the barns up, and brought Shep inside. I had overridden Hank's rule of no animals in the house. Nowadays, it was just as important to have the dog at my side as it was to have a loaded .22 rifle next to the kitchen door.

Hank had taken his evening broth, and I stared at the strips of bacon on my plate and the bowl of canned fruit that sat next to it. We ate a big dinner at noon and a smaller supper in the evening. It had always been that way, and I was in no mood for any more changes in my life, even given Hank's condition.

I brought my dishes to the sink, turned off all of the lights in the house, padded easily to the bedroom, and climbed into bed next to Hank. He smelled of baby oil—to keep the bedsores away—instead of the wind and toil. I missed his healthy scent more than I could say.

"You don't know anything is wrong, Marjie." Hank's eyes were open, staring straight up at the ceiling.

"I do. I do know something is wrong. So do you," I said.

Hank didn't answer; he just exhaled as fully as he could and closed his eyes. It was my turn to stare into the darkness. I was afraid of the dreams I would have if I let myself fall asleep.

CHAPTER 5

There were days when I wished Shep was a retriever instead of a border collie. It would've been a fine luxury to have the capability to send the dog out for the morning newspaper, then have him bring it back inside the house and deposit it at my feet. But Shep was not that kind of dog, and I certainly didn't have the time or the inclination to try and convince him why such a duty would have been in his best interest to take on. He was too busy worrying over the wandering chickens that had already been let out of the coop.

The necessities of the morning had been tended to before the sun had broken over the flat horizon. Hank had been fed, bathed, and exercised. Coffee simmered on the stove, and what little livestock was left on the farm had already been seen to.

I had slept fitfully. Sometime during the night exhaustion took over and I let my worry go, or at least set it aside. My question about musk thistle wasn't far away when I woke. And the fact that Calla hadn't answered the phone nagged at me deeply. Even more worrisome was the fact that Guy had answered the phone. Come one minute after nine, I knew I'd be on the phone to the library to see what I could find out. Until then, it was business as usual. It had to be.

I eased my way to the edge of the road where the newspaper lay waiting for me. Morning dew had dampened the outside of the rolled and rubber-banded paper log. It felt like my fingers would push through it when I picked it up. Retrieving the soggy paper was a mindless act that occurred every morning. If I'd had my way, I would have stopped taking the news a long time ago, but Hank liked me to read it to him after lunch. He would drift off soon after I read *Dear Abby* to him.

Typically, I would have made my way back to the house, refilled my coffee cup, put the paper on the kitchen table to dry out, and headed to my desk. But this morning I stopped halfway to the house and considered the paper in my hand. That bad feeling I'd had after the library phone went unanswered persisted like a bad cough that couldn't be cured.

You're being silly, Marjorie, I said to myself, then looked at Shep, who had herded the chickens up next to the garage. There was no way he was ever going to retrieve anything as long as there were chickens to put in their place.

I looked at the newspaper, the *Dickinson Press*, or the *Press*, as everyone around these parts had forever called it. I opened it gingerly, carefully, because of the dampness and because of my fear of what I would find. If something had happened at the library, to Calla, the day before, it would be in the morning paper. There was no question about that.

The headline announced a deep drop in future grain prices, mostly due to the Cuban embargo, the ongoing distrust of the Russians, and the fall of demand in Europe. I was silently relieved, even though dropping grain prices was the first thing I didn't need when it came to our finances. I was accustomed to that kind of news, to the ups and downs of farm life. My father used to say, "Some years are bedder than others, Marjorie. It all evens out," in his sweet North Dakota accent. But there was plenty of shocking news to comprehend, to digest, of late, and that was what I'd been afraid of.

I was about to chastise myself, until my scanning eyes caught a bit of small print at the bottom corner of the paper. Even without my reading glasses, I knew it had to be what I was searching for.

A strong push of wind reared up behind me, nearly tearing the fragile paper from my hand that had, by then, started to shake. I tightened my grasp, but the paper ripped, and the front page soared up into the sky like an errant kite that had broken free from a child's careless hand.

"No!" I yelled. "No." My words chased after the paper, overtook it on the wind, but did nothing to slow its pace. Before I knew it, the front page of the *Press* had disappeared behind the garage, out of sight.

The words that I'd read exploded in my brain and flew about just as unhindered as the newspaper page. The news might have been in small print, but it might as well have been as big as a highway billboard:

Longtime Librarian Found Dead.

My dread and concern had been right, but I didn't know the details. I could only imagine what had happened at the library. Maybe Calla had a heart attack or choked on a piece of chicken. More than anything, I hoped that death had come quick to her, that she hadn't suffered, hadn't had time to be afraid, but honestly, more than anything, I hoped the paper was wrong. I hoped for a retraction, a heartfelt apology from the editor to Calla. But I knew that was magical thinking, too. Calla Eltmore was dead. I could hardly believe it.

My yell had drawn Shep's attention to me, to the flying paper, and for a brief second I made eye contact with the dog, then gave him a little nod.

Shep tore out after the front page of the *Press*, but I was certain that he was on a fool's errand. That paper was most likely in the next county, leaving me with more questions than I needed and a sense of doom and grief that seemed to live close to my heart.

I couldn't imagine my life without Calla Eltmore in it. It was just impossible to consider such a thing. But I knew the words I'd read to be true, and I felt the emptiness of my life grow under my feet like an endless chasm had opened up, determined to draw me into its deep darkness forever.

CHAPTER 6

Betty Walsh had been a counter girl at the Rexall since she'd graduated high school. She also volunteered at the hospital as a candy striper in her spare time, which in theory made her a perfect candidate to look after Hank when an immediate need arose.

Betty was also Jaeger Knudsen's on-again, off-again girlfriend. Thankfully, at the moment, they were on again. Actually, more *on* than they should be as far as I was concerned. It was obvious to me that they were sleeping together. Not that I was a prude; sex had always been a fact of life on the farm—you could see proof of it every day if you cared enough to notice. I certainly didn't blame Jaeger for the need of comfort, but he was young and vulnerable. One mistake could alter the direction of his life in a bad way, force him into something he wasn't prepared for. Betty's life, too, as far as that went. Neither of them was ready to be a parent.

As it was, the two of them couldn't keep their hands off each other. She nearly sat in his lap in the truck as they drove about town, but it wasn't my place to say anything to Jaeger, even though I was certain his mother would have wanted me to.

But I had faith in Betty to have some sense about herself, since she worked the cash register at the drugstore. The sight of a prophylactic had surely lost its ability to embarrass her by now. Unlike some giggly girls, I was confident that she knew how to use one. There was also *the pill* to consider. It had changed everything in the last few years—Betty'd had exposure to that form of contraception, too; I was sure.

The choices created by the pill intrigued me, but they were of no immediate concern. I had no reason to try it. Sex drew none of my attention, except for the longings deep in the night, when Hank slept and I couldn't. As simple as the pill was, I thought it complicated things in ways that some of us weren't ready for, no matter how old we were. I'd never asked Betty about either form of contraception, and I never would.

I was relieved, and not at all surprised, to find Betty Walsh at Jaeger's house when I'd called over to see if Jaeger could call her for me. I needed to make an unplanned trip into town. Plain and simple, I had to go to the library. It was the only way I knew how to calm myself down.

Shep's ears perked up at the sound of Jaeger's pickup truck as it pulled onto our drive. It only took two seconds for the welcome bark to come out of his mouth—he knew the sound of the red International Harvester's engine as well as that of our own truck.

A black and white blur of wavy fur rushed past me and headed to the door, barking and circling as he went. Shep loved Jaeger. He seemed unsure of Betty, but tolerated her presence with cautious distance. He had let her pet him once, but only after she had magically produced a piece of beef jerky out of her pocket. I thought it was a smart thing to do to gain the dog's trust, but I felt the same way about her as Shep to be honest. I didn't know her or her family well at all. She came from out South Heart way, and I didn't mix into that crowd very often. I'd never had need to until now, so I was as leery as I was grateful.

"That'll be Jaeger," I said to Hank.

His eyes were open, fixed on the ceiling. He'd been quieter than normal since I'd told him the news about Calla.

The sequence of the day was changed by an unforeseeable tragedy again, and it was discomforting for both of us, in our own ways. Calla and Hank had never been friends, not like she and I were, but he knew how important Calla was to me. My small circle of friends had grown smaller.

"You didn't bake a pie," he finally said.

I shrugged. "Calla doesn't have any family in town that I know of. Just Herbert, and they're just friends as far as we know. Where would I take a pie?" I had considered baking something to take with me just in case, but I'd plenty to do and didn't want to end up wasting what ingredients I had on hand, which were plenty at the moment. I had a nice mess of green apples, just like Momma liked them, sitting in a basket on the table, that would have made a wonderful pie.

"This'll send Herbert off to the Wild Pony again," Hank said.

"I suppose it will. Whiskey calls to him something dreadful at fragile times." Shep was relentless with his barking. On top of everything else, the demanding sound of the dog's voice grated on my nerves. "Shep, that's enough," I snapped over my shoulder.

My admonishment did nothing to deter the collie. "Some days," I said. My exasperation was hard to miss, and I regretted showing it as soon as I let out the long sigh after I spoke.

"Dog's a nuisance if he doesn't have a job to do. He's not like that outside," Hank said, without moving a muscle.

It was an old argument—no animals in the house—that was not going to be addressed by me. I ignored the comment. The only reason I'd ever won that fight was because Hank Trumaine couldn't pull himself out of our bed and toss the dog out the door with the sole of his boot. Some old ways were hard to break.

I spun around to let Shep out, but I hesitated when I reached the front door. I was almost certain that the truck I'd heard belonged to Jaeger. *Almost certain*, but not sure, just like the lifecycle of the musk thistle. I *thought* Shep's bark was a welcome bark, but I could have been mistaken.

The Remington .22 was behind the kitchen door, and Hank's grouse shotgun was stuffed in the back of the wardrobe, out of sight but not out of mind. The guns were always loaded for varmints, or to ward off an overly persistent lightning rod salesman.

I opened the door slowly, only to see Jaeger and Betty heading my way. Shep bolted outside, and I relaxed my shoulders as the dog circled around Jaeger gleefully.

Betty stood back out of the way of Shep's exuberance. I could see why she appealed to Jaeger. In the soft midmorning light she looked like a young goddess who had just stepped onto the earth for the first time. She was about three inches shorter than Jaeger, making them a perfect pair for slow dancing. Her shoulder-length brunette hair was comfortably combed and could have gone from bouffant to beehive in the matter of an hour, or less, with a gaggle of girlfriends that I was sure she had to help tend to such things.

The modern look was taking over the world and had come to North Dakota via magazines and the television. From what I understood, there was a British invasion descending upon us. I wasn't sure what that meant, since I was more worried about the Russians than a quartet of mop-headed musicians. But even with a hint of the modern, there was no mistaking Betty Walsh for a farm girl. She had on a pair of well-worn denim pants and a red plaid flannel shirt that looked like it might have come straight out of Jaeger's closet. For some reason, I felt a dormant tinge of jealousy awaken and rise deep inside me when I stepped toward the two of them.

I knew I resented Betty's beauty and Jaeger's ability to walk and talk at the same time. It was as simple as that, and I felt bad for the feeling, even though I knew no way of making it go away.

"Thanks for coming over," I said. I met them halfway to the house. "I'm sorry it's on such short notice."

Shep stopped barking and circling and suddenly planted himself at Jaeger's ankle. It was as if he was interested in being obedient instead of the uncontrollable ball of fur that he was most of the time. I knew it was a ploy, a game to gain more attention, and Jaeger would fall for it hook, line, and sinker.

I was glad for the silence, though the wind had a voice all of its own. The wind was so common—omnipresent—and I was so accustomed to it that I barely noticed—at least until it sang in the depths of winter. Just to remind me that it was there, a hard gust pushed up my back, and I instinctively pushed my hand down to trap my simple navy blue dress against my thigh. I'd made the dress myself from a McCall's pattern. It was one of three that I owned that were suitable to go into town in, even though it had seen its better days. I hadn't had time to sit down at the sewing machine lately. Betty looked at me like I was an old lady, and she was probably right, even though I was just shy of thirty-six. I felt old. All of my friends were dying away.

"It's all right," Jaeger said. I loved to hear him talk. He had his father's voice and his mother's eyes. I could always tell if he meant what he said. He did—his eyes never lied, just like Lida's, though he could be misinterpreted sometimes. Jaeger had been born with the pull of forceps, and that had misshaped his face slightly. He had a droopy eye and looked perpetually angry, even though he wasn't. "I was just thinkin' I needed to come over to see what kind of help you needed to store up for winter. Looks like there's some wood missin' there."

I followed his gaze over to the slim pile and nodded. "I was going to hire that out," I said.

"Nonsense," Jaeger said. "I got a new man on my place. Takes more than me these days, especially with Peter away and my dad . . ." He stopped, looked down, and patted the top of Shep's head, shook off the sudden show of emotion, looked me in the eye, and kept on talking: ". . . gone from this world. We'll get you ready. No worry there, Mrs. Trumaine. Nothin' for you to worry about at all."

If dogs could smile, Shep would have done just that, proud of his accomplishment of gaining more attention from Jaeger.

I hadn't known Jaeger had hired anyone, though it made sense that he would. The Knudsens had five times more land than Hank and I owned, and Erik, Jaeger's father, had always aspired to be an ever bigger operation than he already was. It wasn't any of my business, but the words just slipped out of my mouth like it was. "Who'd you hire?"

"Lester Gustaffson, Lloyd's nephew. You know him?"

I shook my head. "Not directly, but I'm sure he'll be a good one. All those Gustaffsons are good workers."

"I hope so. I'm gonna have to hire two more hands in the spring, just to get everything done I need to. I'm sure hopin' Les'll be good enough to be a foreman. I only got so many hours in the day." Jaeger looked back at Betty and smiled.

Betty smiled back but said nothing. She instinctively knew her place. I liked that, at least.

I was about to invite her and Jaeger inside and give her a rundown on Hank's needs, but a hawk flew over. The gliding shadow distracted me and drew Shep's attention.

The hawk, a big red-tailed, flew right for the chickens that had, of course, wandered away from the garage, thanks to Shep's absence. The dog sank low to the ground, eyes to the sky, then launched after the raptor, even though it was twenty-five feet in the air. Shep's fierce bark filled the silence, caught on the wind, and provoked a flap of the wings and an annoyed glance from the hungry hawk as it climbed higher into the sky.

The rise in altitude didn't deter Shep. He chased after it until they were both out of sight. The bark echoed and the hawk's shadow lingered, giving me pause, concerned for the chickens. Predators were always out and about. It was easy to forget sometimes.

CHAPTER 7

It had never been easy to leave Hank since the accident, but it had become even harder after the murders of Lida and Erik Knudsen. In the dark months that followed their deaths, I had floundered like a fish pulled from a slough and left on the bank to die. I stayed closer to home more than I ever had in my life. Plain and simple, I was afraid to leave Hank. I wanted to spend every possible minute I could with him; I was certain that I feared his death far more than he did.

"Doc Huddleston's phone number is on the wall," I said to Betty Walsh. She smelled like twenty-five-cent perfume, lavender with a hint of rubbing alcohol. It smelled foreign for the time of year, and my nose crinkled with discomfort.

Betty nodded and looked over her shoulder. Jaeger lingered in the kitchen, sipping on a cup of leftover coffee that I'd warmed up in a soup pan on the stove. "He won't be far if something comes up, Mrs. Trumaine. Don't worry; I've handled worse than this." She realized immediately how callous her words sounded and apologized the best she could. "That's not what I meant. I'm sorry, it's just that he . . ."

I interrupted her. "It's all right, Betty. I'd worry about leaving here if I were talking to Doc Huddleston himself. I thought I heard a rattle in his chest this morning, but it's gone now. I'm just extra worried, flustered by everything."

Jaeger padded up behind us. "There's nothin' for ya to be worried about, Mrs. Trumaine. We'll call the doc if something comes up. Hank looks fine to me."

"He does to me, too, now." I wrung my hands, more unsure about leaving by the second.

Shep barked outside. He was still worrying over the chickens, trying to keep them safe from the hawk. One of them must have wandered too far away for his liking.

"Nothing's gonna happen, Mrs. Trumaine."

Betty stood staring at Hank, listening to us, but she immediately detached herself from the conversation. It was like she had just shown up for a paid job, and I appreciated that, at the very least. I would be happy to give her some money on my return.

"Those bad days are over," Jaeger said. "Not a thing is gonna go wrong while we're here. I promise you that. We can look after Hank well enough. Now, you go on into town and do what it is you need to." Jaeger had always been a good manager. He knew how to get people to do what needed to be done without coming off like a dictator.

I sighed, relaxed, and nodded my head. I looked over at Hank lying on the bed. His eyes were fixed in their normal spot on the ceiling—only his face showed aggravation, or maybe frustration, it was hard to tell these days. He either wanted to go with me or was angry about the fuss that was being made over him.

I didn't have to think too hard which it was. Hank had never liked being the center of attention or the cause of folks adjusting their lives to line up with his. It was easy to be shy where we lived.

I squared myself. Jaeger was right; nothing was going to happen. I cast my attention to Betty. "There's a list of instructions on the nightstand."

She nodded and forced a smile. "I understand."

"I won't be long, two hours at the most," I said, as I made my way over to kiss Hank goodbye. Such a show of affection would embarrass him even more if he could see.

"It's such a shame about Miss Eltmore," Betty said. Calla was Miss Eltmore to most all of Dickinson. She had always been the spinster librarian who had never married. Miss. Always Miss, never missus.

"It is," I said, then leaned down and pecked Hank quickly on the forehead.

He winced and exhaled slightly at the same time. "I'll be fine. Go on, now. Get your questions answered. It'll do you good to get away from me and your work."

"Try to be kind to this young girl," I ordered him.

Hank squished his forehead together and pursed his lips at the same time, like he was going to say something rash but decided not to. He just nodded slightly.

I pulled back from him and headed toward the door. As I passed by Betty, she said, "I just can't imagine a person doing such a thing."

I stopped dead in my tracks. Ice water shot through my veins. "What do you mean by that?" It was not a gentle question. It was a demand.

Betty drew back. "I didn't mean anything, Mrs. Trumaine; I was just sayin' that I didn't understand is all."

"Understand what, Betty?"

I had stopped so I was shoulder to shoulder with Jaeger. "She thought you knew," he said. "Betty hears a lot of things at the drugstore. You surely had to know that."

"Heard what?" My heart raced, and I suddenly found it very difficult to breathe. All I could smell was Betty's cheap perfume and the antiseptic tang of Hank's skin. I thought I was going to be sick.

"Miss Eltmore killed herself," Jaeger said. "Put a gun to her head right there at her desk and pulled the trigger. A sad act to be sure."

"Was that in the *Press*?" I whispered, trembling.

Jaeger shook his head. "Probably a good thing it wasn't if you ask me. I'm sorry," he said, easing his hand to my shoulder. "I know she was your friend."

I couldn't contain myself any longer. Tears burst out of my eyes and my chest heaved. The truth of Calla's death was too much to bear. The cause of it wasn't something I had considered other than by natural means. There had been no need to. Calla Eltmore had always seemed like the least likely person in the world to commit suicide.

Jaeger spun me around and wrapped his arms around me. I didn't resist the gesture, the comfort of his caring embrace. I couldn't have resisted even if I'd wanted to.

CHAPTER 8

As a mere child I wrote down everything that I saw, what I needed to remember, what I wanted to accomplish in a day and in my life. My childhood writing desk had been constantly littered with all sizes of paper, with lists of ducks and songbirds—the species, the Latin name, the date that I first saw them, and the date I last saw them. The same with mammals and wildflowers. My father could barely restrain his immense pride at my interest in the outside world. He'd encouraged it by filling my bookshelves with beginner field guides, little books bought at the Ben Franklin for a quarter—they still sat on my shelf—and in long walks on the prairie, sharing his stories and knowledge with me. He wouldn't have been surprised a bit by my vocation as an indexer. I could imagine him holding the *Common Plants* book with such pride you would have thought it was a grandson.

There was no question that once I had learned to read and write making lists came as easily to me as breathing. That skill had been perfectly honed long before I knew what an index was. But being organized came later, slowly. Recognizing order, knowing instinctively where one thing fit into the world and another thing didn't, took experience, time, and loads of failed efforts. More than once I'd been admonished by my mother in the kitchen for putting a pan or skillet in the wrong place. Nothing had thrilled Momma more than when I learned the alphabet, at her prodding, so I could retrieve and replace a spice from the cabinet without making a mess of her world. She was the organized one. Everything had its place. Even me.

And so it was that I found myself lost without a way to organize myself into understanding the concept of suicide. The vision of Calla

Eltmore raising a gun to her temple and pulling the trigger was as foreign to me as the inside of a television or a radio. I had no working knowledge of such things. My tenuous relationship with the Lutheran church didn't help matters much. If I had been left to my childhood religious teachings, then I could only consider that Calla Eltmore had committed the gravest of sins and would be damned to hell for all of eternity. It was a thought that I couldn't hold on to, Calla being damned, suffering and burning for an act that none of us knew the reason for.

I couldn't imagine a reason to commit suicide. Calla loved books, her job. I'd always just assumed that she was happy with her life. She never complained, but she didn't readily share details, either. Calla had never truly confided her deepest, darkest thoughts and secrets to me. I suppose I had never expected her to, but there were times when I thought she looked lonely, and I wondered if she'd ever known true love.

My speculation that Calla and Herbert Frakes, the longtime janitor at the library, were having a secret relationship was more for my own comfort than Calla's. I'd always hoped that she had someone to hold in the deep darkness of night, when life was tough and fear was at the door, that she knew love like Elizabeth Barrett, Calla's favorite poet, had known for Robert Browning. *How do I love thee, let me count the ways . . .* But I'd been wrong about Calla. Life was miserable enough for her to end it suddenly and without so much as a goodbye.

I pulled away from the house with an ugly, unsettled feeling in the pit of my stomach. It felt like I had been punched by some invisible force, and the pain of the blow lingered with the threat of staying on permanently. I had no choice but to go into town, not only to get my question answered but to find out as much as I could about Calla's fate. I wasn't going to rely on the *Press* or Betty Walsh for any kind of update or the full story. A story that, truth be told, I wasn't sure I wanted to know. The ending of it, Calla's suicide, was awful. I could only imagine the beginning and the middle.

The Studebaker had always ridden like a hay wagon with a temperamental engine, but the weather was drier than normal lately, and the rutted gravel road that led away from the house bounced and jarred me physically, almost enough to match what I felt inside my mind and in my heart.

I was surrounded by dun brown fields that went on for as far as the eye could see. There were slight rolls in the land, offering a wide vista, but mostly it was flat, unobscured, with the exception of faraway buttes. What trees that did poke up alongside the road had lost their leaves to the pushing wind a month prior. Most of them looked like skeleton hands reaching up to the broad blue sky for help. Spring was a long way off.

The road was lonely except for the sight of an occasional jackrabbit or a hawk gliding in the distance. I had the radio off only because I didn't want to blare the volume. The rumble and roar underneath the truck sounded like a constant explosion. A dust plume spewed from the tail-end of the Studebaker, and it would have taken little imagination to pretend that I was inside a rocket ship, leaving the world once and for all.

I reached over to my purse, pulled it next to me, then opened it—all the while keeping one eye on the road. I grabbed hold of my pack of cigarettes—Salems, the package green and white—then let them go as quickly as I'd grabbed them.

Calla and I had shared a cigarette nearly every time I'd stopped in the library to visit with her or pick up some errant piece of information that I'd needed. That would never happen again. I could hardly bear the thought of it, and I nearly started crying again. I steeled myself, though, mainly from the embarrassment that I'd felt by breaking down in front of Jaeger and Betty.

I picked up the pack of cigarettes again, eased one into my mouth, put the pack back where it belonged, and pushed in the dashboard lighter. I could taste the mint on the edge of my lip and found no calming effect to it at all. I hoped that would come in the form of a puff or two.

Hank had never smoked, though he was fond of a chaw of Redman tobacco on occasion—mostly when there were men about, working on the engine of one machine or another. He would never chew or spit in front of me, or any other woman for that matter. Nor did Hank like it that I smoked. I wasn't regular about it, but it steadied my nerves when I needed it to. I'd hid my smoking from him before Lida and Erik had been murdered, but not so much anymore—though I would go outside when I felt the need to light one up.

The lighter clicked and ejected outward. I grabbed it and put the red hot coil to the end of the Salem and sucked in as deep as I could. Something needed to calm me down before I got into town. Smoking was the only thing I could think of.

"To Calla," I said aloud as I exhaled, obscuring my vision for a second, filling it with a gray cloud that lingered, then blew back and stung my eyes. It was a good thing I wasn't in downtown Dickinson or I might've wrecked the truck and really found myself up a tree.

CHAPTER 9

The Dickinson Public Library sat on a tree-lined street at the very edge of the residential and business district of town. I'd always thought that the people who lived within walking distance of the library were the luckiest people in the world, especially in winter when all they had to do was bundle up and make an easy trek to the warm, old building. For me, a trip into town could take an hour or two in the middle of January, a half hour at most other times of the year. Time spent at the library was usually tagged onto some other reason for making the journey to town; a doctor's appointment, stocking up on meat, or running into the Rexall for a necessity of one kind or another. Except today. This trip was all about the library, all about Calla Eltmore.

The library, like so many, had been built with the help of a financial gift from Andrew Carnegie. It had opened to readers in 1910. The building was a simple design, yellow brick, a large window on each side of a grand set of steps that led up to the door, the interior was two thousand square feet at the most. The inside ceiling was high, intricately tapped tin that had weathered the years beautifully. Not quite a cathedral, but as close as there was to one as far as I was concerned. A west wing with a full basement had been added on in 1938 by Roosevelt's WPA program. Father called the WPA the We Poke Along Society, and for years that's exactly what I thought the acronym stood for. Some men were offended by the suggestion that they didn't work hard for their relief during the Depression, but others agreed with Father. Still, the craftsmanship of the building had endured, so the task had been undertaken with a high amount of skill and respect. I was glad of that.

Calla had become the librarian a year after the renovation and was just as much a fixture at the library, as were the bookshelves that held a multitude of volumes of pleasure and knowledge. The library was hallowed ground to me, even though the Lutheran church was a few blocks away. My soul had been nourished far more by the time I'd spent in the library than it had in the time I had spent in any pew.

I sat in the Studebaker, parked on the opposite side of the street, staring at the building, still unable to believe that Calla was dead, that she wouldn't be there to greet me with a surprised smile when I walked through the front doors unannounced.

I had to look away from the building for fear of tearing up all over again. *Get yourself together, Marjorie.*

I looked in the rearview mirror and flipped a stray strand of hair from my forehead. My hair was cut shoulder-length and had some natural waves to it. A few wiry sprigs of gray had started to sprout at my temples, but I'd never been tempted to pluck them.

A car passed, drawing my attention away from my reflection in the mirror. It went on down to 1st Street and turned right. *You're going to have to face this sooner or later, Marjorie,* I thought to myself as I pushed open the truck door. *Might as well get on with it.*

I wasn't sure if they were my words I was hearing or my mother's. She had little use for dilly-dallying. She was hard as nails on the outside and soft as pudding on the inside. Some of her rigidness was due to the conditions of life on the plains, what it demanded of you. I think she was just born with the rest, determined to pass on her steel spine to me. Most days I appreciated her insistence on character, but on this day I could have used some pudding.

The wind rushed straight down 3rd Street, careening out of the north, bringing with it a push of October cold; a harbinger of things to come. The temperature had dropped a good ten degrees since I'd left home. I immediately glanced up at the sky before crossing the street. The perfect blue dome was being replaced by a sullen gray blanket. The sun glowed like a shimmering white plate hanging by an invisible thread, and I wondered if I would see it clearly again before the coming of spring.

The smell of burning leaves touched my nose, and I worried that someone would be careless with the flames. Grass fires could get out of control easily, especially since it had been dry recently. Fire was a fear the community held in unison, both out in the country and in town—making an exception for Twelfth Night, when we all gathered at the Lutheran church to burn our Christmas trees. Nature didn't just toss its wrath down from the sky—it was a threat at nearly every step, as I well knew. *Damn gopher hole.*

I squared my shoulders, looked up and down the street, and found as much resolve as I could to take a step forward. I clutched my purse with both hands, worried that my lipstick wasn't as fresh as it could be, and hoping that my coat didn't smell of cigarette smoke. I moved on, hurrying toward the front doors of the library.

I was halfway up the stairs when I saw a woman push her way out the front doors of the library. She was shorter than I was, and older by at least twenty years. Her hair was salt and pepper gray, nicely coifed, not a hair out of place, and she was dressed in an outfit that had surely been bought off-the-rack at one of the fine women's stores in Bismarck. Her wool skirt was a lustrous tan, a result of well-fed sheep tended to under a tumultuous Scottish sky, and her jacket was a big brown plaid. Even from a distance the woman was strikingly beautiful—with the exception of her puffy red eyes and the smear of makeup on her right cheek.

The woman noticed me as she stepped off the first step. She put her unmarred heel in a place that wasn't there, and she instantly lurched forward, sending a pile of books straight up into the air. She tried to capture them. Tried to hang onto the ones that she could like they were made of fragile china and would shatter to pieces on impact. But nothing could have been further from the truth. The books rained down with predictable thuds. They sounded like soft rocks falling from the sky, hitting the cement as solidly as if they'd been thrown on purpose.

The wind screamed, but no sound came from the woman's mouth as she relented to the fall and realized that she wasn't capable of saving the books—or herself. She hit the ground with the same soft thud as the books, rolled a bit, then bounced down two steps and came to a stop on her shoulder without a whimper or a moan. It all happened in the blink of an eye, and I didn't know whether to stop or run to her.

Honestly, I thought she was dead.

CHAPTER 10

A pair of rimless glasses landed at my feet. The left lens had cracked from one corner to the other. The right one was missing altogether. There had been all kinds of noise as the woman tumbled my way; soft flesh hitting hard cement, and books flying without wings and landing harshly on the ground.

"Oh, my," I gasped, then hurried to the women without another thought.

She lay on the ground, not moving a muscle, her arm tucked on her right side and her knees pulled up in a fetal position. To my relief, her eyes were fully open, with life still in them. A trickle of fresh blood trailed out of the corner of her mouth.

A car passed on the street behind me, but it went on, leaving only the woman and me. There was no one around as I kneeled beside her and looked for help at the same time.

She began to move her right arm in an awkward and painful attempt to prop herself up and try to stand. Her lips twisted into a grimace. There was only a hint of lipstick remaining on them—probably smeared off for a reason, long before the fall.

"Don't move," I said. My words were soft, overridden by the push of the chilly north wind. I wasn't sure the woman had heard me, so I said it again, more emphatically. "Don't move." It was definitely my mother's voice, commanding, sharp with authority.

The woman nodded and surrendered. I'd always wondered whether Hank would have ended up paralyzed if he had been handled a little more gently. I'd never blamed anyone for helping him, for rushing him out of the grouse field as quickly as they could. He was going to be blind—the angle of the shotgun when it had gone off had made sure of that—but the paralysis, that was another thing entirely.

"Does anything feel broken?" I said.

She didn't answer straight away; she just stared up at me, then at the sky. I didn't think she was reading the clouds for coming weather or wind, just making sure they were still there.

Her lips trembled, then she closed her eyes slowly, softly, like some hidden door for the final time.

"Can you wiggle your toes and fingers?" I said.

"Yes, I'm fine. Really," she said as she opened her eyes again. They were hazel, the tint of an uncertain summer day. Her skin was pale, fragile white alabaster, but the color had started to return to her face. "I need to get home. Claude doesn't know that I left the house. I have a roast in the oven. It'll burn." She stopped speaking, but I knew the fear of a man in another woman's voice when I heard it. And *there'd be hell to pay*, I assumed she would have said, finishing the sentence, if she'd known me better.

"That was a hard fall you took," I said. "You should take a minute. Catch your breath."

I set my purse on the ground, pulled my handkerchief out, and went to dab the blood from the corner of the woman's mouth. She recoiled like a skittish stray dog meeting an overly friendly stranger for the first time.

I pulled back, fearful of crossing an unseen boundary. "I won't hurt you," I whispered.

She nodded with a soft, open stare. "I know you won't. Really, I'm fine. I must get home. You don't understand."

The wind rippled an open book behind me. "If you're sure nothing's broken and you can move everything without pain, then sit up slowly. I'll help you if that's all right?"

"Yes, of course, it's fine."

I lifted the woman up with ease. She helped, was steadier than I'd expected her to be, and I also had the advantage of living my life on the farm. I'd helped to bale hay more times in my life than I could count, carried in countless cords of firewood from the stack to the house in the middle of winter, and tended and turned Hank more times in a day than I cared to count.

She exhaled and stared me in the face once she was fully on her feet again. "Thank you," she said. "I'm lucky the wind isn't any fiercer today."

I handed her my handkerchief, and she took it without a shiver and wiped away the blood from the corner of her lip. It looked swollen, like she might have bit it during the fall.

Certain that she was steady, I looked about and hurried to the closest book. I picked it up and hesitated. The book was an old, red leather-bound, with gilt letters. It was *Men and Women* by Robert Browning. My heart stopped. I'd never read the book and had little personal history with Browning as a poet. I'd never been enamored by the Victorian poets—but Calla Eltmore had been.

The woman tore the book out of my hand. "I really must go. Thank you for your help," she said, then hurried away from me, leaving the other books and her broken glasses behind.

I picked up the fragile frames and called out, "Don't you need these?"

She ignored me, didn't bother to look back, and disappeared from sight in a matter of two shakes. I stared down at the glasses, then went to my purse and put them in the side pocket. I couldn't just leave them there.

The wind rose up again, making me wish I had worn a heavier coat. The pages of the scattered books flipped and tore open again, leaving me no choice but to gather them up like mindless chickens. Where was Shep when I needed him?

CHAPTER 11

Strangers were most often welcomed with open hearts and suspicious minds in North Dakota. It may sound like a contradiction, but the truth of the matter was that the sudden appearance of a new person in town, or anywhere else for that matter, was about as rare as seeing a shooting star blazing across a clear blue sky on a lazy Saturday afternoon.

Under normal circumstances, Calla Eltmore would have served her time at the library, retired with some small comfort, and made sure that a new librarian was properly installed into her previous position, fully trained and completely aware of the nuances the job required. But the circumstances of the moment were hardly normal, and for some reason the possibility of retirement wasn't something that had given Calla hope, or the will to live. I had no idea what to expect of the person standing behind the librarian's desk.

I plopped the recovered books on the counter with a little louder thump than I had intended. The sound shot up to the two-story tin ceiling and echoed throughout the building with a doom-inspired volume that surprised me. It sounded like a gun had gone off, and I immediately regretted not being more careful; more aware of where I was and why I was there.

The unknown woman spun around and faced me with a hard scowl on her face. She was a head taller than I was, but that was mostly due to the deep brunette hair piled high on her graying scalp. Her hair looked like a boll of cotton that had been dyed, grown upward, then started to wither at the roots; there was no hiding her age, no matter how hard she tried. I had little trust in a woman who changed the color of her hair with a potent mixture of magical chemicals that came out of a dime-store box. Her vanity shocked me.

"May I help you?" the woman demanded. She stepped toward me and I saw, too, that her height was aided by three-inch high heels, not the expected comfortable, sensible shoes like Calla had always worn. She looked me up and down and a judgmental sneer flickered across her face. You would have thought I was wearing a flour sack dress.

"The woman who just left . . ." I flicked my head over my shoulder, then turned back quickly to meet the steel, unchanged gaze of the new librarian. "She dropped these on the way out and went off without them."

"You mean she just left them there?" the woman demanded, twisting her lip up further in disdain.

"Um, yes, she did."

"These books are library property, bought and paid for with tax dollars, or by donations from generous patrons. There's a fine for that." There were wrinkles above the woman's lips that couldn't be filled in by any amount of foundation. They were flared wide open. I guessed she was about ten years older than I was and wound up tighter than barbed wire freshly strung.

I shifted my weight, unprepared for an attack of any kind. "I have no idea who that woman was, and I am fully aware of the rules and policies that govern this library. I have been coming here since I was a child. I'm sure you have the name of the borrower. You can take up the violation with her, not me."

"Well . . ." the woman said, snapping her head back. She wore glasses, not unlike Calla's really—black plastic, pointed at the tips, with a gold chain that attached at the shafts. The chain dangled loosely, and the glasses threatened to fall away.

I said nothing more. I just stood there staring at the woman, numb to my toes, sadder than I had been in months because I wasn't talking to Calla.

There didn't seem to be anyone else in the library but the two of us. I had seen hide nor hair of Herbert Frakes.

There was no other sound—except for the persistent wind outside, but no one heard that noise unless it wasn't there. It was cool inside, just a little warmer than a tomb, and the comforting smell of books and paper wafted about casually, expectedly. Only I found no comfort in anything about being inside the library. It was the first time that had ever happened to me.

"Do you have a name?" I finally asked.

"You may call me Miss Finch," the woman snapped. "I am Delia Finch."

"I don't know any Finches around here."

"I suppose you don't. My family hails from Minnesota. I'm on loan from Bismarck for the foreseeable future."

"Because of Calla."

Delia Finch lowered her head and for the first time showed a modicum of humanity. "Yes, because of the unfortunate circumstances this facility has found itself in."

For the first time since I had arrived, I looked past the woman, Miss Finch, to the closed door that led into Calla's office. It had a frosted glass window marked LIBRARIAN, and it was easy to tell that the room was dark. I imagined that the door was locked, but there was no outward sign of that or that it was blocked off by the police for any reason. Everything looked normal.

Miss Finch caught my gaze. "May I help you? Or did you just come in here to return these books you say you found?"

I didn't know how to answer her. Tears welled up in my eyes as the reality of Calla's death became more and more apparent. The tips of my fingers trembled, and I suddenly felt like I was standing out in an open wheat field in the middle of January.

"I had a question," I whispered, as a tear escaped my right eye and trailed down my cheek. *So much for keeping a stiff upper lip.*

"Oh, dear," Miss Finch said. She leaned down and almost magically produced a box of paper tissues. There wasn't an annoyed look on her face, but it was obvious that she was uncomfortable with such a show of emotion.

I took the tissue she offered and blotted away the tears the best I could. "I'm sorry," I said. "I'm usually not like this."

Miss Finch stared at me like she didn't believe me, but said nothing. I wondered if she'd always been so rigid.

"Calla was my friend," I continued. "I just can't imagine what made her do what she did. It's unthinkable. She never indicated that she was unhappy or capable of doing such a thing."

Capable of doing such a thing . . . echoed inside my mind and in the empty library at the same time. The words flew away from me on wings of disbelief. I couldn't bring myself to accept that Calla Eltmore had killed herself. Especially not at the library, on hallowed ground. It would be the last place I would have expected her to taint with the memory of a desperate, final act. I shook my head and said nothing else. I was tempted to turn around and walk out of the library and never come back. It was such an unimaginable impulse that my feet hesitated and failed to react to what my mind and my heart wanted to do. I was frozen in place, as lifeless as a fence post.

Miss Finch cleared her throat, then said, "It is a difficult day for the library, ma'am. As you would think it would be, but it is business as usual. The calendar was not marked for this tragedy, and the doors must remain open. Now, what was your question?" Her humanity fell away almost as quickly as it had appeared.

"I'm sorry?" I couldn't believe the callous tone emitting from the woman's tight lips. She was moving me along. It was almost like she was tired of my presence and wanted me to leave.

"Your question, the one that brought you here." Miss Finch paused, then said, "You could have called."

"I guess I had to see for myself that Calla really wasn't here."

"The street has been full of traffic this morning. Curiosity seekers, I suppose, driving past, hoping to see something awful. It is just unnerving," she said, pointing toward the window.

I nodded. I'd had some experience with increased traffic, with gawkers, slowing by the house after the Knudsen tragedy a few months back. I didn't like it then, either, being the object of focused attention and speculation.

"It's morbid and rude, if you ask me," Miss Finch continued, staring directly into my eyes. "They should all receive a traffic ticket for driving too slow."

What a hateful woman. I gripped the tissue in my hand tight. "People are just afraid," I said.

"Your question?" she said again, tapping her fingers on the counter.

Right, my question. It took me back to my reality, to the task I had to face once I left here. I had an index to finish, and I had completely detached from that prospect. The work seemed distant, impossible to approach, but I knew I had no choice but to continue on. "Is musk thistle a perennial plant or a biennial plant?" I said.

"I wasn't expecting that," Miss Finch said.

"I'm an indexer," I said, feeling the need to explain myself for some reason.

"A what?"

"I write back-of-the-book indexes. Calla has a shelf of all of the books that have my indexes in them."

"A star is among us."

"Hardly," I said.

"Well, I've never met an indexer any more than I've met a real writer. I'm impressed." Miss Finch's tone had changed, and she was suddenly leaning toward me, almost half over the counter. "Tell me, do you make real money at this job, at writing indexes for books?"

I stepped back unconsciously. It was rude to ask about money. I wasn't accustomed to such a thing. "My question," I stuttered, trying to deflect the query.

"Well, then, how does one become an indexer?" Miss Finch persisted.

"I took a course, then sent off some letters to New York. I've been very lucky to find steady work," I said. "I have an index that's due soon, and I need to answer this question so I can move on. Of course, *I did try to call.* So, if you could please . . ."

Delia Finch nodded and smiled slightly. She spoke without taking a visible breath. "Musk thistle. *Carduus nutans.* A native of North Africa and brought to this country in the early nineteenth century. It is a biennial plant here in North Dakota, though in warmer climates it can germinate and flower in a single year," Miss Finch said, standing back to her original position. A haughty look settled on her face just as she crossed her arms across her chest, proud of her dissertation.

I did not like this woman. "I need a source," I said. "I can't just take your word for it." I *was* mildly impressed by her hair-trigger knowledge, but it would be a cold day when I showed it.

Miss Finch started to say something, then spun around and exited from behind the counter as if her heels had been lit on fire. I just stood there and watched, reasonably satisfied that I had annoyed her as much as she had annoyed me. Her footsteps echoed throughout the library, hard taps on tile floor that almost sounded like a war drum being pounded over and over again.

I stood patiently, hoping for sight of Herbert Frakes, but fearing the worst for him, that he'd gone off on a bender again. Losing Calla would be impossible for him to bear. I was certain of it. Just as I was certain in my hope that Miss Delia Finch was only the temporary librarian and not a permanent replacement for Calla Eltmore. If that were the case, my indexing life would be miserable for the foreseeable future.

Miss Finch returned quickly with a small field guide open in her hands. A satisfied look had replaced her earlier disdain, and I was certain her makeup was going to melt right off her face. She thrust the book toward me and said, "As I said, it *is* a biennial plant. See for yourself if you must."

"I must." I glanced down to the little print, strained my eyes, and read what she wanted me to. She was right, but I really had not doubted that she would be. "Thank you, that will help," I said, offering a feigned smile.

Miss Finch withdrew the book and set it on the counter. "This indexing course you took, did you take it at the local college?"

"No," I said. "The extension agent brought it out. It's a correspondence course facilitated by the USDA."

"The United States Department of Agriculture?"

"Yes, the very one," I said. I had encountered enough academic snobbery since I started indexing to know it when I heard it, so I didn't restrain myself in my own defense. I had nothing to be ashamed of, and I damn well knew it. I was an experienced indexer and proud of it.

"I should have known," she said.

"You can contact Curtis Henderson, the extension agent for information if you'd like." I shook my head, squared my shoulders, and prepared to leave. I opened my purse to put the tissue in and I saw the woman's glasses that I had picked up. "By any chance can you tell me the woman's name who checked out the books I brought in?"

"I beg your pardon?"

"I was just wondering..." I said, staring at the glasses. Returning them seemed the right thing to do.

"That is private information. I cannot give out that name for any reason." Miss Finch had raised her voice. It was as loud as a bank vault slamming shut. Calla would not have done that; at least with me...

My immediate instinct was to shush her, but I thought better of it. "I'm sorry, you're right, of course." I dropped the tissue in my purse and closed it. "Thank you for your time. I hope the coming days are easier for you." And with that, I turned and hurried out of the library, glad to be free of Miss Delia Finch's presence, satisfied that I had obtained what I'd come for. I was past ready to be home with my dog and my husband where I belonged.

CHAPTER 12

I had to drive right past the Wild Pony tavern on my way out of town. I could have bypassed it, gone around the block and avoided it altogether, but I couldn't bring myself to do that. Instead, I slowed as the building came into view, nearly as curious and intentional as the gawkers that I had come to loath.

The Wild Pony was a single-level, brick-front building that had been in business for as long as I could remember. I wasn't sure that the building had always been a tavern; the memory of it was mostly a blur, coming and going to and from town.

Small bungalows populated the cottonwood-lined street and beyond; small, simple well-kept houses that were the most common in Dickinson. I suppose a man could have gotten himself more than drunk and still found his way home if he had been inclined. I was not one for liquor, but a tavern was just as important to some folks as a library was to me. We all needed a place to go, there was no denying that. The luxuries of town-life weren't lost on me. But I wasn't looking for just any man. I was hoping to catch a glimpse of Herbert Frakes.

Like most men of his generation, Herbert had served overseas in World War II and had never been the same since he'd returned home. It was easy to tell that he'd been shattered by the experience of combat, even twenty years later. I feared what the shock of Calla's death had done to him. Previous stresses had sent Herbert straight to the Wild Pony, and my suspicion was that his pattern of behavior hadn't changed.

A few unattended cars sat in front of the Wild Pony. There was no one to be seen milling about. Even though it was late morning, a red neon OPEN sign buzzed brightly in the window next to the door. All the windows, including the door, were blacked out from the inside. It was a dark place even on a sunny day. There was no way I was going to catch a glimpse of Herbert Frakes unless I went inside.

I glanced down at my watch, fully aware that if I stopped I was going to be away from Hank longer than I should be, but I couldn't keep a growing thought from overtaking my mind: *Calla would want you to check on Herbert.*

And then, as I steered the Studebaker over to the curb to park, I felt the first hint of anger erupt in the deepest part of my stomach. "If that were true, she wouldn't have killed herself. Calla would still be here to look after Herbert like she always had," I said aloud to no one but myself.

I let my angry words dissipate inside the cab of the truck as I brought it to a halt, put it in park, and shut off the engine. The engine shimmied and protested like it had developed a cold, but I knew better. The Studebaker needed its points and plugs changed. I was behind on everything.

I sighed and suddenly felt ashamed of my anger toward Calla. But I was angry with her. If she had just ended her life without reaching out for help, without calling me, then I had a right to be angry. At least I thought I did. I didn't even know if she'd left a note explaining her reasons, what had led her down the path to do such a thing. No one— no one being Delia Finch, the only person I'd talked to who might know such a thing—had said whether she'd communicated anything. And I hadn't asked. That woman had left me unnerved.

Regardless of Calla's unknown wishes, I needed to see if Herbert was inside the Wild Pony. If he was, maybe he'd have some information that would make sense of everything. Maybe he knew why Calla Eltmore had killed herself. If anyone knew, it would be Herbert.

I took a quick second to put aside everything I was thinking and feeling. I peeked at myself in the rearview mirror and wondered if I was presentable enough to walk into a tavern. My face was pale and my lipstick, what there was of it, had nearly vanished. My lips looked like a newborn's instead of a lady about town. I was embarrassed by the state

of my hair, by my appearance as a whole, but I wasn't sure that it mattered. I had never been a regular visitor to taverns. I hoped the inside
was as black as the windows were on the outside.

I straightened myself up the best I could, squared my shoulders,
and pushed out of the truck. Hank Trumaine would be furious with me
if he knew what I was about to do, but I couldn't stop myself. I was as
worried about Herbert as much as I wanted to find out what had happened to Calla.

I hurried to the door of the Wild Pony, ignoring any traffic that
passed by. I hunched down, hoping that no one would see me, recognize me. In a town where everyone seemed to know everyone's business, the last thing I wanted to get around was that I was frequenting
the Wild Pony while Hank lay paralyzed and blind in his bed.

I stepped inside a closed vestibule, and garbled music met my
ears. I recognized the song immediately—"I Guess I'm Crazy" by Jim
Reeves. It was the number-one song in the nation, even though poor
Jim had died in a plane crash in July. You couldn't turn on the radio
without hearing that song.

Airplanes and musicians seemed like a deadly combination to me.
I remembered the Buddy Holly tragedy in Clear Lake, Iowa. Death and
wreckage in a cornfield. The fates had no sense of decency as far as I was
concerned, but the irony that I was hearing a ghost singing a love song
was not lost on me.

I stopped before pushing through the second door that led directly
into the tavern. I could smell thick cigarette smoke and the yeasty smell
that came from the ancient presence of beer. I figured the drains were
alive with the stuff. The Wild Pony served food, too, so there was a
mixture of grease and burned meat in the air that did nothing to
provoke my appetite. I wanted to go in, look around, see if Herbert was
there, and get out as quickly as I could.

Never one to back off a decision easily, I stepped inside the Wild
Pony and stopped just beyond the threshold.

The door brushed the back of my behind, encouraging me to go
farther inside, but I held fast. My eyes had to adjust to the darkness

and smoke. I was on unfamiliar ground, and I wasn't so dim as to not know that my entrance would be met with a scrutiny that I was unaccustomed to.

Two lonely pinball machines sat butted up against the far wall with bright carnival lights flashing repetitively, begging lazily, trying to entice someone, anyone, to drop a nickel in their hungry slots. Black-topped tables surrounded by empty orange vinyl covered chairs dotted the floor to my right; a maze that would need to be traversed all the way to the bar. The ornate bar, hand-carved walnut that looked like it belonged in the last century, stretched the length of the entire wall. Sconces haphazardly lit the walls, and the overhead lights were turned off.

A big bearded man glanced up at me from drying dull glass mugs. He hesitated a second, looked me up and down, passing judgment or assessing a threat, I wasn't sure. I wasn't looking to drag an errant husband home and had no intention of making a scene. I stared the bartender in the eye, then turned my attention to a man sitting at the south end of the bar. Satisfied that I wasn't going to cause trouble, the bartender went back to drying the mug.

The man at the end of the bar made two of Herbert and was talking with a blonde waitress, barmaid, whatever she was called, who looked a few years younger than me from the neck down. Her face had miles on it that I would never travel. It was easy to tell, even in the muted light, that she'd had a worrisome, hard life. I immediately felt sad for the woman, even though I didn't know her or remember ever seeing her. She looked up at me, met my stare, and I looked down as quickly as I could, embarrassed.

When I looked up and directed my attention to the other end of the bar, I sighed with relief. I'd found what I'd come looking for: Herbert Frakes hunched over a highball glass half filled with an amber liquid that I assumed was whiskey. He looked like he had been planted in the seat, but his roots were shallow. It was obvious that one tap on the shoulder, one little gust of wind, one more surprise would topple him over and, perhaps, destroy him.

CHAPTER 13

I wasn't quite sure how to approach Herbert. I'd been around enough injured animals in my life to know to be calm and aware of every move they made. I took a deep breath of the sour tavern air and made my way to the stool next to him as gently as I could.

"Herbert," I said, sliding onto the stool, as I clutched my purse with one hand and tucked the back of my dress with the other. "Are you all right?"

He turned to me and my gaze met his swollen, red, sorrowful eyes, and I knew I had just asked the stupidest, most insensitive question I could have asked.

It took a second before any kind of recognition lit up in Herbert's eyes. They were pale blue, a faded late summer sky that was saying goodbye to the swallows and hello to winter. It was the end of one season for Herbert and the beginning of another.

"What are you doin' here, Marjorie?" he said.

The bartender moved my way gracefully, like he was roller skating, floating on air. He slid a cardboard coaster advertising Carling's Black Label beer in front of me with the skill of a lifelong bowler. The round coaster stopped directly in front of me, exactly where it should have.

"A drink, ma'am?" It didn't seem to matter to the bartender that he'd interrupted the start of our conversation. His voice boomed up to the ceiling just as the Jim Reeves song came to a sad end.

I looked over at Herbert's glass, could smell the burning strength of the whiskey, and shook my head. "Just a glass of water and an ashtray."

He nodded and eased away just as smoothly as he came. The waitress eyed me knowingly, like she'd known what I was going to order before I did. There was no money to be made off me.

"I was worried about you," I said to Herbert. My first instinct was to reach over and touch him on the shoulder, offer him what solace I could, but I restrained myself. It didn't take a fool to know that the man didn't like to be touched.

"You heard?"

"It was in the paper."

"I suppose it was. I was afraid to look. That would make it real." He was far from drunk. His words were not slurred, and he seemed lucid, aware.

I stared at him, and he stared back at me. His eyes were already glassy, so it was hard to tell if he was about to cry or had been crying all morning. Just as a tear was about to escape him, he looked away to the wall, to the past, to someplace I had no idea of.

Don't press, Marjorie, my inside voice warned, so I said nothing, nodded as the bartender delivered my requested items, and watched him go back to the task of drying glasses with a white bleached towel.

I dug into my purse and pulled out my cigarettes, a half pack of Salems, and a book of matches from the Ivanhoe. Herbert needed his time, so I went about lighting a cigarette.

The first bit of smoke hit my lungs as I inhaled and it was a nice relief. I needed something to calm me down as much as Herbert did. I exhaled slowly.

"That was Calla's brand, too," he said.

I glanced down to the pack and realized how thoughtless I'd been. "I'm sorry," I said, grabbing up the green and white pack.

Herbert stopped me and grabbed my wrist causally with an easy grip. "It's okay, Marjorie. You can't erase her. She's everywhere I look. Always will be, I suppose."

I heard a familiar love and loss in Herbert's voice. We were kindred spirits at that moment. Something I could never have imagined. I let the silence settle between us and took another draw off my cigarette. Since I wasn't a regular smoker, my throat protested briefly and I let out a small cough.

"How 'bout you, Marjorie? You all right?"

I shook my head. "No, I don't think I am. I can hardly believe she's gone, Herbert."

He agreed silently with a sip of the whiskey. I watched him closely. His hair was still slicked back with yesterday's Brylcreem, pomade made of beeswax and mineral oil. It had lost its smell, or was overwhelmed by all of the circulating aromas inside the Wild Pony. He still had on his janitor's uniform, too. Dark gray Dickie work pants with a shirt to match. His name was stitched over the right pocket.

"Have you been home?" I asked. I sat the Salem down in the ashtray and watched the smoke waft upward until it joined the rest of the tobacco that lingered in the air.

"It's hard to go down there. I don't know what's going to happen now."

Herbert lived in the basement of the library, had for as long as I could remember. There had always been speculation and gossip about a relationship between Herbert and Calla, but no one knew for sure the extent of it. Not even me.

"I met Delia Finch," I said.

Herbert shook his head and his lip twisted up as if he had smelled something dead. "She's a treat."

I started to agree, but didn't want to add to the sourness. I bit my lip instead. "I'm sure it's difficult for her being a stranger in town under the circumstances."

Herbert turned and stared at me. "Why would she do something like this, Marjorie? Why?"

All of the sound in the room ceased. Even the pinball machine quieted, held its breath in sadness or respect, I wasn't sure which.

"I don't know, Herbert. I was hoping you could tell me."

He shook his head, but he could not speak another word. Tears flowed from his eyes in torrents worthy of Niagara Falls. I could do nothing but pull him to me and cradle his head to my chest as he let his emotions go unhindered, unrestrained, and unexplained.

CHAPTER 14

I had a lot to ponder as I pointed the Studebaker toward home.
I'd found the answer to my question about musk thistle early on,
which only left me more unsettled by my encounter with the hard as
nails stranger in Calla's place, Delia Finch. If I had been the praying
kind, the kind of woman who asked for things from the empty sky and
meant it, I would ask for Miss Finch to be an extremely temporary presence at the library. That, of course, would be a shallow thing to ask of a
greater power, and one of the larger reasons why I had always restrained
myself from doing such things. If there were that kind of magic in the
world I would ask for Calla to be restored to her proper place in good
physical and mental health. But that was not to be. Calla was dead,
removed from her station in life, and I was faced with learning to live—
and find respect for—a new librarian.

Even though the trip had been a success, I still carried a nagging
feeling about Calla's death as I left town. I only knew a little more than
I had before I'd left Hank to satisfy my uncontrollable need for information. After Herbert had regained his composure, he'd said there was
no suicide note that he knew of. But the hardest part of what he had to
tell, which further explained the state I'd found him in, was that he had
been the one to find Calla.

He'd found her collapsed at her desk, cold as an iron spigot in deep
winter, blood splattered everywhere, a pistol on the floor at her finger-
tips. There was no saving Calla, even though he had tried. Herbert had
been certain that she'd been dead for hours. Just the thought of it left
me empty and numb.

I looked at my watch and found that I was two hours later than

I'd told Betty Walsh I'd be. I panicked and scanned the street ahead of me for a phone booth. There was nothing but houses. The closest pay phone that I knew of was over on Villard Street in front of the Ivanhoe.

I tapped my fingers on the top of the steering wheel. Usually it took two hands to handle the truck since it lacked power steering, but the street was free of any serious traffic and there were no ruts of snow to battle, not yet anyway. We were in the midst of a dry spell and, for once, I found that to be a pleasant development. I wasn't ready to do battle with Old Man Winter anytime soon, but I knew there would be consequences for the land, and ultimately me, if the rain and snow didn't show up when it was supposed to.

I had hated to leave Herbert behind, especially after he'd told me that he had no plans for staying at the library and really wasn't sure where he was going to go, or what he was going to do. "I can't step foot in that office ever again," he'd said.

I'd told Herbert to check with me if things got tough, if he had no place to go, but he'd said he'd get by, and I had to leave it at that. He hadn't lost his pride, just the center of his universe.

The phone booth on Villard came into view and I was relieved to see an open parking spot in front of it. I guided the Studebaker to the curb and hurried to the pay phone, digging into my purse for a dime. I always had plenty of change, especially when I went into town, so the coin was handy. My hand grazed the pair of broken glasses, another souvenir from this trip, but I tried to ignore them the best I could. I had plenty to do in my life. Tracking down the woman they belonged to was low on my list of things to do at the moment, if ever.

I dialed the phone as quickly as I could and waited for it to ring on the other end. The wind careened up the street, and I was glad to be inside the glass phone booth. Dust and small pebbles pinged at the sides every few seconds. The air turned brown, then the sun cut through the clouds before disappearing again. There was no precipitation, even though the sky was moody, just more wind. I watched a small dirt devil whiz down the street like it was late for an appointment of some kind. Sometimes, I wished the wind would just tire itself out, quit blowing—

just shut up—but I knew that would never happen. The wind was as much a continued presence in my life as the library had always been.

The phone didn't ring. Instead, a cold, surprising busy signal buzzed in my ear. I gritted my teeth, looked at the receiver in disbelief, hung up, retrieved my coin, and dialed the number to my house again. Same thing. Busy: beep, beep, beep.

I knew it had been a mistake charging Betty Walsh with Hank's care. She was nothing more than an irresponsible teenager. She was probably talking to one of her girlfriends or Jaeger, if he had gone back home for something. I didn't know what I had been thinking.

Of course, since my phone was on a party line, the culprit talking up a storm could have been any of my neighbors. A busy signal was as common as a purple martin swooping over a freshly mowed hay field.

I took my dime back again and called Jaeger's house. I had dialed the Knudsens' phone number a thousand times over the years, and I knew it as well as I knew my own. I was relieved when the phone began to ring. But my hope didn't last long, as the phone rang and rang. No one was home. I wanted to scream, but I couldn't find it in myself to let out the frustration I felt.

I tried the number to my house again, but the busy signal persisted, mocking me and chastising me at the same time. I had no choice but to hurry home and give Betty Walsh a good piece of my mind.

I started to calm down a bit as soon as I was free of town. I had always thought that the Ivanhoe was the tallest building in Dickinson, but according to a recent article in the *Press* it was two feet shorter than St. Joseph's Hospital, making it the second tallest building in town. I wasn't sure how that made the proprietor's feel, but the Ivanhoe cast a long and enduring shadow over the business section of town. It was six stories tall, made of brick and concrete, and built in 1952. It had the character of a cardboard box, but it looked sturdy enough to survive the wind and weather for the next couple of centuries. It was a hotel with the best restaurant around, a place where special occasions were celebrated and the most delicious bread to ever slide across your tongue lived deep in the memory of nearly everyone who'd tasted it. Hank and I had eaten there once, a celebration of sorts for a long ago profitable wheat season, but he'd been so uncomfortable with the fanciness of the place that I'd never suggested a return visit. I hadn't ever wanted to see him fidget like that again. Calla and I'd had lunch there more times than I could count, and now I was more like Hank than I'd ever hoped to be. If I never saw the inside of that building again, I would be happier than I could possibly say.

It didn't take long to be back out into the emptiness of open fields, low-lying buttes, and rolling hills, the place where I could breathe, see what was coming, and have plenty of time to react to it. There were no thermals for a hawk to ride, with the sky as gray and unsettled as it was. I spotted a red-tail, most likely a big female, sitting on top of a telephone pole, staring down, waiting for some poor unsuspecting rodent to move about when it shouldn't.

I looked into the rearview mirror, found that I was on the road alone, and pressed down the accelerator as close to the floorboard as I could without jamming the toe of my good shoe through the firewall. The Studebaker shimmied and groaned, then bolted forward with an annoyed lurch. I really needed to talk to Jaeger about giving the old truck a tune-up.

A half hour on an empty road in the middle of land and sky that goes on forever seemed like an exercise in futility. Even though I recognized familiar landmarks, it felt like I wasn't any closer to home than I had been when I'd left town. The roof of my mouth was as dry as the road, and I could taste gravel dust over everything else. It was a wonder that my throat hadn't been cemented shut. A cigarette would have only made things worse, so I passed. Besides, I could still smell the inside of the tavern on my clothes. Hank would be able to smell it, too, but I was sure he'd understand why I felt the need to stop and see to Herbert Frakes once I explained my reasons for going into the tavern. He would have done the same thing, if he'd had the chance, or ability, to do it.

The radio was silent. I had no desire to hear the news or another sad song by a dead singer.

I slowed the truck as the turn to the house came into view. Our property was marked with four-foot cones of rocks as big as pumpkins on both sides of the road. My grandfather had stacked them there one by one, a monument to the work he'd done clearing the first field to plow. Digging rocks was how my father had developed his endurance and strength as a boy, and there had been a time when folks thought this land wouldn't grow anything but boulders and worry. Rocks still rose to the surface like pieces of flotsam in a calm and tamed sea—rocks that could do, and had done, serious damage to a sturdy plow.

I brought the truck to a stop even though I hadn't planned on it. I noticed a six-foot tall plant growing behind the cone of rocks on the north side of the road. It was a dead thistle plant, one like so many others that I hadn't noticed before I started indexing the *Common Plants* book. The weed looked like it belonged there, like it had been growing there since the prehistoric seabed had receded and vanished from sight and memory. But it was possible that I didn't know what I was looking at. It could have been another immigrant, anxious to flee the old country and spread seeds all across the new land, from New York to North Dakota and beyond, just like the rest of us.

Curious, I made my way out of the truck. The wind pushed my dress up as the dry dirt crunched under my feet. I made a halfhearted attempt to pin down my hemline. I was alone, out of view of any house or car for miles; I could have been naked and it wouldn't have mattered. At least to any human. A nearby jackrabbit popped its head up and froze, hoping to blend into the dun landscape like everything else. I didn't let on that I saw it. No use ramping up its heart rate any more than it already was.

Thistle had no practical use that I knew of, which, of course, meant that there was no money to be made from its presence by a farmer or a seed salesman. Just the opposite. The thistle, especially invasive—immigrant—thistle could take over a pasture or field and choke out the healthy, more desirable, grasses and wildflowers. I felt fairly comfortable that I could identify the thistle before me, and upon reaching it I determined fairly quickly that the plant was my illusive and troubling musk thistle.

The plant's spent head drooped, and the brown, crispy bracts looked like little pine cones. The stems were heavily branched, with spiny wings that fluttered outward without interruption. If they had been interrupted, this plant would have been plumeless or bull thistle. The leaves weren't pubescent, and most of the seedless flowers were gone, eaten by birds or other wildlife. There was no doubt in my mind that this was musk thistle.

I reached down and carefully touched *Carduus nutans*. My identification of it was a gift from Leonard Adler's incomplete and maddening description of the plant. Biennial or perennial wasn't obvious. All of the plant was dry and withered, but the spines remained capable of a piercing jab. The tip of my finger immediately itched with warning, and I pulled back in fear of being injured.

I trembled at the thought, at the vision that streamed behind my eyes. Peter and Jaeger had given me the amulet that had been at the heart of their tragedy. It was a souvenir of a time that I wished did not exist. The amulet, too, had been said to offer protection. I was in no mood to revisit Norse mythology, alter my belief system, or consider my past with that amulet any more than I had to, but it seemed to be the right thing to do to take a sprig of the musk thistle with me. I quickly made my way to the Studebaker and grabbed a pair of Hank's faded yellow leather work gloves and trusty pocket Western Auto knife out of the glove box—everything was just where he had left it—then I went back and cut the terminal, the top flower, off the thistle.

Satisfied, I stuck the sprig under the driver's seat and settled back into the truck to go home. I knew that I was being silly, but the musk thistle gave me a little bit of comfort and I needed that, especially after my visit to the Wild Pony with Herbert. Funny thing was, that weed had most likely been here all my life and I'd never noticed it, never had reason to, until now. I wondered if I needed to acknowledge its presence to ignite its magical powers, to call forth Thor's protection.

Maybe that's why my life had taken a horrible turn. I hadn't employed the magic that was on my land. I lacked faith, which was no revelation—and the rest was just drivel. I was sure of it.

I put the truck in gear and drove on.

Shep was waiting for me at the mailbox, overseeing the land like he always had when there was no one home, no one else to worry about. My heart raced a bit as I brought the Studebaker to a hard stop and watched the border collie make his way to me in the rearview mirror. He was slow on the return, casting a glance to and fro, not barking happily—or with warning. My sense of alertness and dread heightened as soon as I realized that there was no sign of Jaeger Knudsen's red International Harvester truck anywhere.

I jumped out of the truck, ignoring Shep, who pushed at my hand for attention of one kind or another, and hurried to the house.

"Betty!" I called out. No answer came, so I called out again and was met with the same silence.

I pushed into the house and made a beeline for the bedroom, screaming for Hank the whole way. I nearly collapsed when I saw that the bed was empty and he was gone.

Gone. Hank was gone. How was that possible?

In his place on the ruffled bed was a note that I could barely read because my hands were shaking so violently:

Mrs. Trumaine, Hank is at the hospital. He was having a hard time breathing so I called Doc Huddleston and he said to get Hank to St. Joseph's as quick as possible. Jaeger put Hank in the truck and we're taking him instead of waiting for the ambulance. I will be there waiting for you. ~~Betty Walsh.

CHAPTER 15

I had spent enough time at St. Joseph's Hospital to suit me for three lifetimes. I was born there, instead of at home like most of the children of the time; I'd watched helplessly as my mother and father died there; and I'd worried over Hank as he hovered between life and death in the long, endless days that followed the accident. It was not a place of happy memories, but then I guess a hospital rarely is.

I could have driven to the hospital with my eyes closed, even in a panic. But not in a panic mixed with rage, fear, and fury. The speed limit wasn't a concern because I could only go as fast as the Studebaker would allow. A speeding ticket was the least of my worries.

I couldn't believe that Hank's breathing had failed enough since I'd left him with Betty Walsh that he needed to be hospitalized. I found myself annoyed with her, but I would have to control my temper, or at least swallow it. I feared telling Betty off, for no other reason than alienating and upsetting Jaeger. I knew him well enough to know that he wouldn't take too kindly to someone yelling at his girlfriend. Not even me. And I needed him more now than ever before. I would be lost without Jaeger Knudsen looking after our farm.

I wheeled the truck into the hospital parking lot, squealing the tires on the turn. I'm sure that wasn't uncommon at the Castle of Life and Death—that's what the six-story red brick building with the green slate-tile roof looked like to me, an old musty castle with a terrible dungeon inside. It was only missing the spires and cathedral roof.

I feared that Hank would be dead by the time I arrived, and I would be left with the guilt of him dying without me at his side. I'd promised him I would be there no matter what. *I'm sorry, I was at the*

Wild Pony, consoling Herbert Frakes instead of looking after you. I didn't want to have to live with that.

Of all that could happen to hasten Hank's demise, I think I feared pneumonia the most. It was an invisible killer that always seemed to be lurking just outside our bedroom door, waiting like a snake in the grass for just the right time to strike. And it looked like it had waited until I left, until I wasn't there to shoo it away, cut its head off once and for all. Warding off pneumonia was out of my power.

I should have never left him with Betty Walsh . . .

It didn't matter to me that St. Joseph's was the tallest building in Dickinson. To me, at that moment, it was the *only* building in Dickinson.

I parked in the closest spot I could find and hurried inside the door marked EMERGENCY. I whizzed past two nuns in full black habits without acknowledging them. They looked at me in unison, with a glare that I didn't care to understand, and kept on walking.

A dainty older woman, with hair as silver as a brand new car bumper looked up from a crossword puzzle as I hurried to the information desk. I knew her. She was a cousin to Burlene Standish. Her name was Olga Olafson, and she had a similar reputation as Burlene when it came to being interested in all of the gossip that went on about town. I was in no mood for idle chitchat.

"I was a wonderin' where you were, Marjorie," Olga said. She had on a white crocheted sweater that looked like it had just been bought at the church bazaar. It was buttoned all the way to the top, pinching the wrinkles that had come naturally with age on her throat. With her glasses and pursed lips, she looked like an old fish about to exhale or explode, I couldn't tell which. She smelled of prune juice and moth balls.

"Hank's here then?" I said.

Olga nodded. Her glasses had a chain on the shafts just like Calla's always had. A pang of recognition flickered in the pit of my stomach.

"Came in with that Knudsen boy. Doc Huddleston just came in, too. Must've got the call that Hank was dire."

Dire? "He was fine when I left home." I glanced at a set of double doors marked NO ADMITTANCE that I'd passed through more than once and knew that Hank was in one of three emergency bays. "Which one's he in?"

"Oh, I can't let you just wander back there, Marjorie. I have to call first and get permission. New rules. The sisters don't want just anyone walking in and out. There's awful things goin' on from time to time back there. You don't know what you might see, and it would be a sin for them to inflict any undue suffering on you. You have to sign in, too." Olga produced a clipboard with a log on it. "Print your name and then sign it. I'll call back and let them know you're here."

I took the clipboard but made no effort to pick up the pen that was on the front lip of Olga's neatly organized desk. "If I don't get an answer in one minute flat, I'm walking through those doors regardless of permission. I'm not afraid of a nun."

"Like to see you try, Marjorie. Those doors are locked. No one gets in or out without me pressing this newfangled buzzer to open the door." Olga pointed underneath the desk like a child with a new toy.

I shook my head, exhaled, and stared at the ceiling. "Can you call back?" I said through gritted teeth.

"Of course I can." She picked up the phone, stuck her gnarled index finger in the rotary hole marked three, and dialed it quickly.

It was one of those moments where seconds felt like hours. I was trapped, kept from Hank with no way that I could see to reach him without making a full-blown scene—which I was on the very edge of anyway. All things considered, the events of the day had left my emotions dry and out of check. I preferred to think of myself as weathered, able to withstand the most difficult of circumstances without losing my head, but the requirement of patience and tact, at the moment, was the least of my concerns.

"Mrs. Trumaine is here," Olga said into the black plastic mouthpiece of the telephone. She waited a second, and then said, "Of course," and put the receiver back in its cradle.

She looked at me, feigned a smile, and punched the buzzer. It echoed throughout the empty waiting room. "You can go back, Marjorie."

"It's about damn time," I said, spinning on my heels and marching away without offering so much as a thank you.

I was certain my reputation and lack of social skills was going to get spread across Dickinson, but to be honest I didn't care. I didn't care at all what that old biddy thought of me at that very moment.

CHAPTER 16

H ank had been easy to find. There were no other patients in the emergency room, and Jaeger and Betty Walsh stood sentinel outside the last bay. The hospital bed was enclosed with a thick blue curtain, and there was no one else to be seen. The lights were dim, and distant sounds of monitors beeped. An air conditioner or rooftop machine of some other kind groaned through the vents. It was like I had just stepped back in time. Nothing in the emergency room had changed since the last time I'd been there—except the presence of Jaeger Knudsen and Betty Walsh.

The full force of the antiseptic hospital aroma that I had come to expect hit my nose. It seemed thicker with ammonia than I remembered, and my eyes started to water almost immediately. I was sure the reaction was from the smell; I'd done everything I could to hold myself together.

This is a mistake. I'll just pack Hank up and take him home where he belongs.

Jaeger looked up as I rushed down the corridor toward him. I'm sure I looked like I was on a mission. The idea of rescue was fully planted in my mind and heart, even though the reality around me suggested just the opposite. Hospitals were temples of change, of mortality. You never left as the same person you were when you entered it, patient or visitor.

Jaeger's face was pale and grim. He looked like all of the summer sun had been drained from him and left outside the hospital door. I made it to him in record time.

"Doc Huddleston's in with him now," Jaeger said, averting his eyes from mine as quickly as he could. He glanced at the slit in the curtain.

Words bubbled at the tip of my tongue, and I could feel the hateful acid that had brewed and was ready to pour out of my mouth as I took note of Betty Walsh. She didn't look as grim as Jaeger. As a matter of fact, she didn't look grim at all; she stood tall, with her shoulders straight and a satisfied turn on her bright red, recently refreshed lips. She looked entirely pleased with herself. Which only infuriated me more. Sexy red was not the color I had hoped to see.

"I'll deal with you in a minute," I said to Betty, as I turned to push my way through the curtains.

Betty Walsh started to say something and that stopped me dead in my tracks. "Don't," I ordered, pointing my index finger at her at the same time. "Just don't." And without waiting for a smug response, or something that I would consider to be throwing gas on a growing fire, I nearly jumped through the blue curtains. The truth was, I was saying "don't" as much to myself as I was to Betty Walsh.

I nearly tackled Doc Huddleston with my entrance into the room, if it could have been called that. He was standing at the foot of the hospital bed, writing on a chart, and he had to use all of his balancing skills not to drop the clipboard and pen onto the sparkling clean white floor. The overhead light nearly blinded me and was such a shock to my retinas that I feared joining Hank in his blindness. Fortunately, my vision returned almost immediately.

Doc was a tall man, a few inches over six feet, of Danish descent, with hair as white and thick as a cotton ball, and a beard that looked like it belonged on a nineteenth-century president's stern face. The beard was long and wavy, always meticulously combed, and stopped mid-chest; I knew no other man that wore such a beard. If he'd had a belly and puffy cheeks, Doc would have made a great Santa, but neither was the case. He was thin as a rail, and I had never seen him be jolly.

"Marjorie," Doc said, regaining his composure. There was no annoyance in his voice. Just surprise. "I've been expecting you."

The collision with Doc had been as much of a surprise to me as it was to him. It was like running headlong into the side of an Angus bull. It took me a second to recover. When I did, I couldn't believe what I was seeing.

Hank was encased in a clear plastic tent. It looked like a see-through coffin, and I didn't like that idea at all. The image of him was blurry, like I was looking at him through tearful eyes—which I wasn't. Yet.

A plastic dome-shaped hood sealed the outside environment away from Hank. Oxygen-rich air was being pumped into the tent, forcing the regular atmosphere to the top, into the dome. A noisy pump, regular as a ticking clock, sat at the side of the bed, along with three tall green canisters of oxygen. NO SMOKING signs were posted everywhere—which explained why there was no cigarette dangling from the corner of Doc's lip. He was rarely without a Tareyton, even in the hospital. There were no ashtrays anywhere to be seen, either. A series of tubes ran out of the tent, all leading to a set of controls that looked more suited to a spaceship than a hospital room. My mind wondered for a second, curious about the buildup of carbon dioxide inside the tent—where it went—but that question would have to wait.

"Is this necessary?" I said to Doc. "He was fine when I left the house. I mean, I heard a rattle this morning, but it was distant, and I just heard it once. I wasn't sure . . ."

Doc Huddleston looked at me curiously. He was not the most easygoing man I had ever met, but there was no sign that he had taken offense at my questioning him. He had dealt with me enough to know that I was born without the capability of holding my tongue or hiding my attitude.

"Of course it is necessary, Marjorie; otherwise I would have driven Hank home myself. It's a precaution that I hope wards off any further deterioration in Hank's condition. Those kids did the right thing by calling me. You just relax a bit now. He's fine. Exactly where he needs to be." Doc went silent and looked over at Hank. His tone and eyes finished saying, "I know what's best for Hank, trust me." But I wasn't convinced. I didn't trust anybody when it came to Hank's care. Not even myself.

I followed Doc's gaze and walked to the side of the bed and looked in at Hank, who was wide awake and staring back at me like a goldfish in a giant aquarium. He looked so small, distant, withered, but there was no mistaking his eyes and the fact that he wasn't afraid or worried about himself, but he was concerned about me. You stay married long enough, you know that look.

"Are you all right, Marjorie?" Doc asked. It was a concerned, low-key tone, one that had nothing to do with Hank. I'd known Doc Huddleston all of my married life and before, so we had a past to refer to. He knew me like a book.

I looked away from Hank and shrugged. "I wasn't home. I was at the library," I said.

"You're upset about Calla Eltmore." It wasn't a question.

"How could I not be?"

"It is a sad situation, Marjorie. One I don't have any more comprehension of than anyone else."

"It *was* suicide then?"

"It appears so. Why would you think it's not?"

I shrugged again. "It just doesn't seem like something Calla would do."

"You knew her well?"

"Maybe not as well as I thought. We shared knowledge, not secrets."

"These kinds of things are always a shock to the system," Doc said. "You question yourself, how good of a friend you were and why you weren't a better one, why you didn't see it coming, weren't there to help. But the truth is, Marjorie, none of us know another human being's true pain unless they reach out for help. Calla didn't do that. The only knowledge we have now is that she is no longer in any kind of pain."

"No, I guess she's not." I turned my attention back to Hank, back to the oxygen tent. I wanted to reach inside and take his hand, crawl into bed with him, and forget about the hole in my heart that belonged to Calla Eltmore.

I knew Hank was uncomfortable, even though he wouldn't show it. But I couldn't touch him. I was barred from that, and just the thought of such a thing agitated me to no end.

"Can I lift this?" I wouldn't have asked, but underneath all of the NO SMOKING signs was another message conveying the severity of the situation. The oxygen was highly explosive. I'd read enough to know that it wasn't as unstable as nitroglycerin, but still, I hesitated. I didn't want to blow Hank up.

"No," Doc said. "Not now. We'll change out the dome every three hours to clear the bad air; you can touch him and talk to him then. He'll be in his own room by then. Chances are the tent is temporary."

"What am I supposed to do between now and then?"

"Wait. You have to wait in the waiting room, Marjorie. You can't stay in here with Hank. I'll let you know if you're needed . . . or the nurses will," Doc said, then turned and exited the bay in a hurry. I'm sure there was a Tareyton in his mouth the second he was free of the explosion zone.

I watched the curtains settle, then turned my attention back to Hank.

"Go," he mouthed. "I'll be fine."

I sighed, lowered my head, and nodded that I would. I had no choice but to do as he ordered. This wasn't the time to put up a fight.

CHAPTER 17

"I'll look after Shep and the place while you're here," Jaeger said. He stood in the same place I'd left him. There was no sign of Betty Walsh, and for the moment I was thankful for that.

I nodded and looked past Jaeger, into the waiting room I had been relegated to by Doc Huddleston. It was small, a little over twice the size of the mudroom in our house, packed with chairs that bore orange cushions made of hard plastic and miserable to sit on for any length of time. They squeaked like a mouse every time you shifted your weight. I knew that from my last stint waiting outside the emergency room. The only change in the room was that a television set had been added. It sat on an aluminum stand and was turned off at the moment. It was like a gray twenty-inch eye staring at me. I looked away from it, back to Jaeger.

"I don't plan on being here long," I said. "No need to trouble yourself." It was a typical defense, even though I didn't know if it was the truth or not. "Shep will be happy to see you," I said, trying not to sound discouraging.

"Is there anything I can bring you?" Jaeger said.

"No, I had enough sense about me after reading your note to grab up the few things I'll need." That was the truth. I had a bag packed just for such occasions, with all of my necessaries in it. It was in the truck, along with a stack of page proofs for the *Common Plants* book and a couple of unopened packets of index cards. I could do my work anywhere, though I would have to write the entries on the index cards instead of typing them. I didn't have the best cursive writing in the world, but I could print as well as anyone. I could read my own writing when it came to compiling the index, and it didn't really matter in the end if the cards were typed or handwritten. My editor would never see them. All I sent him was the freshly typed index. I had a closet full of shoeboxes with index cards in them. I couldn't bear the thought of throwing them out or burning them in the trash barrel, even though they were as useless as thistle.

"You can call to the house if you think of something," Jaeger said. He turned and started to walk away after I offered a silent okay.

"Jaeger?" I said.

He stopped. "Yes?"

"Where's Betty?"

Jaeger looked down and kicked some imaginary dirt off the Linoleum floor. "She's waitin' out in the truck for me."

"Why's that? I wanted to thank her for having the good sense to call Doc Huddleston."

Jaeger looked up and stared me in the eye. "She thinks you're mad at her, Mrs. Trumaine. Mad for bringin' Hank here. But it was my idea to call the doctor. Hank was struggling to breathe like a fish out of water. I just couldn't stand to think of him panicking any more than he already was. I was scared for him. Betty left because she was scared of what you would do or say."

I suddenly felt very ashamed of myself. I stepped up to him and touched his shoulder gently. "I'm sorry. It's been a difficult couple of days. Calla Eltmore's death has come as a shock and shaken me to my core. And I always worry over Hank, over pneumonia. I feared this day would come more than most. I'm sorry. I've acted like a mean old harpy. I'll apologize to Betty the next time I see her. I've been without my manners for a few days."

"It's okay."

"No, it's not really okay. It's not okay, Jaeger. I know you're fond of Betty. I didn't mean anything by it."

He hesitated. "You don't like her much do you?"

"I don't know her well enough not to like her, Jaeger. I just worry about you, that's all. Your parents aren't around to give you any advice, and I'm not sure it's my place to. You're a grown man with a grown man's problems. But you lack experience and wisdom. I just don't want to see you make a mistake that'll wreck your life. You've got enough to overcome the way it is."

"I get lonely in that house by myself." It was a whisper, and there was no mistaking the pain in Jaeger's voice.

I pulled him to me and hugged him the best I could. I wasn't his mother, I wasn't Lida, but I could offer him some of the same comfort. If I'd ever had a son, I would have been proud to have had one just like Jaeger Knudsen.

"Just promise me you'll be careful," I said, pulling back, looking him in the eye. "You know what I mean by that, right?"

He nodded. "Yes, yes, ma'am, I think I do." Then he turned away and started down the hall. "Call me if you need anything," he said over his shoulder.

"I will."

Jaeger disappeared, and I was left to myself. It was just me and the television in the waiting room, both of us void of energy and left with nothing to think about but the ghosts in our memory.

Time slipped away. I'd settled into the hard, orange, plastic-cushioned chair and stared at the silent television after Jaeger had left, tempted to turn it on for company, but uncertain of it enough to stay seated, alone.

The hospital remained eerily quiet. Every once in a while, the automatic door opened, and I could hear Olga Olafson talking above everyone else. She must have come from a large brood of children, all vying for attention, the loudest one the victor. But beyond that, I hadn't seen any sign of Doc Huddleston. Just an occasional nurse I didn't know and who didn't bother to stop and chat. They always seemed to be in a hurry. I was glad a nun hadn't wandered through the emergency room without stopping, too. They made me uncomfortable. I was certain I was going to say something wrong. Even though my Lutheran training was closely tied to the Catholic faith, I knew little about nuns and priests, their life of celibacy, and their idols and saints. Martin Luther had fled the church for his own reasons, and I pretty much shared them. I'd been born into a Lutheran household—at Momma's insistence. Left to his own devices, Father would have worshiped at the library first and out on the land second. I most likely would have felt different if I'd been born into a Catholic home. But I hadn't, and the cold sternness of the nuns who roamed the halls of St. Joseph had always unsettled me and most likely always would. I lacked the ability to understand their sacrifice, their faith, their humanity.

I was tired, and, while I should have been working on the *Common Plants* index, I sat there and dozed in and out, my mind fluttering from the events of the day. I couldn't have slept if I'd wanted to, but it felt good to close my eyes and give them a rest.

The emergency room doors groaned open and startled me out of my torpid state. I opened my eyes, hoping to see Doc ready to go in and change out the dome, but that's not who it was.

It was Guy Reinhardt, the Stark County deputy sheriff I'd spoken to last when I'd called the library. He had a deep, concerned look on his face as he made his way over to me.

CHAPTER 18

I stood up to meet Guy's approach. My gaze looked directly into his chest, since he was at least a head and a half taller than me. The silver star over his heart glimmered in the fluorescent light. He had his campaign hat off and carried it with his right hand. The hat resembled a Mountie's hat, only dark brown instead of Canadian tan. It matched his Stark County sheriff's department uniform.

Guy's head bore a red indented rim in the flesh, like the hat had been permanently attached—or done permanent damage to his skull. Gray flecks peppered his perfectly trimmed sideburns and hair, a few shades lighter brown than the hat, which was neatly parted and recently cut. I couldn't remember a time when I'd ever seen Guy and he hadn't been wearing his uniform. But if I had, I would have recognized him anywhere. He was hard to miss, as tall as he was. The Gary Cooper limp that accompanied his easy gait was even harder to mistake.

"I was hopin' you'd still be here, Marjorie," Guy said.

He stopped a few feet from me, but I could smell his aftershave—Old Spice mixed with a healthy dose of vim and vigor. At that moment, I preferred the antiseptic hospital smell I'd grown accustomed to.

"Doesn't look like I'll be going anywhere anytime soon, Guy. Is something the matter?" I said.

"No, I just ran into Jaeger Knudsen earlier, and he told me about Hank. How is he?"

I looked at my feet, trying the best I could to conjure a lie, but I lacked the desire and the creativity to make something up. Besides, there was no hiding anything from Guy. "I don't know. Doc Huddleston has him in an oxygen tent as a precaution. Everything seems to be all right, but you never know with someone who's in a condition like Hank is."

"It's a hard road, Marjorie."

I'd heard that phrase so many times in the last year, I could've screamed. But I didn't say a word and tried not to show my discomfort on my face. Guy meant no harm, and he couldn't have known what he'd said was a bad thing. It just was to me. One full year of it. *Happy Anniversary.*

I looked up at Guy and at that second I wasn't sure if he meant it was a hard road for Hank, for me, or for both of us. He had striking blue eyes, the color of a clear summer sky, and they seemed sincere. I was being sensitive because I really didn't know how to take Guy. I really didn't know him that well, even though we'd been though a trying time together a few months back.

"I'm sure Hank'll be fine. He's always bounced back before," I said.

"I suppose it's hard not to hope so," Guy said. He darted his eyes away and hid his ringless left hand behind the campaign hat like a hawk afraid to lose its supper to an approaching coyote. He seemed suddenly flustered, nervous for some reason.

I held back mentioning anything about his personal life. I'd heard that Guy and his second wife, Ruth, had finalized their divorce. A second divorce was a scandal in these parts and proof that Guy Reinhardt was damaged goods—regardless of who was at fault in either divorce. It would be a difficult character flaw to overcome in an election—since I knew that Guy had ambitions to become the sheriff. Though Duke Parsons held that position now and would most likely run in the upcoming emergency election.

"If there's anything you need, Marjorie . . ." Guy continued.

"Thanks, Guy. Jaeger's helping out at our place. He's picked up as much extra work as he could and has been a big help. He's got a new hand now, too."

"I heard he took on Lester Gustaffson. That's a good move, but he'll need more'n Les come spring."

I agreed with a nod. "He knows that." I paused, trying my best not to bring up a bad subject, but I knew I had no choice. Even with my current situation focused on Hank, I was still bereft about Calla. "Last time I talked to you," I said, "you were at the library."

"A sad day," Guy said. "I sure liked Miss Eltmore, and I was surprised to find her like that."

"You found her?"

"Well, no, not right off. That was Herbert. He came in for the day, and she was at her desk. Wasn't no use tryin' to save her from what Herb said. I'd just come on duty, got the call, and wasn't but a couple of minutes away."

That made sense. Herbert had told me he'd found Calla. I sighed and shook my head.

"What's the matter, Marjorie?"

"You really think she did it, Guy? Do you really think that Calla stuck that gun to her head and killed herself?"

"Well, what else would it be, Marjorie? Lord, it was a hard thing to see. I gotta tell you that, but it looked plain and simple to me and Duke, and to the coroner, Pete McClandon, too. What else are you sayin', Marjorie?"

"I'm not saying anything; I'm just wondering, that's all. Asking a question, right? I can't help myself. It just doesn't make any sense to me that Calla would have done such a thing."

"It's a shock, Marjorie."

"Everybody keeps saying that. But it's more than a shock; it's a puzzle piece that doesn't fit anywhere. Did she leave a note, Guy? Herbert didn't see one."

"You talked to Herbert?"

"I was worried about him. Found him at the Wild Pony. He's tore up, Guy, and just as confused as I am. Calla was my friend, and she didn't give me the slightest hint that she would ever do something like this. *Ever*, Guy. *Ever*. Calla Eltmore loved life, her job, books. All you had to do was watch her. She wasn't a depressed person. She was smart, engaged, well-read, and never ever mentioned that she was unhappy. I talked to her frequently. I would have picked up on something wrong. I'm sure of it."

"We don't know people as well as we think we do, Marjorie."

"Did she leave a note, Guy?"

He stepped back, looked up and down the hall, then back to me. "You know I can't say anything about that, Marjorie. Duke would fire me quicker than a happy dog waggin' its tail if he knew I told you something about an ongoing investigation."

"It's ongoing? Why?"

"Just a practical matter, Marjorie, until the coroner signs off on the death. Standard operating procedure. Just the rules, that's all." He stared at me with some pity. "Don't you have enough burdens to carry? Why are you all worried about something like this? It looks like Calla Eltmore committed suicide, plain and simple, except I can't say that officially till everybody else says it. I'm sorry, it's just that way. You just have to accept that there's eyes on this that know exactly what they are looking at. Calla Eltmore is dead, and there's nothin' we can do to put things back the way they was. As hard as it is to believe, she's gone, Marjorie. I'm sorry about that. I really am."

A pulse of anger shot up my spine. Guy's tone was typical. A man telling a woman what to do, what to think, because he said so. Hank took that tone with me on occasion, but he'd been fool enough to do it more than he should have after we'd first married, and he'd learned the hard way that I wasn't the kind of woman who bowed to the status of a man just because he said so. I was raised by both of my parents to have my own mind, to stand up for myself. I was the son my father never had and the daughter my mother had hoped for. I was no doormat, even if I was a woman.

"Is that the sheriff department's official stand?" I demanded.

Guy blew out a deep breath and tensed up at the same time. "There's nothing for you to question here, Marjorie. I'm sure of it. I'm sorry to have bothered you." He turned to leave, then stopped short of breaking into a run. "Give my regards to Hank. I hope he gets to go home soon." He completed his turn, put his Mountie hat back on, and scurried away.

I was left again with my thoughts and regrets. But no matter how I looked at it, I couldn't just accept what someone told me to accept because it looked like the plain and simple truth. Calla's death deserved more respect than that.

CHAPTER 19

The real world and the time it abided by ceased to exist inside the confines of the hospital. Schedules and routines were clear as long as everything moved as it should, without a crisis, without an alarm that brought nurses and doctors running to save the day. But beyond that, the minutes dragged into hours, and the hours quickly accumulated, promising to turn into long, exhausting days. The dull white walls, acoustic tiled ceilings, and white shiny linoleum floors never changed, never offered a hint of weather. They were void of any emotion or cheer. I could never predict what was next, though I constantly sat on the edge of my chair waiting for bad news. I couldn't outrun this pure white storm. It was early winter without the deep freeze.

For someone accustomed to seven hundred acres of open space and solitude, it didn't take long for the walls to start closing in, for claustrophobia to set in. I paced the halls, toured the cafeteria, wished for a library, dodged the nuns, and read all of the *Life* and *Field and Stream* magazines that I could find, constantly looking for a distraction. I'd never been enamored with Hollywood, but I found pictures of the deceased Marilyn Monroe to be sad and lonely, no help at all in propelling me out of the doldrums that I was stuck in. Other magazines were devoted to President Kennedy. I avoided them like they were infected with a disease I could easily catch. I understood all too well the loss of a vibrant, healthy man in his prime—or just the loss of the simplicity of living a full life and dying of old age.

Hank had stabilized and the rattle in his chest had subsided, thanks to the miracles of modern medicine—an oxygen tent and consistent doses of penicillin and other more mundane drugs to boost his strength. Doc Huddleston assured me more than once that if his body had been left to its own devices, Hank would never have survived this latest battle to breathe, to live, to stay on this earth with me. I'd asked him not to tell Hank that for fear that he would swear off the medicine and treatment without my knowledge. There was no question in my mind that he was capable of that. No matter how withered and frail he was, Hank Trumaine was still fully in charge of what came next—at least verbally.

In between visits with Hank, usually ten minutes at a time, every three hours; consultations with Doc Huddleston, who remained optimistic that Hank would get to go home soon; and appropriate and expected visits from Pastor John Mark Llewellyn from the Lutheran church where Hank and I were still members, although not regular attendees, two days passed before I had fully realized it.

I'd slept in the waiting room on a dull and lifeless mattress thrown over two chairs that I had pushed together. I was glad I wasn't as tall as Guy Reinhardt; I would never have found any comfort at all. And I was aided by a few sweet nurses who had brought me pillows, sheets, and a blanket to stay warm.

The hospital was as cold as the tip of an iceberg at night, and I had failed to plan for the onset of October weather. I could hardly believe it was mid-fall, nearly winter, even though the skies were constantly gray and filled with the threat of turmoil when I looked out the windows. Winter was never far away, and summer was always too brief a reprieve. I'd seen it snow in June once and knew from then on that the coldest season of the year never fully retreated; it was like a bug under a rock just waiting for the right time or right opportunity to make its presence known, to sneak out and sting when you least expected it.

I worked in that small room, too, occasionally accompanied by visitors there to see their own sick relatives and to do their duty just like me. A few times I'd been asked, "What are you doing?" and without any thought, I replied, "Writing an index." To which the response was almost always, "How do you do that?" or "What is that?"

I should have just kept my mouth shut, but I think there were times when I was glad to have a conversation with someone that didn't concern death and dying.

I had finished going through all the pages of the *Common Plants* book, and I hadn't come across any more questions that I couldn't answer for myself. The last thing I wanted to do was call the library and speak with Delia Finch. I'd tried to put that woman as far out of my mind as possible. Now all I had to do was find the time to go home, compile the entries that I'd already typed or written into one document, edit it, and then send it to my editor, Richard Rothstein.

It was early afternoon, and Hank was out from under the tent for his longest stretch since he'd been admitted to the hospital. Doc was weaning him off the oxygen, and Hank really was doing well, looking forward to going home in the next couple of days.

I was free of the waiting room, which smelled more like cigarette smoke—with a few contributions from me—than the antiseptic room that Hank was moored in, when Hank looked over at me and asked, "When is Calla's funeral?"

I knew; I had looked at her obituary in the *Press*, but I had tried not to read it too closely. I had just scanned it to make sure it really was about Calla. Guy had gotten to me—I had decided he was right. I had enough burdens of my own to deal with. But it was a fool's game I was playing with myself. I knew I wouldn't be able to stay away from my questions about Calla's death any more than a June bug could stay away from the dusk-to-dawn light at the peak of the garage roof.

"Tomorrow," I finally said.

"Is there calling?"

I nodded. "This evening for a few hours."

"And you're going, aye?"

I stood up and walked to the door of the room, which was closed. I pressed my head against it for a long second, trying to convince myself to say "yes," then made my way back to Hank's bed so I could hear him speak. "I hadn't planned on it," I said, gripping the bed rails with both of my hands to steady myself. I couldn't lie to Hank. Blind as he was, he could see it from a mile away.

He cocked his head at me and offered a furtive glance with his blank eyes. It was more habit than anything else, and as much as he could read me, I could still read him, too. Blindness had been a recent malady, and I was sure his body still responded just like it always had. "I think you should go," he said. "You've been holed up in this hospital since I came in, and to be honest, I think it's getting to you. You're snippy and prone to bite the head off of anyone who disagrees with you. Some fresh air will do you good."

"I am not snippy." I let go of the bedrails and planted both of my hands on my hips.

After a long beat, he said, "My point exactly, Marjorie. You need to go to the calling, but more than anything, you need to get out of this hospital for a little while. It'll do me some good too, to know you're still doing the things that you need to. I hate it that I crippled both of us."

I let those words drift away and relaxed my arms at the same time. I wanted to ask him who the patient was and who the concerned spouse was, but I held my tongue. "I'm not leaving you," I whispered.

"I'm not going anywhere." Hank's voice was weak but certainly stronger than it had been in days. There was no mistaking the sincerity of his words. He had just fought a battle and won, had come out on the other side with the ability to breathe on his own quicker than anyone thought he would be able to. But I knew how fleeting those victories could be. I had left him at the house with Betty Walsh, only to come back and find him gone. I feared finding the same thing all over again when I returned to the hospital room.

"Do you promise?" I demanded, trying to push the image of an empty hospital bed from my mind.

"Yes," Hank said. "I promise. Scout's honor. I'd make a cross over my chest if I could."

"Don't do that; the nuns will tell you you're doing it wrong."

"Maybe I am. Maybe that's the problem." He forced a smile, then looked away from me for a quick second. "I'll be right here when you get back, Marjorie. Go pay your respects to Calla for both of us. I know she was your friend, not mine, but she made *our* life better. She was always there for you. What would you have done without her with all of your book work?"

Book work. That was what Hank always called my indexing jobs. It was like farm work to him, the only way he could understand it. An index was a tool that Hank seldom used, and he had no interest in knowing how it worked or how to create one. He just wanted it when he needed it—like the horribly written one in the back of the owner's manual for the combine. He'd used that one over and over learning the ins and outs of the new machine.

"Besides," he continued, "I'm sure Herbert'll be happy to see you."

I sighed. "All right. You're right; I *should* go. But I didn't bring my good clothes to town with me. I'll need to go out to the house and get ready."

"I'm sure Shep'll be happy to see you, too. That dog likes you more than he ever did me."

I ignored the comment because it was true. I looked up at the clock over Hank's bed and calculated the time it would take to drive home, dress, then drive back to the funeral home. "If I'm going to go to the calling, then I need to leave now," I said.

"Then you better get going," Hank said. "Or you'll be late and miss it altogether."

CHAPTER 20

T he house looked the same as it had when I'd left it last, only Jaeger had brought in the mail and stacked it neatly on the kitchen table. Shep danced around my feet, trying to fill up on the attention he had lost out on since I'd been away. I ignored him the best I could and riffled through the pile of envelopes, hoping for a check for the last index I'd written, but I only found more bills than I cared to admit ownership of. There was seed debt, the combine payment, and overdue medical bills to pay. Along with the bills in my hands, there was a mortgage and the expenses of daily living to contend with. We'd barely broke even on last season's crop, and the dry spell we were in the midst of didn't foretell a positive cash flow for the winter wheat that was already in the ground—and not yet paid for. The truth was, my indexing income barely kept the lights on. One of these days, all of our debts were going to catch up with us and come due all at once—but not right now. Not today, not while Hank still breathed and fought to live. I tried to make money the least of my concerns. Hank worried enough in his silence for both of us.

I dropped the bills on the table and set about getting myself prepared to leave again, even though I wished I could have just stayed home with my dog at my feet, doing the work I loved—all while Hank tended to a bounty crop on the back forty. It was a fantasy that would never come true—more magical thinking, more wasted time on wishing for something that could never be. Those days were gone, and just like I had to accept Calla's fate I knew I had to accept my own whether I liked it or not.

Time ticked away with each breath. As much as I wanted to ignore the clock, I knew I couldn't. Calla's calling was in an hour, and Hank was lying in his hospital bed awaiting my return.

It wasn't long before I was back in the Studebaker, rattling my way toward Dickinson, feeling like a yo-yo. I was loaded down with proof pages from the *Zhanzheng* book—which I began to fully consider now that all of the entries for the *Common Plants* book were written—enough clothes and essentials to last three days, and a heavy heart for leaving Shep behind again. I was certain that the nuns would cart him off to the dog pound if they found him snuggled up with me in my makeshift bed in the waiting room. It was a nice thought, but not worth the risk. I needed Shep and he needed me. If I was sure of anything at that moment, it was that.

"I'll be home soon, boy, I promise," I heard myself saying. *I'll be home soon . . .*

The parking lot to McClandon's Funeral Home was nearly empty. I didn't know what I had been expecting, but I certainly didn't think that I would be the only library patron in town who felt that Calla Eltmore held one of the most important jobs in the entire county. But maybe I was wrong. Maybe Calla was just the old, dried-up woman who checked out their books when they wanted them. I was filled with a deep, uncomfortable sadness as I parked the truck up near the front door.

When Erik and Lida Knudsen were shown in the funeral home, there hadn't been a parking spot to be found. Guy Reinhardt had had to direct traffic. But I guess folks were curious because that was a murder and this was a suicide. Even though there wasn't an official word on the cause of Calla's death, the gossip chain in town had pronounced it to be true. Betty Walsh's original pronouncement at the house was proof of that.

Suicide made everything different, and I knew it. Murder was an unprovoked nightmare, and suicide was a self-inflicted sin. The darkest sin. A commandment broken with blatant disregard for anything that was believed or held in faith—or outside of it, for that matter.

Thou shall not kill was the highest order in the land—unless it was lamb season—and Calla Eltmore had broken that commandment. Her memory would be forever shunned, or at the very least ignored, not spoken of in polite company from here on out. It was almost as if suicide was contagious, a disease transmitted by touch or thought.

I was in no mood for such thinking, and for that I was glad of the sparse showing of mourners' cars in the parking lot. I wouldn't have to face the gossip and the judgmental sneers as I made my way up to the casket to say my goodbyes.

Without another moment of thought, or giving in to the temptation of putting the truck in reverse and speeding back to the hospital, I squared myself, glanced in the mirror to make sure my face and hair were presentable, then pushed the creaky driver's door open and marched toward the entrance to the funeral home. It opened upon my approach almost on command, as if someone had been watching me the entire time—just waiting. The solemn act unsettled me.

I stepped over the threshold and stopped just inside the foyer. The overbearing and unwanted smell of the funeral home hit my nose in a floral explosion of blossoming life that could only be associated with death. It was such a mix of scents that my mind, usually prone to sorting and listing identifiable substances, was confused and scattered. I knew it was more than the jumble of flowers all vying for my attention, demanding to be categorized. It was the fact that I was about see to Calla in her final state. Unless the casket was closed. *Please let it be closed . . .*

"Miss Eltmore, I presume," a man's familiar voice said.

I looked over and made eye contact with Pete McClandon, proprietor of the funeral home and the current Stark County coroner. I had known Pete for most of my life, and to be honest he looked the same now as he did when I was a young girl. He had to be in his early eighties, and his hair was still as black as the underbelly of a crow. I wondered if he colored it with shoe polish. It looked like it—either that or Rit dye. His face held deep worry lines, rivulets of time cut through weathered flesh that made him look hard, like a marble sculpture had been set on his shoulders instead of a soft human face. His gray eyes were cloudy but still as warm and comforting as they could be in any circumstance. Pete McClandon had a quick smile and a hearty handshake on most days, except when he was working the front of the funeral home; then he was the tower of sadness, quiet and respectful. Like now, like he had been for both my parents and Hank's and for so many of our friends.

"Yes, of course, I'm here to see Calla Eltmore," I said to Pete, never breaking eye contact with him. I wondered if there were any other funerals in the coming days. I hadn't checked the paper to see.

"Straight ahead." Pete pointed the way. He was wearing his signature black suit, which made him look the same as always. I'd never seen him dressed any other way. Always in black, like it was a cloak he couldn't escape or a military uniform he refused to discard.

I hesitated; I had a flood of questions that I wanted to ask Pete, but I knew he wouldn't answer them, couldn't answer them. *Did she really kill herself? Why does a person do that? You've seen it before, you have to know . . .* I exhaled instead and walked slowly toward the open double doors that led into the parlor that held Calla's casket. The walk was lined with bouquets of colorful flowers, but one thing was missing from each of them: a card. It was like no one wanted to be associated with a suicide but had sent flowers out of respect anyway—or the funeral home had put them there so the showing, the funeral, would appear normal for those who did attend. That made sense.

The parlor was long and narrow and also served as a chapel for those that chose not to have their funerals in a church. The walls were stark white and the ceiling was arched, the rafters dark walnut with a high sheen. The center of the room was filled with folding chairs, all spaced evenly, row after row, waiting to be filled. The floral fragrance—carnations, chrysanthemums, heather, lilies, and more—followed me inside the room and was accompanied by distant music, an instrumental organ hymn that I knew the words to but tried to ignore. The promise of salvation, of a perfect eternity, was out of place, distasteful, a discussion I didn't want to have. I couldn't imagine heaven at that moment—if ever. Hell was easier. I never thought of Calla as a tortured soul, but I must have been wrong.

I gasped and stopped when I realized that the lid to the casket was open. It was a simple oak coffin like I had seen more times than I wanted to admit, with a white satin interior. When I focused, I could make out Calla's profile, her face angled upward, her glasses on like she was staring into the sky at a forty-five degree angle, her head propped up on a soft virgin pillow. I was certain that her eyes were closed. As certain as I could be at that moment.

At the thought, I closed my own eyes, and then opened them again to make sure I wasn't imagining the vision of Calla dead, lying in a casket. I wasn't. She was there for all the world to see.

There was only one other person in the parlor, which surprised me, since there had been a few cars in the parking lot. It only took me a second to recognize Herbert Frakes, sitting alone in the front row, dressed in his best moth-eaten suit, his head bowed like he was praying, or counting the threads in the lush, gold-sculptured carpet under his feet. I made my way to him, never taking my eyes off of Calla. I couldn't believe that Pete had left the lid open. I just couldn't believe it.

"Herbert," I whispered, putting my hand on his shoulder as I came to a stop. There was no mistaking that it was Calla in the casket. I was less than eight feet away from her, and she looked just like herself, not a waxy, unrecognizable, embalmed face.

"Marjorie." Herbert reached up and clasped my hand on his shoulder. It was like ice jamming into ice. It was a miracle that we both didn't shatter. "How's Hank?"

"Getting better," I said. Only this time it wasn't a lie to placate curiosity. It was the truth, and what I fully believed. "I hope to have him home in a few days."

"That'd be good." Herbert's voice echoed up into the rafters and then mixed with the hymn, "Awake, My Heart, with Gladness." Even though I hadn't been to church in ages, I figured I would remember the Lutheran hymns in any circumstance. They were engrained in me, wedged deep in a part of myself that I barely knew any longer. I still thought the hymn was inappropriate, but I supposed Pete didn't have a record for suicides to trumpet through the oversized speakers in each corner of the room, just records for a death that promised hope and eternal life, streets paved of gold and the reunion of souls who had passed the test of time and faith.

Herbert looked up at me. "It looks just like her, doesn't it?"

I nodded, then leaned down and whispered, "Why is it open?"

Herbert looked at me, so that we were eye to eye. "I asked Pete to do that. I wanted to see her one last time. He didn't figure it'd be a problem since there was no one here and it wasn't like her head was . . ." He stopped and looked down again. "Broken open," he said with a quiver. "He'll close it if I ask him to, if people start to come." He hesitated and said, "It'll be closed for the funeral, so you best go see her now."

"Okay," I said. He looked on the verge of tears, but restrained himself. I sighed, patted his shoulder, and stood up at the sound of voices coming in the door. Truth was, I wanted to see her, too, say goodbye one last time.

I took a deep breath, ignored the incoming visitors the best I could, and made my way to the casket alone. An unannounced shiver trembled up my spine, and I suddenly realized how cold it was in the parlor. I wanted to stop and run to the nearest fire to warm myself, to feel alive, to be warm, but I couldn't. I had to see her.

Tears flowed down my cheeks, obscured my vision, and Calla looked distant, asleep, at peace, which I had not expected. Her hands were clasped over an old book bound in worn brown leather—*Poems*, by Elizabeth Barrett Browning. More of Herbert's doing, I was sure. Browning was Calla's favorite poet. She had on a soft pink sweater, a color I'd never seen her in before—she wore mostly grays, blacks, and browns—and figured she would balk if she could. It probably wasn't even her sweater, but a piece of spare clothing out of Pete's wardrobe for the dead.

I cleared my eyes and stood over Calla as *Why? Why? Why?* circulated through my mind and heart. I studied her face, looking for an answer that I knew would never come. I had to accept that she had had her reasons for doing what she did, and no matter how much I protested she wasn't ever going to be able to answer my questions.

Slowly, with shame and curiosity, my vision drifted to her right temple, expecting to see something of note, something that would look like a cake of makeup to cover up a scar, or a bullet hole in this case. But nothing was there.

A quick glance at her left temple gave me what I was looking for, and at that moment I knew something was wrong. Something was horribly wrong.

CHAPTER 21

I had to consider that my immediate perception of the truth was completely wrong. But first I had to catch my breath, slow my heart from jumping out of my chest. I felt like all of the blood in my head had drained to my feet. I couldn't move. Each toe felt chained to the soft carpeted floor. I was a prisoner of my vision, to the horror of the sudden reality that I was certain of: *Calla Eltmore had not committed suicide.* If I fully understood what I had seen, then I had been right all along. I had never believed that Calla could do such a thing, and now that I had seen her, I was almost certain that I knew that to be true. As true as the sun rose in the east and set in the west.

I looked at Calla again and what I saw made sense—or made no sense at all. Calla had been right-handed. The bullet wound should have been at her right temple, not her left. *Calla had been right-handed, damn it.*

Frozen in place, locked in my own imagination, I raised my right hand to my head. It instinctively went to the same side, to my right temple. My hand did not cross over to the left side of my head. But if she had done that, then why? What difference would it have made? Why not just take the path of least resistance and get it over with? *Just get it over with*—unless she hadn't been the one to pull the trigger.

I hadn't wanted to believe that Calla had killed herself from the very beginning. But maybe she did cross her hand and the gun over to her left temple. It was possible that she had done exactly that—and impossible to know for sure.

Questioning everything had always been a way of life for me. I questioned myself, but in that single moment I couldn't come up with one reason why a right-handed person would shoot themselves on the left side of their head.

Somehow, I staggered backward, away from the casket and made my way to Herbert.

He reached out to steady me. "You alright, there, Marjorie? You look pale as a fresh bleached sheet hung on the line. It's hard to take, I'll tell you that. Sure is hard to take seein' her like that."

"I'm fine." I welcomed Herbert's touch, even though up close to him I realized he smelled of whiskey. The overwhelming fragrance of funeral flowers had completely hidden it when I'd spoken to him before. "I need to find Pete McClandon," I said.

"I saw him leave."

"What time is it?" I asked, befuddled that Pete had left the building, that he would leave his post at the door during a viewing.

Herbert looked down at his bare wrist. "It's the funniest thing, Marjorie, I can't seem to find my watch. I take it off every evening when I wash up after work. It's not waterproof like those new-fangled ones. I must've left it on the sink, but when I reached for it, it was gone, like it had never been there." He shook his head in disbelief. "But it's hard to say; maybe I left it somewhere else. The last few days have been a blur. That was my Navy watch. I bought it in the Philippines when I was on leave the first time. I'll never find another one like it. Nope, I sure won't. I can't believe it's gone any more than I can believe Calla's gone."

"I'm sure it'll turn up." I tried to sound hopeful but I didn't believe myself, and I was pretty sure that Herbert wasn't comforted at all by my meager offering.

"Everything's lost," Herbert said, turning away from me, facing Calla's presentation in the casket.

I didn't know what else to say to that. He was right. *Everything* is *lost*. I felt exactly the same way.

My feet suddenly moved underneath me, away from the casket, away from my puzzling assumption as quickly as they could go. It felt like I wasn't in control of any part of my body. I was being propelled out of the parlor by an unseen force: fear, dread, panic, and righteousness. I had to find Pete.

If I was right, that the bullet hole was on the wrong side of Calla's head, then it meant there was a possibility that Calla Eltmore hadn't killed herself at all. That would only mean one thing. Being right would mean that she had been murdered, killed in her office for some unknown reason, by some unknown person, who, as I thought about it, was still walking around free of any suspicion.

The killer could be anyone.

I shuddered at the thought and came to the quick conclusion that I hoped I was wrong. Now, I hoped that Calla *had* killed herself. I couldn't bear the thought of another murderer loose in Dickinson. My stomach tied itself up in knots so tight I feared they would never be undone.

I was at the front door of the funeral home before I knew it. Pete had been replaced by his wife, Helen, a tall thin woman with perfectly coifed hair the same color as Pete's shoe-polish-black. Pete had an easier time hiding his age than she did; her face was a map of deep worry lines. She smelled like a garden of flowers, too, like the fragrance inside the funeral home was permanently housed inside every pore in her skin. But unlike Pete, Helen was a perpetually stoic woman. Her smiles took effort. The muscles in her face protested openly every time she smiled, making the map more canyons than roads. She wore a modest, knee-length, black skirt and a blouse and jacket the same color, with a red rose pinned to the right lapel. There was not one speck of lint on her anywhere to be seen. Her eyes were nearly as dark as her hair and outfit, and, if I had to guess, it was her steel spine that navigated the business side of things, while Pete was left to the politics of the coroner's office and glad-handing at the front door. I had always preferred to deal with Pete. He was the gentler of the two. Helen always looked uncomfortable at her public post at the door—and at Pete's side.

I stopped before her almost like I would if I were a lesser human being. "Could I speak to Pete?" It was almost a whisper.

Helen flicked a quick smile at me. I shivered. "He's been called out on business," she said. There was no hint of emotion on her face. Just matter of fact, even though Pete's business was death. I suppose she was accustomed to it. Someone's bad news was good news for their coffers. I didn't know how a person managed such a life, but it was not my place to consider it anything other than it was. I was only speculating anyway. I had no idea what Helen meant by "business," and truth be told, I didn't want to know.

"Is there something I can help you with?" Helen asked, at the same time glancing out the door, calculating, I was sure, how soon to open the door for a small crowd of incoming mourners.

"It's just that . . . no, I suppose not. I'll wait until I see Pete and ask him."

"He's a busy man. There's nothing he knows that I don't. We share everything." Another quick smile, another quick shiver.

"No, that's all right, I'll wait, thank you." And with that I moved toward the door.

Helen didn't object or try to convince me any further. "Thank you for coming," she said, as I was halfway out the door.

I hurried away from the funeral home as quickly as I could, ignoring the mourners walking up to the door. They could have been my best friends in the world and I wouldn't have noticed. I wanted to get as far away from there as possible. I wanted the world to be right again, but I knew that wasn't going to be possible, no matter how much I desired it. I was just going to have to figure out how to live in it, and with this new truth I thought I had discovered. If that were possible. How did you live with murder?

CHAPTER 22

I couldn't believe what I was hearing. The foreign sound echoed down the hall like a siren out of place on a cloudless day. Hank's laugh was as distinct and unmistakable as a returning meadowlark's trill, celebrating spring, happy to be alive, relieved to be home on the breeding ground it had known and loved all of its life. I would have known that laugh anywhere, even though it had been ages—another lifetime—since I'd heard it.

The laugh nearly crumpled me to my knees. It was the most unexpected sound in the world. One I thought I would never ever hear again, and for a moment the joyousness of the sound lifted my spirits, made me forget the discovery that I'd made and the dire implications that came with it—if I was right.

I hurried down the long sterile hospital hall, propelled by curiosity and hope—but any of that gleeful emotion I felt disappeared the second I walked into the hospital room. Betty Walsh stood next to Hank's bed, holding his hand, laughing just like he was.

"And then, Mrs. Gordon got all flustered when she realized that she'd picked up Lloyd Kramer's pack of Trojans instead of her breath mints, which she was in serious need of. Heavens, you shoulda seen the look on her face. It was like she was going to go straight to hell right then and there," Betty said, without detecting my entrance into the room.

They both laughed like eighth graders who had shared a private joke at someone else's expense. In this case I assumed that someone had to be Charlotte Gordon, one of the most pious, persistently religious women I had ever met in my life. I would have given anything to have seen her mistakenly pick up a pack of prophylactics instead of breath mints.

I stood solemn as a flagpole, as quiet as possible. As surprised and annoyed as I was to find Betty Walsh in the hospital room sharing infantile gossip, I didn't want to ruin Hank's laugh.

Hank cleared his throat and nodded in my direction. He must have smelled me or heard me with his sharp as a tack sense of hearing—all of his senses had improved since the loss of his sight. It was no consolation.

Betty followed Hank's lead and turned in my direction. The blood ran from her face as soon as she realized it was me she was looking at. "Oh, Mrs. Trumaine, I wasn't expecting you to be back so soon."

"I can see that." I walked to the opposite side of the bed. My nose was pointed straight up at the ceiling as pious as Charlotte Gordon, but I didn't care. Something about Betty Walsh set me on edge, and I couldn't find it in myself to overcome whatever that something was.

Betty was stuffed into her candy striper uniform, dressed red and white like a Christmas candy cane from head to toe, every perfect curve of her young body noticeable and demanding attention. Even her little nurse's cap was striped and cocked a little to the side rebelliously. The truth was, Betty looked cute as a button, like the dress and its colors had been designed just for her. And maybe it had been, maybe her mother was an expert seamstress. Somebody was—though for some reason, I doubted it was Betty herself. I could see Jaeger's attraction to her, and for a brief second I was relieved that Hank was blind. Even when Betty was being catty, she was delightful about it, not mean-spirited. Somehow she had got to know Hank quick enough to figure out that he liked to hear tales about people getting their comeuppances. It had been a long time since I'd been jealous of a woman around Hank. . . . There was that *something*. I was jealous of Betty Walsh, as silly as that is.

"Really, Mrs. Trumaine, I was just here spending time with Hank, checking on him and all. I've just been worried sick about him since me and Jaeger brought him in."

"Relax, Betty," I said. "I'm glad you're here, and I'm not mad at you at all. Jaeger said you thought I was." I looked down to Hank, who was watching me as intently as Shep ever did—even though he couldn't see me, at least with his eyes. I was sure he saw me plain and clear in his mind, though. I could tell he was trying to gauge my mood, my reaction to Betty being in the room with him, but I couldn't tell him why I was unsettled and out of sorts, at least not until we were alone. The last thing I wanted to do was tell him my theory about Calla in front of Betty. Lord, before sunset the whole town would think I'd gone off my rocker.

"Thank you, I'm glad to hear that Mrs. Trumaine." Betty deflated, believing me, which I was glad of, mostly. I was still a little perturbed that *she* had been able to make Hank laugh and not me. The jealousy had not subsided. But I guess I hadn't given Hank much to laugh at recently. I'd been stuck in the doldrums, and Calla's death hadn't helped me out of them one bit. If anything, I was worse off now than I had been in months.

"Are you all right?" Hank said, attempting to change the subject. He knew better than anyone that I wouldn't say a word about what was troubling me until we were alone.

"I'm fine."

"McClandon's must have been packed," Hank said.

Betty stepped away from the hospital bed, but she didn't take her eyes off me.

"There was hardly anyone there." I lowered my head, then turned my attention to Betty. "Did people talk about Calla, Betty?"

"I beg your pardon?" The question obviously took her by surprise. She stepped back and almost plastered herself against the wall.

Hank exhaled and turned his head from me, annoyed.

"Did people talk about her? You know, in a bad way, or a good way as far as that goes?"

"She *was* the librarian, Mrs. Trumaine," Betty said.

"What's that supposed to mean?"

"She could be terse, shush you if you talked just a little loud, or be snobby about the books that you checked out, even though it wasn't any of her business. You could tell if she liked you, and you sure knew it if she didn't. Everybody knew that. But it was just the way of things. She was what she was supposed to be, I guess, just like we all are."

I sighed. Betty was right on the money about Calla. I couldn't dispute a word she said. "Is that what people said about her?" I persisted.

Betty shook her head. "People didn't talk much about her at all, Mrs. Trumaine. There was really nothing to talk about. She was the same, day in and day out, for years. I mean, I always wondered if she ever changed clothes because they all looked alike every time I went in the library," Betty said.

I wondered how often Betty actually visited the library, then batted the thought away and focused on what she'd said. Calla *did* always look the same. She would have been mortified if she'd known she was going to be buried in a pink sweater—that I was sure hadn't belonged to her in the first place. That was a small tragedy in itself.

"I better go, Mrs. Trumaine," Betty said, stepping forward.

I nodded and watched her move to the side of Hank's bed. "You stay out of trouble now, Hank. I'll check on you before I leave."

Hank smiled. "I'll look forward to it," he said, his voice as strong as ever. That jealous streak shot down my back like a miniature bolt of lightning had exploded out of my cloudy, conflicted brain.

Betty walked away, but I stopped her as she met the door. "Betty," I said.

She turned and faced me. "Yes, Mrs. Trumaine?"

"Thank you," I offered.

"You're welcome." A slight smile flickered across Betty's young face, then she disappeared out the door and down the hall. She didn't bother to ask me what I meant, and to be honest, I was glad of that.

I turned back to Hank, and I could tell straight away that he wasn't pleased with me. "You should take it easier on that girl."

"I thanked her for looking after you, what else do you want?"

"I want you to be nice to her."

"I'll try."

Hank rolled his head back on the pillow like he was looking up at the sky, then he guffawed. "Good Lord, Marjorie Trumaine, you're jealous."

"I am not."

He laughed harder, and it only took me a long second to see how ridiculous I had been acting, and I joined in with him.

It was a moment I knew I'd treasure for the rest of my life.

CHAPTER 23

Iclosed the door to the hospital room so Hank and I could have some privacy. He watched me walk toward him with his blank eyes—his head was tilted more to the floor than directed at my face. I knew he was listening to my feet. I was almost glad he couldn't see my face. What little makeup I'd brushed on wore through the moment I'd stared down at Calla. My hair was a rat's nest that needed a good brushing and a professional set. I just hadn't had the time or the emotion to be any more concerned than I'd ever been, if the truth be told.

"What's wrong, Marjorie?" Hank said, with an easy, knowing tone. The distance in his voice had returned, and I realized at that moment that he had been exerting himself with Betty, that he was showing his best side. I wanted to be angry with him for it, but I couldn't be. What I really wanted to do was climb into the bed with him, push away the intravenous tubes and cords attached to the monitor next to the bed, snuggle into his arms, and feel safe and normal. But the monitor beeped every time Hank's heart took a beat. It was a constant reminder that he was still fragile, that we both were, and that I could wish as much as I wanted to and nothing would ever change the circumstance I stood in at that moment—or the one earlier, at McClandon's Funeral Home.

I sighed and bit my lip. "I don't think Calla killed herself, Hank. I don't think she committed suicide at all. I've been right all along."

"Oh, Marjorie, you've just got to let go of that notion." Hank was exasperated without the energy to fully show it. His throat tensed up, and I was sure in his mind he clenched his fists in frustration. Sadly, I saw no movement from the neck down.

"No, you don't understand," I said. "Calla was right-handed, and the bullet wound was at her left temple. Why would she cross her hand over to the other side of her head? You've handled guns all of your life, Hank, and you're right-handed, too. Think about it, picture it. If you were going to raise a pistol to your temple, it'd be to your right temple, not to your left one. You know I'm right about that. It would take a fool not to see it." I almost regretted saying those words as soon as they left my mouth, but Hank and I had agreed a long time ago not to restrain ourselves, not to dance tepidly around the fact that he was blind, an invalid. Still, I tried not to remind him of it any more than necessary.

Hank said nothing. He just stared upward, but I knew he could still see, still imagine, actions and images. His blindness was recent, not a malady he had been born with, his darkness was still alive with dancing memories. *He could still imagine . . . he could still see.*

"Did you talk to Pete at the funeral home?" he finally said.

"He was called away on business. I didn't want to discuss this with Helen."

"What about the sheriff, the police? Don't you think they could figure out the same thing as you?"

I shrugged my shoulders. "I don't know. It seems like they've accepted her death as a suicide and don't want to stir up any trouble. Guy said the investigation was still open, that I should let it alone and accept that Calla was dead. He never came right out and said it was *officially* a suicide."

Hank's throat tensed up even more. "When did you talk to Guy?" I had to strain my ears to hear him clearly, his voice had faded drastically.

"He was here, a few days ago."

"Oh."

More silence. The consistent beat of the monitor and the rumble of a distant boiler coming to life worked their way between us. Hank was as jealous of Guy Reinhardt as I was of Betty Walsh, and his fears were just as unfounded and ridiculous as my own, but far more serious. Hank couldn't take any kind of action with his impulses, if they existed, but I could. He had always trusted me, and I'd never given him reason not to, but it was easy to see in his darkness where his mind and fear might take him if he allowed himself to question me, to question my love and devotion to him. I hoped he'd never taken that journey, but I couldn't be sure. He had a lot of idle time on his hands.

I remained quiet, let him consider that I was standing next to him, that I was there. No sense throwing a match on dried grass with words I might regret later.

"The police are smart men, Marjorie," Hank whispered. "They have to know what you know, had to see what you saw. Probably more. But I think you should say something to Duke if it would make you feel better. You won't be able to restrain yourself."

"I don't trust the police," I offered. "What if I really am right, what if Calla didn't kill herself and they let it go, don't do anything about it? Someone is out there who did a bad, bad thing, Hank, and they will get away with it scot-free. Someone is getting away with murder."

"Then you should let the police do their job and keep your nose out of it once you've raised your suspicions to Duke. It's not your business, Marjorie. You've enough to worry about."

"You sound like Guy." *Damn it, no filters are dangerous.*

"For good reason, Marjorie," Hank snapped back at me. "That ugliness over the summer came too close to us the last time. I could have lost you. Do you realize what *my life* would be like without you? Do you? If there's someone out there that hurt Calla, Duke and his boys'll figure it out. I know you don't think much of him, but he's smarter than you think he is."

"I never said such a thing."

Hank relaxed his throat and rolled his head to me so we were facing each other. I couldn't hide how I felt about Duke Parsons. I thought Guy would have made a better sheriff. Hank knew that, and agreed, even though he'd never come right out and said it. "Promise me two things," he said.

I had to resist the urge to be angry about being treated like a child. Hank's tone was not malicious or demeaning in any way, but I was frustrated by being warned off of something so important. "What?"

He ignored my petulance. "That you'll talk to Duke if you feel like you have to and leave it at that and let him do his job."

"Is that it?"

Hank shook his head. "No, I want you to go home and get some rest. You have a long day tomorrow with Calla's funeral and all. Sleeping in your own bed will do you good."

"I'm not leaving you."

"Marjorie, you're exhausted. You need some rest, some familiar surroundings. I'm fine. I feel better than I have in months."

"It's those shots Doc's been giving you."

"I don't care what it is. I feel fine. I'll sleep better if I know you're resting."

"You're sure?"

"As sure as anything I've been of before. I'm fine. Go home. Get some rest," Hank said, with as much of a smile and nod as he could muster. It wasn't an order. He knew better than that, but it was as close as he could get without demanding that I leave. He was concerned about me. His desire was out of love. I understood that. I wanted to resist, but I couldn't. All I could do was nod, then without regard to where I was, I eased into the hospital bed and snuggled up as close to Hank as I could get until he drifted off to sleep.

CHAPTER 24

I wrote an index for a book about the stages of paranoia early on in my indexing career. The book was a dissertation and had all of the bells and whistles of academic writing—loads of footnotes and an extensive bibliography that led to ramblings that were distantly relevant to the reader but somehow very relevant to the pompous author. Mostly, the book was a really boring read, clinical and dry, but I never minded that kind of reading, really, especially when I was being paid for it. The troubling part of that book had been the personal information that I came away with after I'd finished indexing it. Plain and simple: I had identified with nearly every stage of paranoia that was described in the pages of the book.

I had, at times in my life, suspected that I was being exploited or deceived by people around me without sufficient cause. Strangers showed up on the doorstep trying to sell something all of the time. It didn't matter whether it was the *Encyclopedia Britannica* or Jesus, the truth was I'd always suspected that they were just trying to find their way into my purse and nothing more with their sales pitches. And, of course, I'd always been reluctant to confide in others. I doubted the loyalty of friends and family and constantly read demeaning or threatening meanings into remarks that could not be mistaken for anything other than benign. I supposed it might be different if I held a library sciences or teaching degree instead of a correspondence course certificate from the USDA. The sting of my father's disappointment of me for not finishing college, for marrying Hank and becoming a farmer's wife, still chased after me like a hungry piglet missing its teat all these years later.

Questioning everything in my life had had its price, I supposed. There were more stages of paranoia, but I'd taken away more doubts about myself than I'd needed to from that book, and I swore right then and there that if I ever had the luxury to say no to an indexing project, say no to an editor, I would definitely do so if there was any kind of medical content included in the text. I was sure I would recognize the symptoms of dengue fever at the bare mention of it, and a new strain of paranoia and fear would send me running to Doc Huddleston at full speed for a cure. I didn't need that kind of madness in my life, and neither did Hank.

Of course, at that moment, dengue fever was not a major concern. The dry weather and the time of year had thankfully sent North Dakota's squadrons of mosquitoes into retreat. Paranoia, on the other hand, remained a concern.

It didn't take long to drive from the hospital to the courthouse. The building that housed most all of Stark County's government offices sat off of 3rd Street and had been built in the mid-1930s to help keep the men in Dickinson employed—a WPA project that had stood the test of time. It looked like a square, four-story wedding cake, fortified with blonde brick and accented with limestone-inlaid columns. It was an understated building, like most others in town, and I didn't think it was Art Deco at all, even though it was purported to be. The courthouse looked like a normal North Dakota building to me.

The building sat on a couple of grassy acres, surrounded by a few pine trees and a thin copse of tall cottonwoods that had lost their leaves weeks ago. I wheeled the Studebaker into the parking lot hoping to see Duke Parsons's squad car sitting in its normal spot but was immediately disappointed. There wasn't a police car to be seen for miles.

A few cars that I didn't recognize sat next to the side entrance of the building, and I had no idea what Duke's civilian car looked like, so I held out hope that he was still inside the building, even though the day had gotten long and evening was swiftly falling into the dark of night. I wasn't so sure of or familiar with Duke Parsons. But he was the man to express my concerns about Calla's death to and no other. Guy Reinhardt had no power, and, to be honest, after our last uncomfortable encounter I was in no mood to speak with him anytime soon.

I glanced in the mirror. I was still dressed in my second-best, go-to-the-funeral-home clothes, but there was no mistaking that I was a farmer's wife, that I was as frugal as the day was long, not because I wanted to be, but because I had to be. I looked tired and so did my clothes, my hair, and my eyes, and there wasn't a darn thing I could do about any of it other than give a wit less what Duke Parsons thought of me. He needed to hear what I had to say.

I pushed out of the truck and made my way to the courthouse. I was hardly aware of my surroundings, too busy practicing what I was going to say to Duke inside my head. The last thing I wanted to do was come off like some nutcase or put myself in a position to be told to mind my own business and go home, bake a cake, and forget about it like a good woman should. I swear, if Duke Parsons even so much as suggested such a thing, I was going to stomp on his toe. Of course, that'd probably land me in jail, the last place I needed to be.

The inside of the courthouse was lit with dim overhead lights that hadn't seen a duster in ages. The air smelled stale, and distantly like wet paper, another institutional aroma but not sterile like the hospital. Government smelled incapable, broken, struggling.

A pair of footsteps coming my way pulled me up out of my rehearsal for Duke. I blinked my eyes, cleared my vision, and saw a well-dressed woman rushing toward me, I assumed toward the exit. At first glance, I didn't know the woman. She could have been a clerk, a secretary working late in a hurry to get home. More and more women worked outside the house these days. But as she got closer, I recognized her. She was the woman who had taken a tumble down the stairs at the library. I still had her glasses in my purse.

CHAPTER 25

I knew anger and rage when I saw it. The woman raced toward me, her fists balled, her eyes red with emotion, and her teeth clenched tight, holding back a storm of unknown origins. I stopped and turned my back to the wall as if to parry a strike or to give way to a rumbling avalanche, I wasn't sure which. For a moment, I wondered if the woman even saw me, knew that I shared the hallway with her.

Her intention seemed to be to escape the sterile courthouse hallway as quickly as possible. But she stopped when she was even with me. With a deliberate lock step she turned to face me but said nothing, just craned her neck toward my face, examining it, looking for some sign of recognition. She looked bug-eyed, like an insect trying to decide whether I was worthy prey or an attacker, something to be threatened by.

The woman smelled of expensive perfume, a variety and brand unknown to me. It surely had to come from some faraway department store that had a fancy family name, like Macy's in New York City or the A.W. Lucas store in Bismarck. I held my breath, stood frozen like a jackrabbit on alert, and tried not to breathe in the fragrance of her.

"You look familiar," the woman said, retreating backward a step as her shoulders and jaw relaxed. The clouds in her eyes seemed to dissipate.

I exhaled, relaxing as much as I could. I hadn't been afraid so much as I had been uncomfortable. Still, the woman seemed unpredictable or unstable, I wasn't sure which. Her perfume lingered between us. She looked like she had just stepped off the page of a Montgomery Ward's catalog.

"I was at the library when you took the tumble down the steps,"

I said, eyeing a bit of heavily caked foundation under her right eye. It was there to hide a recent bruise, most likely from the fall, I assumed—hoped. "Are you all right?"

She caught my gaze on the flaw on her face and turned her head away from me for a brief second, breaking my line of sight, with a direct attempt to avoid my inquiry as well. Her profile was equine, in a gentle, beautiful sort of way. But there was something else lingering on her face that caught my attention. I knew shame, too, but not as well as I knew anger. That emotion had ceded to something else in this woman, something unknown to me. I needed a field guide to human emotions, just like I needed one to identify musk thistle. My lack of social understanding was one of the many consequences of the isolation of my work as an indexer and my life on the farm.

"Ah, yes," the woman said, as a softness in her tone appeared for the first time. There had been no denying her perfect put-together-beauty the first time I saw her, but it was the internal glow of her eyes that complimented her choice in clothes, in shoes—which I was envious of and demeaned by at the same time. They probably cost a week's wages for most folks in and around Dickinson. "I'm sorry, I must look a mess to you," she went on. "That was a terribly difficult day, and I'm sorry to say this one is worse than that, not better like I'd hoped."

I clutched the strap of my purse a little tighter. I'd felt exactly the same way. "I have your glasses."

"What a relief. I'm nearly blind as a bat without them. I have an old pair to rely on when I drive, but even at that, the distance is blurry."

"One lens is shattered. The other is missing. I'm afraid they won't do you much good."

"Well, that's the way of things right now, isn't it? I'll just have to wait another week for the new pair to come in. Perhaps I'm better off not being able to see things as clearly."

We had the empty hallway to ourselves. The day of law and justice was over. Only the sheriff's office remained open and unlocked twenty-four hours a day—as far as I knew. I supposed there were other agencies that needed to be staffed around the clock, but the courthouse was dismally quiet, with no distant footsteps, no whirling fans or mumbled voices.

I unlatched my purse, grabbed the woman's glasses, and handed them to her as carefully as I could. I was glad to be rid of them, to be honest. "My name's Marjorie, by the way. Marjorie Trumaine."

"The indexer?" The woman didn't look at me directly, but took the glasses and handled them as if they were as fragile as an eggshell, threatening to turn to dust at her touch. She stuffed them into her own purse, a leather clutch that looked brand new and unmarred with use and matched her outfit and shoes perfectly. I was certain I could smell tanning oil past her perfume.

A slight smile flickered across my face. "Yes, how did you know?"

A black drape returned to the woman's face, and her eyes charged red, angrily, with an electricity, a power source I had clicked on with a simple question. "I'm sorry, I really must go," she said.

I reached out and took her wrist as she turned. "Please don't. It was Calla, wasn't it? Calla told you that I was an indexer, didn't she?" I wondered what else Calla had told this woman, how well she had known her.

The woman stopped and froze, uncomfortable with my physical intrusion, but she didn't try to pull away from me. She just stood there like a helpless child, caught by an adult who refused to let her go. "Yes," she whispered. "It was Calla. Dear, sweet, Calla."

The dry, red rage that I initially saw in her eyes suddenly turned moist. Tears escaped the corner of each eye, and she just stared at me without apology or effort to wipe them away. I knew the look. She was as broken up and confused by Calla's death as I was.

"She didn't do it," the woman said angrily, her lip twisted upward in a fit. "I know it as certain as the moon is rising as we speak. Calla Eltmore didn't kill herself. I know it; I just know it to be true." Then her lip broke and quivered, an initial shock that trailed down her throat and grew in intensity as it did. I was certain that she was going to collapse, to shatter into a million pieces. I let go of her wrist and reached out to her, to catch her in case she fell—but the woman stood fast, her mood changing completely and assuredly in the blink of an eye. She suddenly looked afraid, like she had spoken out loud when she shouldn't have, like she had let out a deep, dark, secret, or, even worse, that I was going to judge her as some crazy loon who should be feared.

"I know," I offered her. "That's why I'm here. I don't think Calla killed herself, either, and the sheriff needs to know what I think, what I saw when I looked at Calla."

"They won't listen," the woman said, as a relieved look fell across her face—*I'm not the only one*. "They will just send you on your way like you don't know a thing."

"Calla was right-handed," I said.

The woman nodded. "And the wound was on her left temple. I told him that. I told him, and he stared at me with a blank face and pursed lips. I'm not even sure he really heard me." She stopped, caught her breath, and pulled a handkerchief out of her clutch and wiped her eyes. "I really must get home. Claude will be worried about me."

"There must be a way we can convince them that they're overlooking something. If Calla didn't kill herself, then someone . . ."

". . . Killed her," the woman said. "I told him that, too, and I was hustled out the door. 'A murderer is free,' I yelled like a mad harpy sent over the cliffs to meet my fate."

"By the sheriff?"

"No, he wasn't in. It was some deputy."

I glanced down the hall and imagined Guy standing there, waiting to tell me the same thing he had told this woman. He already had once, and I was sure he would send me packing again, too. But today wasn't the day. I'd have to come back when Duke was in.

"I'll talk to them," I said.

The woman dropped her handkerchief into her clutch and snapped it shut. "It won't do you a bit of good. We're just two nosy women who shouldn't leave the kitchen. We should just shut up and mind our own *goddamned* business."

The swear word resounded sharply in the empty hallway. She spun and departed without saying another word, exiting toward the entrance of the courthouse without so much as a goodbye or good day.

I watched her hurry off for a long second and considered what she had said, until I realized that I didn't even know her name.

We had both come to the same conclusion, had come to the same place to restore Calla's reputation, if that were possible, and had shared a fear and knowledge that needed to be spread to the rest of the world, and yet, I didn't know who she was. Plain and simple, I had never seen her before, not until she'd fallen down the stairs of the library, fleeing it like she was fleeing the courthouse—in a fit of emotion that suggested she was capable of saying or doing anything.

CHAPTER 26

Darkness had not drained the wind of any of its power. Just the opposite, it seemed, as I made my way out of the building. There was a brutal force to the heavy gusts, along with a cold undercurrent, a familiar gift from the upper reaches of Alberta. Winter's blunt calling card made me shiver, and I was forced to acknowledge the changing season.

A pair of headlights swept across my waist at the same time as I pinned down my dress so it wouldn't blow up to my neck. One of these days I was going to set aside my pride and expectations and wear my worn Levi's and muck boots into town instead of my handmade dress and best shoes. To heck with expectations and social demands.

The car edged alongside me almost close enough that I could touch it, close enough that I could see it clearly in all of its glory in the parking lot lights. The engine purred like a kitten sated on fresh milk. The car looked like a brand new Cadillac, a 1965 model, a two-door coupe, beige, but most likely called something fancy like champagne. Hank would have known for sure. He knew all of the cars and models, which by default, sitting next to him in the truck as he drove and identified them, so did I.

The woman with the broken glasses was behind the steering wheel. She was alone, sobbing, her face aglow from the instrument panel, lost in a world of her own. I wondered how she could see to drive.

I put my hand out like I was hailing a cab to stop her, but she ignored me, pressed on the accelerator, and sped out of the parking lot. As she passed, I saw the flaw in the beautiful, expensive Cadillac: The windshield had been shattered, although not broken completely through, and there was a basketball-sized dent in the front driver's-side fender. The damage seemed out of place, but not surprising for some reason. The woman had looked broken the first time we'd met, and this time had been no different.

I stood and watched as the red taillights disappeared into the night. The wind buffeted me, all the while my ears were cocked for any sign of danger. A sad feeling grew in the pit of my stomach. There was more to this woman than met the eye. I was sure of it, and I had to consider what she really knew about Calla's life and, ultimately, her death.

My first inclination had been to drive straight back to St. Joseph's and tell Hank about my conversation with the woman. Afterward, I imagined, I would climb into a spot in his bed and be lulled to sleep by the constant beep of the monitors that gave proof that my one true love in this life still breathed, still lived. But I knew he would send me off, certain that I needed to walk and sleep in the purified air of our home. Shep would dance and rest at my feet, and the call of an open book lying on my desk would be too strong to resist. Hank was right. I did need to be home, to feel safe inside my house, restoring as much of my energy as I could, even though leaving him pained me more than I could say.

The coming day demanded my attendance at a funeral I did not want to attend, or even believe was occurring, but I had no choice. I hoped to see Calla one more time. I hoped to wish her a good journey and promise her that I would find her killer—especially since no one else seemed interested in doing such a thing except for me and a harried, unnamed women. Once there, I hoped to look a little closer at Calla's temple, just to make sure I saw what I had the first time. I honestly needed to reinforce my thinking, convince myself that I wasn't crazy as an exhausted loon mistaking the shimmering wet road for a lake after a long flight to nowhere. It would be a hard landing.

I climbed into the Studebaker reluctantly. In the blink of an eye,

I was free of the confines of town. The headlights cut into the darkness and led me home like a leash, lighting just enough of the way and its landmarks for me to know that I was on the right path. I smoked one cigarette after another, lighting the tip of a new one with the dying cinder of the old one. I felt like I had to keep the flame going, like I couldn't let the hot orange tip die out, even though the dashboard lighter offered an unlimited amount of fire.

I had the window cracked to vent the smoke and the heater on to keep my feet warm in my dress shoes. The radio sang distantly, turned down low just so I wouldn't feel like I was the only human being in the world. Even in space, in that odd-looking, claustrophobic capsule, John Glenn had had radio contact with another human, at least until he burned through the atmosphere. I had read that everyone in Houston held their breath during that period of silence, fearing the worst, that he had been burned alive. I felt like that, like I was holding my breath until I arrived home, on my land, where I could be human, myself.

Shep, of course, was happy to see me again. I thought he was going to knock me down as I dug into my purse for the house key. Jaeger had left on the stoop light and a lamp burning inside the house so it appeared as if someone was home while I was away. I rarely used the key, since the front door was hardly ever locked, so it wasn't in a handy or specific place in my purse. I noticed immediately that the woman's glasses were gone, and for a brief second I regretted returning them to her. They were my only link to finding out who she was.

I stepped into the house, and Shep pushed past me, barking and circling in the front room, his bushy black and white tail wagging a million miles an hour. You would have thought I'd been gone a month. But I understood. It felt like that to me, too.

The house was just like I'd left it, a museum dedicated to my life and Hank's, the warmth of our family memorabilia all in its place. It was easy to tell that the house had been closed up longer than it normally was. The air was still, and the smell of it was thick with the frass of the box-elder bugs, who'd most likely had a heyday in my absence, burrowing into places I could only imagine to survive the winter. But there was a smell that was missing, one that I noticed right away. It was the antiseptic, medical smell that came with Hank's condition. It was gone when he was, which was something I didn't think I could get used to, now or ever.

CHAPTER 27

S ometime in the middle of the night I woke up and couldn't go
back to sleep. I could have sworn I'd heard a coyote, that a nearby
yip had roused me from my fitful attempt to rest, but Shep still lay at
my feet with his ears relaxed, his sleepy eyes searching mine for the
reason that I had stirred awake. If trouble lurked nearby, Shep would
be the first to know it.

The bedroom was dark, along with the rest of the house, and there
was no moon to offer a glow of light beyond the windows. I was covered
in *the* black, confining shroud of night. Out of habit, I reached over
to touch Hank's chest, but my hand sank to the down filled mattress.
There was nothing to comfort me other than Shep's watchful presence
and the Remington .22 stuffed behind the kitchen door. *I needed more
than that . . . I needed more.*

I put my head back on the pillow and stared up at the ceiling, listening to the world around me. My ears were met with dead silence.
The wind had retreated, as it often did at that time of the night, and
no other creature stirred. Even the box-elder bugs and mice rested. It
felt like I was the only person in the world, stranded and alone on a
planet of my own making. I knew I was feeling guilty for leaving Hank
at the hospital, but it was more than that. I missed knowing that Calla
Eltmore waited for my queries at the other end of the phone line. I was
surrounded by death, loss, and sickness, and they ate at me in a way I
didn't know how to deal with.

Going back to sleep in such a state was impossible, so I got up,
put my housecoat on, and made my way to my desk, my island of salvation. There was order there, or at least order waiting to be made. I

could cultivate an index, put words where they needed to go so ideas and thoughts could be found by someone with a question. I could give someone else what I needed. That was a small comfort, but the harder questions that life served up were beyond my reach.

My shoebox full of index cards for *Common Plants* sat on the desk next to my Underwood typewriter, along with my red pen and reading glasses. Everything waited on me, and for that I was glad. I needed a bit of normalcy.

There was nothing left to do but compile the index, type up the first draft, and see what it was that I had made. Most of the time, I saw the index forming in my mind, neat rows of words, garden plots that needed to be fertilized and weeded. But I couldn't edit anything until I had all of the entries on the page.

A

amorpha canescens (leadplant),
    2
arctostaphylos (kinni-
    kinnik), 50

K

kinnikinnik (*arctostaph-
    ylos*), 50

L

leadplant (*amorpha canes-
    cens*), 2

G

shrubs, 2, 23, 50, 76, 191
    leadplant (*amorpha canes-
    cens*), 2
    kinnikinnik (*arctostaphylos*),
    50

I worked my way through the As—*arctostaphylos* (kinnikinnik), *amorpha canescens* (leadplant)—leading with the scientific names for the plants, as well as double posting them by their common name under their appropriate letter. Leadplant and kinnikinnik were shrubs, so they were also posted under the shrubs main entry. The more access points the reader had into the text, the better. Questions were as variable as the reader.

Of course, I still had to get through all of the grasses, flowering perennials, perennial ferns, shrubs, trees, and vines, and enter the elusive musk thistle were it belonged. But as I typed the entries onto the page from each index card in the A section, I had to try harder than I usually did to focus my mind on the task.

Compiling the index was the end game in the indexing process, nearly the last task before I sent the document off to New York, never to be seen or thought of again—at least until Calla proudly showed me one of my indexes in the book she'd purchased for the library. And that was where I wavered, of course. I seriously doubted that Delia Finch would be as interested as Calla had been in stocking the library with the books that held my indexes.

I stopped typing once I could get no more entries on the page, stood up from my desk, grabbed my cigarettes, and made my way outside. Shep padded after me with curiosity and confusion in his amber eyes. It was too early to feed the chickens.

The predawn air was cold; the temperature had dipped down into the mid-thirties. A heat wave in winter, but nothing more than a tease in October. The air was dry, which made it seem warmer. After living all of my life in North Dakota, I was hardened, accustomed to the cold. I hadn't thought to grab my robe or a jacket to keep myself warm.

I lit a Salem, drew in the cool menthol, and held it for a second longer than I normally would have. No matter what I did, I couldn't tamp down my agitation.

I exhaled the smoke, and it obscured the black, cloud-free sky, smudged the stars so they looked even more distant and unreachable. That was how I felt about the truth, about what had happened to Calla. My mind was cluttered, and I knew right then what I had to do to calm myself down. I took a couple more quick puffs off the Salem, scanned the dark horizon for anything out of place, then nickered Shep along with a click of the tongue so he would follow me back inside the house. Not that he needed goading; it was just habit. Shep had been happy to be invited to live in the house. I hurried to my desk, slid in a fresh piece of paper, and started typing again. Only this time I was indexing my mind, not the shoebox full of *Common Plants* cards. B was the most obvious section to start at:

B

Browning, Robert
Browning, Elizabeth B.

D

death, surprise of
depression, no sign of

E

Eltmore, Calla
    murder not suicide
    no known enemies
    no note left

F

Frakes, Herbert
    found Calla
    no violent history

G

gun, what kind?

M

Men and Women
    by favorite poet—Calla
    woman dropped
motive?
    What don't I know?
    What to gain?

S

Suspects
    Herbert, found Calla
    woman at library

W

woman at library
    doesn't believe suicide
    dropped *Men and Women*
    need to find

I exhaled deeply and sat back in my chair. I was grasping at straws. A good index was meant to answer questions, but also raise some. Any kind of research typically prompted the researcher into uncharted territory with the information they stumbled across. But I had found no answers. I had only managed to raise more questions.

I had no idea who had killed Calla or why. For the life of me, I couldn't begin to wrap my mind around the fact that that was the truth—that Calla had been murdered. But murder was far more believable than her having killed herself, especially now that someone else had validated my opinion.

I only had two suspects, and they weren't really suspects. I only included Herbert because he'd found Calla, but honestly I couldn't imagine that Herbert Frakes would hurt a fly, much less shoot Calla in the head to make the murder look like suicide. He had no violent history that I was aware of. And the woman with the broken glasses? I didn't even know her name. All I knew was that she believed what I believed, that Calla had been killed. That certainly didn't point toward a cold-blooded killer—she walked into the police department, for heaven's sake. I knew she drove a brand new Cadillac with a broken windshield and a dented fender—a car like that shouldn't be too hard to find in Dickinson—and that she was leaving the library with a book of poetry that was by Calla's favorite poet. That could have been coincidence and nothing more. I really needed to find the woman and find out what she knew about Calla. But that seemed unlikely. I had too much to do.

I kept thinking that Hank and Guy Reinhardt were right, that I should just leave things to the police, tell Duke what I'd seen when I saw him and leave it at that. It was obvious that I wasn't very good at playing Sherlock Holmes—but I owed it to Calla to find out the truth. I know she would have done the same thing for me.

CHAPTER 28

As the sun leapt up from the horizon, I started to feel a little more hopeful. I had been able to type up half of the compiled index for the *Common Plants* book once I'd set aside my own personal index. My lack of information about Calla, her death, and the women with the broken glasses had ended in frustration and sadness.

The deadline to mail the *Common Plants* index to New York was just days away, but I wasn't worried about making it. Well, not too much. I'd always worried about missing deadlines. I needed the indexing money, but I was confident about making this deadline, even with everything that was going on.

I expected to bring Hank home in a day or two, and then I could get things back on a normal routine, finish compiling the *Plants* index, start on the next one, the *Zhanzheng: Five Hundred Years of Chinese War Strategy* book, and do my own chores around the farm.

Jaeger had done a fine job of keeping up with the minimal October demands, and I was grateful for that. The hay had been brought in in September, along with the planting of winter wheat. About the only harvesting going on now was for sugar beets, and Hank and I had never planted them. They seemed to fair better in the eastern part of the state, not around our area. My woodpile had grown since the last time I had paid attention to it, which meant I could relax a bit about feeding the Franklin stove in the middle of January. I imagined that Jaeger's life had gotten a little easier since he'd taken on Lester Gustaffson as a hand around his own farm, but I needed to slide some money into Jaeger's pocket, too. I didn't expect him to do work around our place for free, even though I knew he wouldn't ask for a dime—and would refuse to take it when I offered.

Shep happily followed me as I made my way around morning chores. I'd saved retrieving the newspaper for last. I was in no hurry to see the headlines. I'd read enough bad news recently to last me into the next lifetime.

Oddly, I felt refreshed, invigorated, even though I hadn't slept much—I'd laid my head down on the desk and drifted off for a bit just as the sun was cutting away the darkness, but I'd woken up not long after. My neck felt a little stiff, but I was accustomed to the discomfort. I'd slept at my desk more times than I could count. I thought working on both of the indexes had helped me set my mind right. And it felt good to be home, though I missed Hank's presence terribly. The house was just a shell without him, something I never wanted to get used to.

All of the chickens were accounted for, and I was happy that none of them had been lost to hawks or foxes in my absence. Shep had done a fine job of keeping an eye on things. I didn't know what I would have done without him.

I made my way to the road to get the paper, greeted by a hard gust of the ever-present wind. I had on Hank's flannel jacket, which was a little long in the sleeves for me but was comfortable and warm enough to wear in the chill of October—and kept Hank near me in a way. I kept on walking, undeterred by the wind. I was used to that fight, though I did have to shield my eyes. The dust was loose from the lack of rain; little pellets peppered me relentlessly. I was glad for the coat, that my skin was covered; otherwise I would have been covered in welts. Not the look I wanted to carry with me to Calla's funeral. It was hard enough to shake the farm off me in proper clothes.

The sky was pink on the horizon, but as the fingers of color reached up it grew darker, angrier. The taller reaches of light made the sky look blood red where it met the retreating darkness, although there were no obvious clouds. This dry spell was quickly turning into a drought, and I'd hardly noticed. If it kept up, all of Montana was going to blow onto North Dakota's fields.

I grabbed up the newspaper and started to head back to the house, but something stopped me. Something I saw didn't make sense. My heart nearly jumped into my throat. Shep followed suit and stopped at my ankle. He looked up at me curiously, wondering what I was going to do next since it didn't seem obvious, even to me.

I had left the Studebaker parked up next to the door when I'd returned home the night before. Normally, I would have parked the truck in the garage, but that effort had been the last thing on my mind once I'd made my way inside the house.

The front tire was flat. And on second glance, so was the rear one. The truck sat low to the ground, like it was hunkering down, trying to avoid the wind and dirt just like Shep and I.

"What the hell?" I offered to no one. My words slipped away on the wind and Shep followed my gaze with his amber eyes, stopping where mine stopped: on the truck.

I took off and stalked straight to the front tire. Shep remained on my heels, silent, his ears up, his tail stiff, on alert. I was sure he felt my fear, my concern.

I leaned down and examined the tire, and there was no mistaking that the tire had been slashed. A twelve-inch gouge was slit from the air valve to the top of the tire in a perfect curve. I touched it, cold black rubber to finger, like I would touch the wound on a human, wondering if I could fix it somehow. I knew immediately that I couldn't.

I spun away from the tire and made my way to the rear axle. Same exact thing, same exact slit. I stood up, numb, my mind swirling, trying to comprehend what had happened, what I was seeing.

I surveyed the truck from bumper to bumper and it didn't take long to realize that the truck was sitting evenly, not tilted, which prompted me to hurry to the other side. Just as I'd feared, both of those tires were flat, too. All four tires were flat. Slashed. Deflated and destroyed on purpose, with intention.

A wave of panic washed over me. We didn't have four spare tires for the truck. There was only one that I knew of. Thanks to Hank's insistence, I knew how to change a tire; I wasn't going to be stranded between home and town on a flat tire. But this was something else. I didn't know how to fix this.

Someone had been here. Might still be here.

Someone didn't want me to leave.

I looked around quickly and saw nothing out of place. There was no sign of anyone or evidence that anyone had been at the house. Then I looked down to Shep. "How'd you let this happen?"

The dog just looked at me, unable to answer, unable to understand my question. But I was sure he could smell my fear. I knew I could.

"Come on, Shep." I hurried inside the house, pelted by the dirt and urged on by my discomfort of standing out in the wide open alone. *Alone. All alone*, I thought. *I'm stranded. Trapped. Alone.*

On the way inside, I grabbed up the .22 from behind the kitchen door and headed to the phone. I didn't hesitate to pick up the receiver, wasn't the least bit concerned that Burlene Standish might be listening in on the party line. The only person I knew to call was Jaeger. He was close by, would know how to fix the tires or would be able to help get new ones on, and he would come running once I told him what was going on. I wouldn't be alone then. But I couldn't call Jaeger. There was no dial tone.

The phone was dead.

CHAPTER 29

I made my way outside, staying as close to the house as I could, and found the telephone line had been slashed just like the tires. It had been cut as cleanly as a shaft of wheat at the stalk for harvesting. The sight of the line in two parts numbed me even more than I already was. I was completely cut off from the outer world.

You get used to being stranded when you live on a farm on the edge of western North Dakota. Losing power, or the use of the phone, happened from time to time, especially in winter, when ice, wind, or a combination of both, brought down the lines. Days could pass before the lights came back, which was one of the reasons that Hank and I still relied on the two Franklin stoves to keep us warm in the winter instead of a modern furnace of some kind that required a spark of electricity to light it.

It wasn't that long ago that none of the modern conveniences were available to us this far from town. My grandparents and parents survived most of their lives with minimal intervention from technology, no electricity and no phone, and they got along just fine from what I could tell. But those kinds of survival skills fade fast. You got used to the power being there when you turned on a light switch or picked up the telephone to call the librarian in town for a quick answer to a question. Modern technology seemed to disappear into the daily routine and brainwash you into believing that it had always been there, that you couldn't live without it.

At least it was morning. The darkness of night would have only added to the confinement, fear, and loss that I felt as I stared at that cut line. Just considering such a thing nearly pushed me off balance and sent me into a fit of sheer terror. I took a deep breath instead and tried to calm myself.

I had no choice but to hurry back inside the house. I felt like a rabbit fleeing from the shadow of a hawk as I edged along the siding, hoping the house would protect me with its power of love and its persistence at surviving the winters since my grandparents had built it, would save me from whomever lurked out of my sight—but not out of my mind.

Shep followed along and charged past me and ran circles around me as I stepped foot inside the house. He didn't bark, just eyed me with a stern look that said to stop and stay. I'd always trusted him, so I did.

I closed the front door and locked it. But I kept hold of the .22. That gun wasn't going to leave my sight until I figured out what was going on and what I was going to do.

"Stay," I said to Shep. Then I went around to all of the windows, peered out of them, and closed the blinds. I knew I was closing myself in more by doing so, but I didn't want anybody seeing me move about. If they had a knife, they might have a gun, too. One shot through the window and that would be the end of me. I had to think like that. I had to get back to Hank somehow.

I gripped the .22 tighter as I made my way through the house closing the blinds. The odd red light in the early morning sky had faded, but there was still a pink glow penetrating the slats of the blinds.

What had I done?

I got to the bedroom last and, as I closed the blind and put the house into a sullen, stormy, gray darkness, I started to feel something else. Another emotion sprouted from deep inside me and began to overcome the fear I felt. I was starting to get mad. Mad at the crazy world I lived in, mad at the situation I found myself in, and mad at the person who'd sent me into a state of terror. I answered my own question then: I hadn't done a damn thing. Not a damn thing. I didn't deserve this. I didn't deserve this at all.

I have a funeral to go to, damn it! I wanted to scream, but I didn't. I was afraid someone would hear me, afraid that I would snap. Instead, I allowed a single tear to run down my cheek. One. It was all I had left.

CHAPTER 30

The idea of having two functional vehicles to maintain and look after was absurd, a luxury that Hank and I would never consider or be able to afford. The Studebaker had been our one and only means of personal transportation for nearly as long as I could remember. A single pickup truck to meet all of our needs, whether it was to pull a hay wagon loaded down with bales or drive to a funeral in our best clothes.

The only other operational vehicles on the farm were an old Farmall tractor that I was unsure of and the Allis-Chalmers Gleaner Model E combine that I was still making payments on. I had never driven the Gleaner. That machine had been Hank's pride and joy, and the care and operation of it had fallen to Erik Knudsen after the accident. Now that task was another thing Jaeger had taken on. I didn't even know how to start the darn thing. I'd have to check the index in the operator's manual and hope to good heavens that the indexer had put an entry in for starting it—if not, I'd have to write it in.

The Model E had no driver's enclosure, meaning I would be exposed to the world while I hunted for the ignition. Another bad plan. It'd be my luck that I'd get shot using the index. I almost smiled at the irony of the thought. Almost. There was nothing funny about murder as far as I was concerned.

Get ahold of yourself, Marjorie. Think. You can find a way out of this. You have to.

I took a deep breath and looked down at Shep. I wished I had trained him to run to the Knudsens' on command, used him like a passenger pigeon with a note asking Jaeger to come rescue me, but I hadn't.

Shep had never been that kind of dog. Instead, he sat staring up at me, waiting to see what I was going to do next. He was always trying to figure it out before I did. If only I had his talents. But I didn't; I had no clue about what to do next.

I was about to go peek out the window and see if I could see any-thing—or anyone—moving about, when Shep's ears shot straight up. He turned his attention to the front door and ran to it, barking.

I panicked. "Shep, shut up. Shut up, boy," I said through gritted teeth, as quietly, but as demandingly, as I possibly could. As usual, the dog paid me no mind. I didn't have the commanding tone that Hank had. All that man had to do was utter a syllable in a deeper than normal voice and Shep would freeze at attention no matter what he'd been doing. I guess I was a pushover.

And now, whatever—or whoever—had gotten Shep's attention, was alerted to the fact that we were inside the house. But I guess if they'd been watching all along then they already knew that . . . didn't they?

Shep continued to bark, then he spun in circles like he always did when someone drove onto the land. I hadn't moved an inch, and I wasn't sure that I was going to be able to unless I had to, so I stood there and strained my ears to hear what the dog heard. And I did hear. At least distantly. A vehicle of some kind had turned off the road and was rumbling toward the house. It was either that or a tornado. I doubted that Shep had a different dance for bad storms. Besides, the sky had been red not green.

I repeated my demand again for Shep to shut up, but he ignored me, actually heightening the pitch of his bark. I knew the only way he was going to quiet down was to let him out so he could see for himself who had trespassed onto his territory without permission.

I sighed and made my way to the picture window that looked out on the road. Slowly, carefully, so I didn't ripple my mother's handmade curtains. I peered out.

A dusty, black, ten-year-old Ford sedan rolled to a stop behind the Studebaker and a familiar man stepped out of it, intent on making his way to the door. I sighed again, only this time in relief. It wasn't a killer, or a bad man set on doing me further harm. The man was Pastor John Mark Llewellyn from the Lutheran Church in Dickinson. And then another wave of stress hit me. I had chicken shit on my shoes from doing chores, and I was sure that I smelled of fear and panic from everything that had transpired since discovering my tires had been slashed. I was in no way ready for—or expecting—company from a man of God. But I was, at the very least, certain that he hadn't come to kill me, though even that was hard to be sure of these days. The truth was, everybody I encountered was likely to find their way onto my suspect list. At least until I, and the rest of the world, figured out why somebody had killed Calla Eltmore.

I took a deep breath, half ashamed of myself for thinking Pastor John Mark could kill someone. He was no more than a gentle boy just a few years out of the seminary. No, I was certain that Pastor John Mark had come to save me in one way or another. And for once, I was grateful for the idea of salvation.

There were five Lutheran churches in town. I never understood the difference between them, and the truth was I suspected that it didn't much matter. My father always said that humans made God a lot more complicated than they needed to. And then he'd say, "All a man has to do is to stand in the middle of a North Dakota wheat field to know he isn't alone in this universe, Marjorie."

I agreed with him for the most part, but I'd had my own arguments with God long before Hank stepped into a gopher hole. That incident had only deepened the schism. Still, I had to say I was never more relieved to see a man of the cloth on my front stoop than I was at that moment.

The first knock came as I was halfway between the picture window and the door. Shep was spinning so fast that I thought for sure he was going to blend his black and white fur into a permanent gray. He was barking his fool head off, too.

I had just about given up trying to shush him. "Shep!" I yelled. "Be nice!" To my surprise, the dog stopped barking and sat down properly at my ankle without making another sound.

The second knock came as I slowly opened the door. I judged how long it would take for me to slam the door closed and lock it if I felt threatened. I couldn't help myself.

"Marjorie?" Pastor John Mark said. "Are you all right?" His voice was as soft as his sweet blue eyes. If he meant me harm, then there was no escaping it; I was sure of it. Pastor was a tall man, with hair as yellow as the best straw around, and he was lean and fit. He could have muscled his way into the house before I could raise the .22 to fire.

I couldn't answer him. All I could do was shake my head and open the door a little wider to let him inside.

CHAPTER 31

Putting Pastor John Mark Llewellyn on my personal suspect list seemed like the worst kind of sin I could have committed at that moment. He was a calm, serene man, young, but wise in ways I would never understand, and he always seemed happy as a lark. And he should be. He was married to a beautiful girl—well, girl to me—Connie, who was pregnant with their second child. She was the perfect pastor's wife—calm but energetic, comfortable in the shadow of a religious man, and amazingly unfazed by jealousy. Pastor garnered a lot of attention that could be misinterpreted by a less confident woman. Connie Llewellyn seemed completely comfortable in her skin, and every time I had been around her I'd been completely at ease. The two of them took pleasure in building a life in Dickinson after being transferred from another church—his first—in Minnesota. Their firstborn son, Paul Mark, was the spitting image of his father and just as happy. They lived in a well-kept bungalow behind the Redeemer's Lutheran Church just off 10th Street. It was a Free Lutheran affiliation. As far as I knew, everybody in the congregation loved Pastor John Mark. My time in the pew had been sparse since his arrival, so I had been dependent on subtle gossip. Everyone at church hoped Pastor planned on staying on for the rest of his life—but no one believed that he would. A handsome, gregarious pastor like him was bound to be promoted to a larger church at some point in the future. The religious life suited him well, and even though he was fair-haired and fair-skinned, he looked good in black, not faded, pale, or weighed down by the color or the position at all.

"What on earth is the matter, Marjorie?" Pastor asked, as he stepped cautiously inside the house. He glanced down at Shep quickly,

I think just to make sure he knew where the dog was, then turned his attention back to me a little more warily.

I could barely form the words to answer him. I knew I must have looked crazed, all disheveled like Medusa, with my work clothes on and the Remington .22 clutched tightly in my hand. All I could do was keep shaking my head from side to side.

"Marjorie," Pastor said, stopping just inside the threshold, "you're concerning me. Is everything all right?" I didn't blame him for not wanting to come inside the house any farther. He was a trained observer, but it was my guess that he'd never walked into a situation like this before.

As usual, he was dressed head to toe in black, including his perfectly starched shirt. His dog collar was nothing but a white square perched directly and perfectly under his Adam's apple. I was reminded of Pete McClandon's outfit, but Pete didn't emit authentic grace like Pastor did.

"I'm not all right, Pastor. I can't tell you how happy I am to see you."

"Is something the matter with Hank?"

"Not that I know of. But I wouldn't know. The telephone line's cut."

"Cut? On purpose? Are you sure, Marjorie?" He looked at me like I was a child prone to making things up. It was a practiced look for such a young man.

"I'm certain of it." I still had hold of the .22. I wasn't letting go of the rifle just yet. Shep had calmed down. He hadn't taken his eyes off of Pastor since he'd walked in the door, and he sensed, I guess, that Pastor, like Hank, frowned on animals in the house.

"Who would do such a thing?" he asked.

"The same person who slashed all four of my truck tires, that's who." I was angry and scared and did nothing to hide it.

Pastor swallowed hard. "You're certain of that?"

"As certain as we are both standing here."

"Did you call the police?"

I glared at Pastor, then realized what I'd done and tried my best to make the look go away. I'm sure the question was just a gut reaction.

"Oh," he said, two seconds later. "You couldn't, could you?"

I shook my head again. "No. I didn't know what I was going to do. I need to get to the hospital to check on Hank, and I had planned on attending Calla Eltmore's funeral." I glanced over at the clock on the wall. I wasn't surprised to see that it had quit running. There'd been no one home to wind it.

He looked at the .22 approvingly. "We need to get you out of here." I sighed. "If you could just take me to the Knudsens' that'd be fine." "Do you think it's safe to leave?"

"I don't know, but I can't stay here. I'm taking this," I nodded at the .22, "and Shep with me. I've shot at varmints before, and I'll do it again if I have to."

"All right," Pastor John Mark said, "let's go." He turned toward door, then stopped to allow me to go first. I wasn't sure if it was because I was a woman or because I had the gun, but it didn't matter. I'd protect us both. But the first thing I had to do was trust that the man who had my back wasn't a killer. I had no choice but to suspect him and everyone else who showed up on my doorstep.

<hr />

Shep was happy to sit in the backseat and stick his head out of Pastor's Ford and ignore us completely. Even though it was ten years old, the interior of the car was pristine. The floor mats were so clean you could have eaten off them, and there wasn't a speck of dirt or dust to be seen on the dashboard . The chrome push-buttons on the front of the radio gleamed like freshly brushed teeth. And if it hadn't been for Shep's presence and the shit ground into the soles of my shoes, I could have sworn I smelled that new car smell distantly, still embedded in the black vinyl seats.

The sky had threatened to bleach itself white as the sun rose. A clean bedsheet that went on for as far as the eye could see, the edges tinged with color. The wind had returned, and any promise of precipitation was farther off than I could see. We needed rain—or snow, as much as I hated to say it.

There had been no one waiting to stop us, but I'd yet to relax. Every nerve in my body sizzled with awareness and restrained panic. I looked over at Pastor, who had both hands gripping the black metal steering wheel tightly; there was a line of sweat resting on his upper lip. His eyes were starting to turn red, too, irritated or on the verge of an emotion he dared not speak of.

"Are you sure that you don't want me to take you into town?" Pastor asked, not taking his eyes off the road. "I think you should talk to the police."

I shook my head. "I want to leave Shep with Jaeger. He'll be safe there. Besides, I want to make sure Jaeger's all right, all things considered."

"I understand."

"I don't want to hold you up."

Pastor glanced over at me quickly, then focused back on the road ahead—all the while keeping an eye on the rearview mirror. The road behind us was obscured by an eruption of brown dust coming out from underneath the car. We weren't going fast, but Pastor wasn't driving like a grandma, either.

"You're not holding me up," Pastor said. He sniffled.

"Are *you* all right?"

He ticked his head toward Shep. "I'm allergic to dogs."

I immediately felt awful. "I'm sorry; I didn't know."

"You couldn't leave him behind."

"No, I couldn't. It must be hard with your job and all."

He flashed a quick smile. "It's a small burden that I pay to visit with folks. Besides, most people around here don't keep their dogs inside."

"I need Shep's company," I snapped.

"I wasn't judging, Marjorie. Just saying, that's all."

"I'm sorry."

"No need."

Silence suddenly settled between us. The only sound inside the car was the roar of the engine, the unsettled gravel hitting the chassis underneath, and the wind pushing in through Shep's open window. The dog was in pure heaven, enjoying the ride, in a new place, content with watching the world go by. He had no chores to do, nothing to worry about. I was envious.

"Will you be officiating at Calla's funeral?" I finally asked. I wasn't sure why. I knew Calla wasn't a Lutheran. I didn't know exactly what she was. We hardly discussed her personal views on religion, which were vague and nondenominational. God and Jesus in any setting seemed an uncomfortable topic for her, so I tended to avoid it.

Pastor shook his head. "She wasn't a member at our church. Not any church as far as I know. Pete McClandon called and asked if I would conduct the service, but I had to tell him no."

"Why?" It was not an inquisitive question. I knew why. I just wanted him to tell me to be sure.

"You know why, Marjorie. Suicide is the gravest of all sins. I couldn't bargain with God to allow Miss Eltmore into heaven. All I could do would be to preach to the mourners, try to ward them off doing such a thing themselves, and that seemed inappropriate, so I declined. I think Pete's going to say some words."

"No one would do it?" I was exasperated.

Pastor shook his head. "I'm sorry, Marjorie."

"But she didn't do it. She didn't kill herself, Pastor. I'm sure of it."

He looked at me the same way he had when he'd first arrived at the house: Like I was crazed, out of my mind. Then the look faded into sadness. He felt sorry for me; I was deluded.

"I swear to you," I said, defending myself. "Calla Eltmore didn't kill herself. And I'm not the only one who thinks so."

"Do you know what you're saying, Marjorie?"

"Yes. Yes, I do. And I'm not crazy. As God is my witness, I believe Calla Eltmore was murdered in cold blood and that she deserves the same kind of respect as anyone else who's had their life stolen from them. There is nothing to bargain. The sin wasn't hers."

More silence. More rumbling; the engine slowed as we came over a rise. He looked at me curiously and stopped the Ford just at the edge of the Knudsens' lane up to the house. "Why do you believe this, Marjorie?"

I answered by telling him everything I knew. The wound on the wrong side of Calla's head, no note, no sign of depression leading up to the event, and validation from the women with the broken glasses. Everything.

"You have to go to Duke, then. Especially when you consider what has happened at your house," Pastor said. "You have to go to the police right away. If you're right, then whoever did kill Calla must have figured out what you know. You're not safe, Marjorie. Not here. Not in town. Not anywhere."

I sat frozen, listening to Pastor's concerned voice. I knew he was right, that I was in danger. I just didn't want to believe him.

CHAPTER 32

The landscape in North Dakota was so flat and barren that it most often felt like you were the only human on earth, sharing the ground with only antelopes, coyotes, and those ubiquitous and dangerous gophers. And then out of nowhere a house appeared like it had been dropped from the sky. Humans in this topography seemed like an odd add on, like an automobile painted into a picture of cowboys, like they had never belonged there in the first place. But more than the rare oddity of a house sitting in the middle of thousands of unoccupied acres of nothingness, it was the sight of the Knudsens' house in particular that brought me the real shock. I had avoided visiting Jaeger and my dear neighbor's house as much as possible after Erik and Lida's death. I felt guilty about that, but the sight of the small abode that had housed my friends for so many years was more of a heartbreaking sight than I could bear on the best of days.

I expected to see Jaeger's red International Harvester pickup in its normal spot as Pastor pulled up the lane, but the truck wasn't there. There was a different truck parked next to the simple gray clapboard house instead. A white Chevy about as old as my Studebaker, and in far worse shape, sat where Jaeger's truck should have been. The fender wells were rusted so completely that I could see daylight streaming through to the ground. Red bubbles of rust and jagged edges of metal looked like a bad rash had broken out at the weakest points of the battered vehicle's body. The rest of the truck was dented all about, peppered by more than one hailstorm, and it looked like the only wash it had had in the last ten years had come from the rain, and not any human effort. No question, it was a work truck and nothing more.

A familiar young man stood with his back to us, swinging an axe. He stopped chopping wood as we drove up to the house and shielded his eyes from the midmorning sun as he tried to get a look at us. I knew right away that the young man was Lester Gustafson, Jaeger's new hand. He looked like a younger version of our previous extension agent, Lloyd Gustafson. It wasn't hard to tell a Gustafson from any distance. He was of medium height, less than six feet tall, muscular but in a sinewy, trim kind of way, with a head of thick, wheat-colored brown hair. It was like the land had dyed Lester's hair and eyes from so much exposure to it. He was about Jaeger's age and might've even had a few years on him, and all in all, Lester looked to be a fine choice for a hand around the place.

After we parked, I waited for Pastor John Mark to get out of the car before I did. I didn't know Lester, but I suspected his manners were as consistent as his Gustafson looks. He wouldn't look down at me for being the mess that I was, but I still glanced at the mirror and patted my unruly hair into place. Once Pastor was halfway around the car, I got out and followed after him. I made Shep stay in the car.

"Lester," Pastor said, extending his hand for a friendly shake as he made his way to him.

"I thought that was you, Pastor John Mark," Lester said, then looked at me curiously. "Mrs. Trumaine?"

I nodded and offered him no explanation. "Is Jaeger home?"

"No, he just ran Betty Walsh home. She came out to fix us a fine breakfast before we set to work ourselves. I swear, I'm not sure there's anything that girl can't do. Not sure why Jaeger don't go ahead and marry her and get it over with. But it ain't any of my business now is it, aye? She said she had to get ready for some funeral today, I think." Lester propped the axe up against the chopping block, an old ironwood stump that had taken a beating over the years but still looked to have plenty of use ahead of it.

There was only one funeral in town that I knew of and that was Calla's. I wasn't surprised to hear that Betty planned on going. From what I could tell, she liked a spectacle as much, or a little more than, everyone else in town. Though I wasn't quite sure that Calla's funeral was going to be a big draw.

Pastor stuffed his hands into his pockets and a serious look drew on his otherwise sunny face. "You see anything out of the ordinary this morning, Lester?"

"Here?" He shrugged his shoulders.

I stood still and watched Lester as closely as I could. I wasn't surprised that Pastor had questioned him right away. Glad of it, truth be told. It meant he believed me, didn't think I was totally crazy.

"Anywhere in between town and here?" Pastor said.

"Nah, not that I can say," Lester answered. "'Course I wasn't lookin' for nothin' out of the ordinary, either. Why'd you ask?"

"Just some tomfoolery going on about, that's all," Pastor said.

"Over't your place?" Lester asked me.

I nodded. "Somebody slashed all four tires on my truck."

"That don't sound like tomfoolery to me. Sounds like meanness of the worst kind. Too much of that goin' on 'round here of late, you ask me, aye?"

I looked at the ground. Honestly, I was trying my hardest not to look up at the house. I expected Lida to come rushing out the front door at any second with flour on her cheek, wiping it away with the corner of her apron, wondering what was going on. Or Erik to be making his way out of the barn, one hand covered in grease, the other wrapped in a bloody towel because he had busted a knuckle trying to wrench something off a motor. But neither was going to happen. Not now or ever.

Before I could answer Lester, I heard the rev of an engine behind me. I was relieved when I turned around to see Jaeger's red truck cresting the rise of the drive.

"There's Jaeger now," Lester said, glancing back at a wood pile that would hardly last a week in January. "I best get back at it. We got a lot of makin' up to do."

"Jaeger won't mind that you talked to us," I said.

Lester shrugged. "Probably not. But I need this job. I can't afford to mess it up."

"You'll be fine, Lester. I'm proud of you," Pastor said. There was a knowing tone and a lack of information that I didn't seem privy to that passed between the two of them and, for a brief second, made me uncomfortable. Then that feeling evaporated with a warm smile from Lester.

Pastor was a keeper of secrets. I understood that. It was just that I didn't witness it very often—or share any darkness of my own with him. I didn't understand the depth of that trust, of that relationship. Hank was my hope chest and the safe locker of my fears all rolled into one.

Jaeger parked his International Harvester next to Pastor's sedan.

Shep immediately started bouncing between the front and back seats of the Ford, barking his fool head off. I looked over at Pastor, who had a concerned look on his face. I knew he was worried the dog was going to muck up his car.

"Shep!" I yelled. "Settle down!" But the dog paid me no mind.

Jaeger stopped at the back door of the Ford and looked up at me questioningly as he grabbed ahold of the door handle. I nodded yes, and Shep tore out of the car like he'd been caged up half his life. The dog circled happily around Jaeger as he joined the three of us.

"What brings you here, Pastor?" Jaeger asked. He looked back at the Ford, expecting, I think, to see my truck. "And Mrs. Trumaine? Everything all right?"

The air had a dry, static feel to it. The wind wasn't so pushy where we stood, and the sky had lost all of its early morning threat. Thin gray clouds were glued in place high against the white sky overhead.

Pastor offered an answer before I could. "I was heading out to the South Branch for a little fishing this morning and dropped by to see how Marjorie was doing," he said.

I hadn't had the forethought or concern to ask why he'd come by the house in the first place. I'd been in such a state that wondering hadn't crossed my mind. I had just been happy to see him.

I looked at Pastor, all dressed in his everyday preaching clothes, and wondered if he waded into the river like that, or if he ever put on a pair of work pants at all. I wondered if he had his gear and fishing clothes in the trunk of the car. But I didn't say anything. I was sure Pastor had his reasons for saying the things he did.

Jaeger looked at me. "Hank all right?"

"As far as I know," I answered.

He must of heard something in my voice. "You're sure?"

"As sure as I can be. I haven't had the chance to check on him this morning. Somebody cut my phone line."

Jaeger shivered, and his face withdrew into a tight pale retreat. "Cut?" he said. "On purpose?"

"Cut clean through and through. Never knew of any animal or bug who could do such a thing," I said. "I'm sorry, Jaeger; I didn't know where else to go."

"No, of course. I'm glad you came here. What can I do?"

At that second I didn't know how to answer him. I knew there were things coming at me on this day that I would have given anything to avoid, but I knew I couldn't. The truth was, I just wanted to stand there and scream at the world, at Pastor John Mark's loving, plotting, maniacal god for allowing such horrible things to happen, at the wind for not carrying me away, far away to another place and another life that held a dose of happiness and peace in it. But that was impossible. This was my life, and this was the day I had woken up and found myself in.

"Can I use your phone?" I finally said to Jaeger.

He nodded, leaving me no choice but to go inside the house where one of my worst nightmares had begun.

CHAPTER 33

The black plastic phone hung on the wall in between the kitchen and the front room. The perpetually curled cord dangled to the floor, still as a dead snake hanging out to dry. It didn't take much to imagine Lida with the receiver cradled to her ear as she went about making lefse, a Norwegian potato flatbread, for the holidays, or rakfisk from the trout that came out of the Green River out by Gladstone. Pastor had set me thinking about fishing, I suppose, and rakfisk was one of Lida's staple recipes; my mother's, too, as far as that went.

Plain and simple, rakfisk was a salt- and sugar-fermented fish that would last through the winter, served uncooked with onions, sour cream, and dill mustard. It was not a favorite dish of mine, or Hank's, so I hardly ever cooked it, but Erik had loved it; mostly, I think, because he loved to fish nearly as much as he loved to farm. It was difficult being in Lida's kitchen without thinking about rakfisk and lefse. All that was missing was the smell. The kitchen was clean and tidy. Breakfast dishes and skillets were put away but bacon lingered in the air. I was glad that Jaeger was eating.

I picked up the phone and dialed the number from memory. Olga picked up on the first ring. "St. Joseph's Hospital, how may I direct your call?"

"Olga, it's me, Marjorie Trumaine. I need to check in on Hank."

"Just a second, and I'll see if I can get ahold of one of the nurses for ya."

Olga's tone was matter of fact, so I wasn't alarmed. Just uncomfortable because of where I was and what had happened to get the day going. I closed my eyes to help keep the ghosts away, but it didn't help.

Jaeger hadn't changed a thing in the house. Hadn't moved one knick-knack or traded out one picture. I doubted he ever would. The house was a museum to a life that once was.

"Marjorie?" Olga came back on the line, pulling me back into the present.

"Yes?"

"Hank had an easy night. Doc had a baby to deliver this morning, but it's possible he'll get to go home before the end of the day, or first thing in the morning. He sure has rallied since I first saw him come in. Had me worried, he did."

"Thanks for your concern, Olga. Can you get a message to him for me?"

"Sure thing. Whatcha want me to tell him?"

"Let him know I'm running late. It might be after lunch before I make it to the hospital."

"Goin' to *that* funeral, are you?"

I drew in a breath and bit my tongue before I spoke. "Can you please tell him, Olga?"

"Sure thing, Marjorie. I just wouldn't go to . . ."

I cut her off. "Thanks, Olga. I have to go."

I stood in the kitchen, trying to decide what to do next, when Jaeger and Pastor walked in the door. They stopped in unison and stood shoulder to shoulder.

"What's the matter?" I said, looking at them both. They had serious looks on their faces.

Pastor shrugged. "I told Jaeger about your truck. We don't think you should be alone, Marjorie."

"Did you tell him my thinking about Calla?"

Pastor nodded. "All things considered, I thought it was best."

Jaeger stood stoically, the scar over his eye a little more noticeable than it had been outside. He always looked on the verge of anger, but that was only because of the structure of his bones, not the makeup of his heart. At that moment, he seemed timid as a mouse, every fiber of his being on alert. I understood completely.

"I'll be fine. But I have to get ready to go into town. I don't want to miss Calla's funeral because of this. And, of course, I need to get to Hank. He might get to come home later today. I'll need my truck for that."

"Pete'll take him home if need be," Pastor said.

I shook my head. "That's a hearse and an ambulance. Hank'll only ride in the back of it once. He refuses otherwise."

A knowing smile flickered across Pastor's face and disappeared as quickly as it had come. "We don't think going back to your place is a good thing to do. At least until you've had a conversation with the police about what's happened."

I didn't think before I spoke. "Well, I can't go to a funeral dressed like this!"

"You can wear my mother's dress," Jaeger said, then looked at the floor. "She would like that."

I wished I hadn't said a word, but that was no surprise. I was always getting myself into something or other without thinking about the consequences.

❦

Erik and Lida Knudsen had been murdered in their bed as they'd slept. I had never seen the aftermath, just imagined it a million times. I stopped at the closed bedroom door and looked at Jaeger, who had his hand on the glass doorknob.

"It's all right," he said, reading my fears. "We made it look like it always did."

"I'm sorry," I said. "I didn't mean to put you through this."

"It's okay. Once I decided that I was going to stay here, I had to figure out how to live with what was, not just the way things are. I got too much to do to walk in sadness every day. I think you understand what I mean. If I keep this place goin', it keeps them both alive in a way, and that doesn't make everything all right, but it makes me feel better. It would break their hearts if I sold this place off. It's mine and Peter's now, even if he is away, not breaking a sweat to keep up with it. He'll throw a hand in when he can one of these days; I'm sure of it."

I nodded, smiled, then looked past Jaeger to the open door of his bedroom. His bed was unmade, the sheets and blankets a tangled mess that looked like the beginnings of a bird's nest. I still worried about him and Betty, but I wasn't going to say anything. Not now. I'd already said my piece once; that had been enough.

I looked at Jaeger a little more closely; there was something I first noticed as he drove up, but I hadn't put my finger on it until that moment. "You should come by when this all settles down. I'll give you a haircut like I used to when you and Peter were boys."

He reached up to his ear and tugged on the hair. "Nah, that's all right. All of the kids are letting their hair grow a little longer these days."

I sighed. Even without a television set, I'd heard plenty about the boys from Liverpool that played on the Ed Sullivan show back in February, but I hadn't thought about them changing the world. They were a music band, for goodness sakes. A band named after a bug. I still preferred Bing Crosby myself.

Pastor had gone back outside to wait on me. He was going to take me into town while Jaeger set about getting the Studebaker's tires replaced. I could see him through Jaeger's window, standing next to the black Ford in his black clothes, smoking a cigarette. He looked like a smokestack at a distant factory. It was the first time I had ever seen Pastor John Mark smoke. Stumbling across my mess was a far cry from a peaceful morning spent fishing.

I didn't say anything else about a haircut. Jaeger opened the door to Erik and Lida's room and walked in without hesitating. He headed straight to a wardrobe on the opposite side of the room.

I stood at the doorway, blocked by my own fears. The air in the room smelled stale, but that was all. There was no hint of death or blood to detect, and I was glad of that. The bed was covered with a white chenille bedspread, made up perfectly. There wasn't a wrinkle to be seen. I looked away from the two pillows; they were bleached snow white, no sign of murder anywhere to be seen.

Jaeger stood staring at me. "She only had one black dress," he said. "I hope you like it."

Of course she only had one black dress. It was all she needed. I didn't say that, though. I just smiled the best I could and walked to the wardrobe. Luckily, Lida and I were about the same size. I was sure I could wear the dress, even if I didn't want to.

CHAPTER 34

The parking lot of the funeral home was full, but it didn't require a sheriff's deputy to direct traffic. Pastor was able to drive up to the front door without any trouble. He put the Ford in park and left the engine running.

"Aren't you coming in?" I said.

He looked at me sadly, then turned his attention back to the entrance of McClandon's. "I can't condone what Miss Eltmore did, Marjorie. Surely, you must understand what my appearance at her funeral would suggest."

"Then you don't believe me."

"It's not that."

"It's that no one else does. That it's not official that she was murdered, that she didn't kill herself. Pastor, if I'm right, then Calla's basking in the glory of heaven instead of shackled in the bonds of eternal damnation. You should be shouting that victory from the roof of the church."

"I'll pray for her."

"It can't hurt." I wanted to say more than that, but I didn't. Now was not the time to debate the rights and wrongs of Christian behavior more than I already had. I had to stop. It was obvious I wasn't going to change Pastor's position. I grabbed the door handle and pulled it up. "Thank you for stopping by this morning. I don't know what would have happened to me if you hadn't," I said.

"It had been a while, and I thought with all that was going on with Hank that you could use a visit. We haven't seen much of you at services."

I wasn't about to be made to feel guilty for my lack of attendance at church. "Well, I appreciate it." I pushed open the door and a gust of fresh air rushed inside the car, clearing out the last remnants of dog smell. Shep had stayed with Jaeger.

"Don't be a stranger, Marjorie. I know things are hard, but the Lord has a plan for us all."

I stiffened. "Tell that to Erik and Lida, Pastor—or Calla. You tell them that," I snapped, then as sure as Sunday came once a week, my face went pale, and a wave of embarrassment washed over me. Even I was shocked by my own lack of restraint, but I couldn't help myself. I couldn't believe murder was ever planned for the good of anything. That just didn't make any sense to me. The suggestion of such a thing just flat out made me mad.

Too his credit, Pastor smiled as I got out of the car. But before I could apologize, he leaned over and closed the door, put the car in gear, and drove off without saying another word.

I couldn't do anything but stand there and watch the black car disappear out of the parking lot, feeling like I had just irrevocably insulted one of the nicest men on earth.

There were only two or three seats open in the back of the funeral chapel. There were no more floral bouquets than there had been at the viewing, but they were clustered together in strategic spots around the room to make it look like an abundant garden of grief. The fragrance of more varieties of flowers than I could identify, or classify, had been dulled by the presence of humans. It looked like Easter Sunday at church, the pews full, everyone in their best clothes, though darker in nature, the air uncomfortable instead of celebratory.

Before I sat down in one of the remaining seats, I craned my neck forward to get a look at the front of the chapel. On one hand, I was thankful that the lid of the simple wood casket was closed. No one would have to see Calla in her final state, dressed in a borrowed pink sweater and with a bullet hole in the wrong side of her head. But that also meant I would never see her again, or be able to confirm what I had seen at the viewing. I was left with my memory and nothing more.

The front row of seats that faced the casket was empty except for one. Herbert Frakes sat alone, hunched over, staring away from the casket at something unseen. I was tempted to walk up there and sit down next to him, offer him some comfort, but my feet remained planted. That would have to wait. I wasn't family. I didn't belong there.

Organ music whispered over the crowd, who with their fidgeting and discomfort drowned out the peaks and valleys of an unknown hymn. I had nearly been late to the service, and as I finally took my seat the volume of the music began to increase.

I was seated next to a little boy who was about ten years old. He looked at me, then looked away. He had on a light blue, short-sleeved Oxford shirt and a pair of blue dress pants to match; his one and only best summer outfit that he was about to grow out of. He was a towhead, his hair shimmering white like an old man's. His hair was a common sight; I would have been more surprised to see a ginger haired boy next to me, or a black haired boy, like Pete McClandon must have been. I glanced over at his mother, Melba Olafson, and smiled. She smiled back. There were a lot of Olafsons in town, just like there were a lot of Smiths or Joneses in other towns. I was glad to sit next to a child; he had no clue what was going on.

Pete McClandon appeared at the open set of double doors that led into the chapel. He looked like I expected him to. Dressed in black from head to toe, his shoulders erect and his gray eyes curiously aware—searching the crowd or just gazing over it, I wasn't sure which. After a long second, he walked into the room and slowly made his way down the single aisle toward the casket.

But what I didn't expect, and it seemed no one else did, either, was for Pete to be followed into the room by Duke Parsons, Guy Reinhardt, and another sheriff's deputy that I didn't recognize. All three men were dressed in their shiny best brown and tan uniforms, their campaign hats on top of their heads, their guns holstered with the snaps open.

There was no question that they were here on business, not to pay their respects to the deceased town librarian.

A wave of murmurs reached my ears, and the music faded away. Suddenly, I was witness to a confusing spectacle instead of being here just to pay my respects. I was trapped, given no choice but to be part of something I had not intended to be. My whole day had been like that.

Pete and the trio of law officers seemed oblivious of the crowd. They walked straight to the end of the aisle and stopped in front of the casket with their backs to the crowd of mourners. They did not show their intention, and I could only guess at their purpose or reasoning. I should have been able to come up with something, but I couldn't. I was stunned.

The murmurs didn't so much as stop but seemed to take a collective breath, waiting to see what was going to happen next. Everyone, including me, had questions that needed to be answered. The main ones being, *Why here? Why now? Isn't this a sacred place? Couldn't whatever it is have been delayed until after the funeral? Away from the eyes of the whole town? Hadn't Calla's reputation and legacy suffered enough?*

Only the boy next to me seemed not to be interested in what was happening. He stared at the floor, tapping his shoes to some unheard melody. I wished I could have traded places with him, but I couldn't take my eyes off the front of the room.

After a long second at the casket, Duke turned around and walked over to Herbert. Guy and the other deputy followed, stopped an equal step behind. Pete remained at the casket, looking over the crowd.

"Herbert Frakes," Duke Parsons, the acting sheriff, said, "you are under arrest for the murder of Calla Eltmore."

CHAPTER 35

I'd never fainted at bad news, and I wasn't about to start, but I had to admit that my whole body trembled as the word "arrest" echoed to the back of the funeral chapel. There were quite a few groans, some whispering, and then dead silence, as Herbert Frakes was handcuffed and led down the aisle, silent, shoulders slumped, eyes cast to the floor, offering no struggle at all.

The little boy next to me was interested now, and I wanted to do nothing more than shield his eyes. He didn't need to see this. But he had. A childhood memory that would mark this day forever. I resisted, held my hands tight at my side. Anyone in this room was bound to remember this day for a long time to come, not just the boy. Me included.

I thought the roof would erupt off of the funeral home once the police and Herbert were out of sight, but it didn't, not really. People talked, coughed, shifted in their seats, respectful of where they were. I think most folks were just stunned.

Pete McClandon stepped up to take control of the crowd, calm them, shush them; he was ready to get on with the funeral. It was a seemingly impossible task. Pete'd had a lot of experience with crowds, but my guess was he'd never had to face anything like this. I wasn't sure anybody ever had.

Then words and music melded into an unintelligible garble. My mind ran a million miles a second, sorting, searching, organizing—indexing, in an odd way—for any sign that led me to believe that Herbert Frakes was capable of being a killer.

Herbert? How could he have killed Calla? He loved her; I was sure of it. There were, of course, things that I didn't know about their relationship. But what I had just witnessed didn't make any sense to me. At that second, I didn't believe that Herbert had killed Calla any more than I'd believed that Calla had killed herself. But Duke believed it. Duke, the acting sheriff, the deputy intent on winning the upcoming special election. He might have just sealed the win, catching a killer and bringing him to justice in front of everyone. Maybe that was his plan. The *Press* would surely have something to say about the dramatic arrest at the murdered librarian's funeral.

I just couldn't settle my mind to the fact that I had been right. But never in a thousand years would I have thought that Herbert really could have killed Calla—even though he had been on my suspect list in my personal index. Him and the woman with the broken glasses. I hadn't believed that either of them were responsible for murdering Calla. Not really. I had been grasping at straws. But maybe I'd been right about that, as well. Maybe I'd needed to trust my instincts more than I had. Maybe Hank had been right all along, too—right that Duke knew what I knew, that the police were doing their job. Which meant they had evidence and, most likely, more information about Herbert that I didn't, and couldn't, know.

I felt sick at the thought.

I looked over at the towheaded boy, who had gone back to being bored, tapping his toes to that unknown melody, wringing his hands like he was keeping time—or trying to move it along, I wasn't sure which. I wished I could join in with him, because I sure didn't like what I was thinking, or what I was hearing coming from the front of the chapel.

"Death is not an end," Pete McClandon declared loudly, in a deep baritone voice. "It is only a beginning. A sweet peaceful rest from the madness of life as a human being . . ."

I was glad to have my own purse with me. I had a pack of Salems stuck in the side, and if I could have ever used a cigarette, this was the time. Sitting in the back of the chapel had its advantages. I was nearly the first person out of the funeral home at the end of the service. There would be no procession to the cemetery. Calla was to be cremated. And with the casket closed, and no family to console, the long trip to say goodbye had already occurred.

The threat, then dullness, of the morning sky had changed once again, to a nonthreatening blue with a few strokes of feathery cirrus clouds dabbed on it here and there. I had hoped to see rain clouds in the distance as I exited Calla's funeral. I had hoped that the world would show some grief and sadness. Lord knew we needed the rain, and there would be something to mark Calla's passing left behind.

I scanned the parking lot, looking for my Studebaker. Jaeger was supposed to deliver it here once the tires had been repaired, or new ones put on. There weren't many older Studebaker trucks in town, so my truck was usually easy to pick out of a crowd. But I didn't see it anywhere.

I stepped aside, off the walk, and found a comfortable spot out of the sun under a tall cottonwood tree. The grass on the lawn of the funeral home had been meticulously cut. Each blade was the exact same height. It looked like carpet, brown stalks with green tips, life trying to hang on through the seasons, summer stubbornly refusing to give into autumn. The grass would go dormant for the winter, and, to my disappointment, I saw no weeds to identify from where I stood.

No matter where I went, I felt the tug of work. I should be working now, but that was just impossible. I had to be where I was at the moment. No matter what. *Even if someone had tried to stop me.*

I shivered at the thought. Could it have been Herbert who had slashed my tires and cut the phone line, all because he didn't want me to be at the funeral? Did he know what was going to happen? Surely Duke had interrogated him before he'd arrested him, checked to see if Herbert had an alibi, could account for his time? Maybe he didn't want me to see him arrested for the murder of my dear friend.

At the very least, it was an explanation for the incidents at the house this morning. But no matter how hard I tried, I still couldn't quite accept the idea that Herbert was a killer, that he had sneaked onto my land and slashed my tires. Shep would have barked, would have alerted me, and he didn't. The dog hadn't done his job, and something about that simple fact bothered me to no end.

Nothing made sense to me at the moment. I dug into my purse and pulled out my pack of cigarettes, just as the crowd began to push out of the funeral home.

I spotted Delia Finch right away, head above the rest, nose to the air, dressed in an appropriate black dress and hat and in a hurry to get away from the funeral home. She almost marched to the sidewalk and headed straight toward the library. I wondered if she'd closed it for the funeral and deprived the taxpayers of the opportunity to borrow a book. It was a catty thought. But I couldn't help it. I didn't like that woman.

I lit my Salem and, as always, the menthol was a bit of a surprise to the back of my throat. I coughed and exhaled at the same time.

My head had dropped, and when I brought it back up I came face-to-face with the woman with the broken glasses. "Do you mind if I join you?" she said.

CHAPTER 36

I almost choked on the cigarette smoke again, but my lungs were free. I was glad to see the woman, though not under these circumstances. It would have been easy to think that she was just a figment of my imagination. But she stood before me as real as any other human being, and unlike every other time I had encountered her, this time she wasn't alone. An unknown man stood next to her.

"I *would* like some company, thank you" I said, answering her question. Which was the truth. After bearing witness to such a dramatic funeral, I didn't want to be alone. I wanted Hank to lean on, to comfort me, but that, of course, was impossible right now.

The woman was dressed like everyone else, suited for mourning in deep shades of black and gray. A pill box hat sat on her perfectly coifed hair with the netted veil pulled up, so I could look her in the eye. Each stitch of her clothes seemed to be made just for her; the dress fit her like a glove, and she was surprisingly feminine for a woman twenty years my senior. I was immediately aware of the borrowed dress I was wearing; self-conscious and embarrassed.

The woman dug into her purse and pulled out a gold cigarette case. In an orchestrated move that looked like it had been rehearsed a million times, the man produced a shiny silver Zippo lighter, as if by prestidigitation, and rolled the tiny wheel against the flint, producing a steady flame for her.

Before she put the cigarette to the flame, the woman said, "This is my husband, Claude. Professor Claude Tutweiler." There was no pride in the woman's voice. It was just a matter-of-fact statement.

I extended my hand to the man, who looked to have the same

seamstress or tailor as the woman. His suit looked perfect on him, too, like an extra set of black wool skin had been formed over his entire body. Starting with the man, my mind began to count the number of clothing items in my sight that were black. Deep in the recesses of consciousness a list formed:

Ascot instead of a tie
Belt with three holes left to fill
Black shirt instead of white
Fedora (this man would never wear a trilby) with an adorning black
    feather (fake? Or a crow's feather?)
Trousers, double-pleated and cuffed
Umbrella with a smooth black handle and wear marks just starting to
    show
Wingtip shoes (no galoshes), highly polished
Wool overcoat with black buttons made of wood and painted

I had to take a deep breath and close my eyes for a brief second to make the listing stop. Sometimes, my inclination to organize bordered on madness, and I knew the truth was that I couldn't stop it any more than I could stop breathing. Along with the list, the index in my mind had a new main entry: Tutweiler, Claude.

"Are you all right?" the woman said.

I opened my eyes to find them both gazing at me with genuine concern. "Yes, well, as much as I can be." I feigned a quick smile. It was all I could muster. "I'm still in a bit of shock and disbelief," I said, not sure why I felt comfortable enough to say so.

The man relaxed with a nod. "It *was* quite an event, unexpected and saddening." He had a sharp jaw, a Roman nose, and the deepest blue eyes I think I had ever seen. He was a strikingly handsome man, and in appearance perhaps a little younger than the woman, though there were flecks of gray in his perfectly trimmed hair, white wall tires around the ears under the comfortably placed Fedora. He also wore a mustache that was as brown and perfectly edged as a whisk broom. The two of them complimented each other in a planned, paired kind of way, but there were differences between them that I couldn't quite put my finger on.

"A pleasure to meet you, Mr. Tutweiler," I said to the man.

He winced. I'm sure he was accustomed to being called "Professor."

"And you," he said, without a change in expression. His voice could have melted butter. His accent was flat, almost distant, not noticeable. I was certain that he hadn't been born or raised in North Dakota. "Miss?"

"I'm Marjorie Trumaine," I said to Professor Tutweiler, then turned my attention to the woman. "I never caught your name?"

"I'm Nina. Nina Tutweiler, the professor's wife." She gazed up at him with pride, or something else, I couldn't be sure, but when she looked back at me I searched for judgment or superiority and felt none. I was relieved. She made no offer to shake hands or touch me physically in any way. For some reason, I wasn't surprised.

"It's nice to finally have a name to put with a face," I said to Nina Tutweiler.

Before she could say anything, her husband said, "Oh, she must be the one who dusted you off from that nasty fall."

"I was terribly unstable that day," Nina said. She took a drag off her cigarette and looked away.

I had nearly forgotten my own cigarette, transfixed by the Tutweilers as I was. I tapped off a long ash and watched it dissipate in the wind before it hit the ground. I thought of Calla being reduced to nothing more than ash and grit, and a lump formed immediately in my throat.

"I would like to properly repay you for your kindness," Nina said. "There was no announcement of a gathering after the funeral like there normally is."

"Everyone was convinced that Calla had committed the gravest of sins, that she wasn't worthy of respectable treatment," I said with an uncontrollable sneer.

"They were wrong," Claude said. "But you both knew that, didn't you?"

Nina sighed and cast an uncomfortable look at Claude. "Would you care to stop by our home for some tea and cookies? Some company on this dreary day would be grand," she said. "It's not a buffet, but Calla spoke highly of you to me. You were her local celebrity. She was proud of you."

"Oh," Claude said, "*she's* the indexer."

"Yes," Nina answered. "Calla had all of her books on a special shelf. And she kept a list of all of the questions Marjorie had ever asked of her. The indexes were a part of her legacy, of something that would last on in this world long after she had departed it. You were special to her, Marjorie, but surely you knew that."

The lump in my throat vanished, and my face flushed red. "I never knew Calla kept a list."

"She made lots of lists. You and she were more alike than you may know," Nina said.

"How did you know her so well?" I asked bluntly. It was a question that came out of nowhere, except from my own discomfort. I hadn't known Nina Tutweiler existed until she had fallen down the library steps.

"That would be my doing," Claude interjected.

"He's an English professor at the college," Nina said. "He and Calla shared a passion. Robert Browning and Elizabeth Barrett Browning. I was pulled into her orbit because of Claude, of course." She smiled over at her husband, who, oddly, was staring past me. "The Victorians were never my favorites, but after spending time with Calla I came to appreciate the Brownings' poetry and their life together."

"Dear Nina is a little more of a dramatist. She's always been quite taken with Shakespeare."

Nina dropped her cigarette on the ground and smashed the orange coal at the end of it with the toe of her black high-heeled shoe. "To die, to sleep—To sleep, perchance to dream—ay, there's the rub, For in this sleep of death what dreams may come ..."

"Shall I reciprocate a little more from your beloved *Hamlet*?" Claude said.

"Not here," Nina answered, narrowly. She looked at me. "Claude

likes to battle with my memory of verses and sonnets. He finds it enter-
taining. His memory is much better than mine for holding onto things."

I had no idea what was being discussed. A gust of wind pushed
its way around us, bringing with it the noise of departing vehicles, of
people vacating the premises as quickly and dutifully as possible. Along
with those noises came voices and footsteps descending upon us.

"Well, look at this," a familiar voice said from behind me.

I turned around to face Betty Walsh, alone and without an escort,
of course. Jaeger was seeing to my truck. Though I had expected to see
her with her parents, if I saw her at all.

Betty pushed her way in between the Tutweilers and me, con-
tinuing her intrusion—which was how I felt about it. I hoped I'd be
able to keep my mouth shut. "It's Professor Tutweiler and Mrs. Trumaine," Betty went on, as she came to a stop. "I didn't know you two
knew each other."

"We just met," I said coldly.

Betty was about the only person I'd seen since arriving at the
funeral home who wasn't wearing black. She was dressed head to toe
in a deep maroon front-pleated dress with a scoop neck and shirred
skirt. The trim was acetate satin and glinted in the sunlight. She wore
a simple sweater, about two shades darker than her dress, probably to
keep herself warm.

I had already created a memory index for Betty. One that included
an unmade bed and a Candy Striper's uniform. I was about to add ill-
mannered and brash to the index, as well.

"I just love Professor Tutweiler's class," Betty said, then looked at
Nina. "Oh, you must be his wife."

"I am," Nina said. "Nina Tutweiler." She extended her hand to Betty,
who responded in kind and smiled as Nina stared her in the eyes. "I'm
so glad you're in Claude's class. He needs enthusiastic students like you."

"Thank you," Betty said, withdrawing from Nina. "Well, that was a
big surprise in there, wasn't it, Mrs. Trumaine? I can't wait to tell Jaeger
all about it. It's a shame he had to miss this." She stared at me with penetrating eyes, and I looked away, uncomfortable.

The wind subsided, then picked up again, whistling as it went. We all grabbed our skirts, an automatic response that was lost on Claude.

When I looked back at Betty, I could see Claude Tutweiler staring at her. He looked like he had just stepped barefoot on a bee and was trying not to show any pain. It was an unsuccessful attempt at hiding his discomfort.

"Well," Betty said, "I just wanted to say hello. It was nice to meet you, Mrs. Tutweiler. I best be off. I have a shift at the hospital this afternoon." She paused and looked at me. "I'll check on Hank as soon as I get there."

"I'll be there shortly," I said.

"I'm sure you will," Betty replied, then turned and flittered away, disappearing into the parking lot full of departing mourners.

"A first-year, Claude?" Nina said snidely, digging into her purse for something.

"Too early to tell if she's talented or not," Claude said, looking away from the direction where Betty had gone.

"I bet it is," Nina said. She pulled out a piece of paper and offered it to me.

I took it. It was a business card with her name and address on it.

"Please come by for tea this afternoon, if you can," Nina said. "I'm aware of the situation with your husband. I hope everything will work out the best it can for you."

I didn't know what to say to that, so I avoided acknowledging it. "I'll try to come by. It's very nice of both of you." I didn't want to burden them with my worries about Hank. Not after a funeral. Not ever, really.

"It would be our pleasure," Claude said. "Any friend of Calla's is a friend of ours."

CHAPTER 37

I had never been so glad to see the Studebaker. The parking lot was nearly empty, and I hadn't been standing alone long. I should have been happy with myself, smugly satisfied that I had been right all along. Calla Eltmore *had* been murdered. Murdered by Herbert Frakes, according to the Stark County Sheriff's Department. But I wasn't smug at all. I was bewildered.

I still couldn't bring myself to believe that Herbert had killed Calla any more than that Calla had killed herself. It felt like I was right back where I started, adrift in a confusing nightmare that made no sense at all, with no choice but to leave the situation to the authorities. I had to trust that Duke Parsons knew what he was doing. He had to have had evidence and motive to have arrested Herbert in the first place. He had been investigating the suicide the whole time I was questioning it.

Jaeger pulled the truck up to the curb, and Lester pulled in right behind him in the Harvester. A tag team of help and courtesy that lightened my heart.

"I hope you weren't waitin' long, Mrs. Trumaine," Jaeger said, as he slid out from the driver's seat. He left the engine running and the door open. His knuckles were still marred by grease, and I could smell his sweat as he stopped in front of me. I felt bad. He had done so much for me and Hank that I knew I would never be able to repay him. I didn't even know where to start.

"No, I haven't been waiting long. I was talking to a nice couple and that made the time pass."

"Must have been a light funeral," Jaeger said, looking around. Lester remained in the truck. He sat watching us, smoking a nonfiltered Lucky Strike. A pack of the cigarettes sat on top of the dash, just within reach.

"The room was packed. Betty was there," I said.

"I expect she was." Jaeger's left eye winced, and, had I not known him as well as I did, I would have missed the expression of discomfort.

"Is everything all right?"

"I was going to ask you the same thing."

"Yes, well, no, it's not. Are you two having troubles?" I couldn't help myself.

Jaeger sighed. "It's just that she's always got one thing to do after another. One minute she's working at the Rexall, then she's off to class at the college, then it's on to piano lessons, candy striping, or something else. Sometimes, I just wish she had time to walk the fields with me, you know? Get lost on the land and listen to the meadowlarks sing. I just wish she'd slow down a bit, that's all. One day she wants to spend the rest of her life with me, and the next day she won't answer the phone. We've broke up so many times I've lost count."

"She doesn't seem interested in the farm?" I said.

"She was, but she gets bored fast."

"And that worries you?"

"Come winter and the hard times, yeah, it worries me. Both of them always come. You know that, Mrs. Trumaine."

It was clear that Jaeger had doubts about Betty being a good farmer's wife. I was standing before him in his mother's best dress, and that must have made him relax enough to open up to me. I was glad to listen.

Jaeger wasn't going to change, be anything other than what he was—a lover of the land, of the weather, of the seasons—a farmer until the day he died. And I didn't suspect that Betty Walsh was going to change, either. A child might focus her. I'd seen that happen before, but that was a huge risk, and one I wouldn't ever suggest to Jaeger. Only he could figure out whether she was the person for him to marry. I wasn't surprised at his doubt, though. I'd had mine for a little while.

Lester's smoke wafted my way, and I looked at the waiting Studebaker.

"But you're all right?" Jaeger said.

"I need to go see to Hank. It's been a trying day from the start. Thankfully, Olga Olafson said he was doing all right since I'd seen him last." I paused, looked at the sky, then back at Jaeger. "Duke and a few deputies showed up right before the funeral started. They arrested Herbert Frakes for murdering Calla."

It was as if the wind had drawn back and stopped to listen to our hearts beating.

"Herbert Frakes?" Jaeger said. He scrunched his forehead in confusion, just like his father used to. "I would've never thought it."

"Me either."

"You think it's a mistake that they arrested Herbert?"

"I don't know what to think now."

"You should tell Duke about your tires bein' slashed and the phone line bein' cut. See if they think Herbert did that, too. Though I can't figure why he would. Does Herbert even have a car?"

"Not that I know of. He could have used Calla's car, I suppose, but I don't know why on earth he'd do such a thing."

"Maybe he didn't want you to leave the house?"

"I thought of that, but it doesn't settle well. To be honest, that act felt far more nefarious than someone not wanting me to leave. I think I was lucky Pastor John Mark stopped by to check on me."

Jaeger heaved a visible sigh. "Feels familiar, doesn't it?"

"A little too much for my liking. I don't want you to worry. I think the worst of all of this is behind us." I wasn't sure I believed that, but Jaeger's face had gone pale as a new-fallen snow the second I'd mentioned Herbert's arrest. I knew he was reliving all the pain brought on by his parents' murders.

I let silence settle between us for a long second, while the Studebaker sat idling, waiting. I could smell the richness of the exhaust and was reminded that the engine needed maintenance. "I need to get off to see Hank. Thank you, Jaeger. One day soon, you and I are going to sit and talk about how I can repay you for all of your kindness." I wanted to reach up and peck him on the cheek, but I'd never been affectionate with him before, other than a consolatory hug, so I restrained myself even though he looked like he needed comforting.

Jaeger shook his head. "You don't need to worry about anything right now other than what you got right before you, Mrs. Trumaine. I'll be fine. Me and Lester got things under control, and like I told you, come spring I'm gonna bring on some extra hands. Sooner if I have to."

I nodded and turned to go to the truck, but Jaeger stopped me with an unexpected question. "Ma'am—Mrs. Trumaine?" he said.

There was an urgency in his voice that I couldn't deny. I spun around. "Yes?"

"A man from New York called my house. Said he was looking for you."

I went numb. "Was his name Richard Rothstein?"

Jaeger nodded his head. "That sounds right."

"He's my editor from H.P. Howard and Sons. I gave him your mother and father's phone number a long time ago as backup, if he needed to get ahold of me and couldn't reach me at home."

"He wasn't very nice," Jaeger said.

"I'm sure he is nice, Jaeger; it's just that he has a lot of things to do. Did he say what he wanted?"

"He did," Jaeger answered. "He wants you to call him right away. He said that index you're working on is late, and he wanted to know where it was."

It was like the wind had climbed into my ears and jumbled up all of the words. "I'm sorry, what did you say?"

"I said the index you're working on is late, and this Rothstein fella seemed fit to be tied. Like he'd woke up and drank a cup of hornets instead of a cup of coffee."

CHAPTER 38

The last task before I send in a completed index to my editor is to check each and every page reference to make sure that it matches up to the text. It's a tedious task, but I've also marked the reference on the page in red ink so I can easily find it in the end. The index would be a completely unusable document if a reader looked something up and it was supposed to be on page thirty-nine, but it was on page ninety-three instead. I'd done that before, transposed a number in my hurried march to finish a day's work, and had only caught the mistake at the very last moment, when I'd edited and double-checked the index.

With everything that had been going on in my life, now I had to wonder if I'd written down the wrong deadline or transposed a date or number for the *Common Plants of the Western Plains: North Dakota* index. It was the only quick explanation that I could come up with for Richard Rothstein's call. *Late? How could I be late?*

I couldn't imagine being deemed unreliable, and, even more, I feared losing what steady income I had coming in. Punctuality was a matter of pride, as well as a necessity and requirement by the publisher—any publisher, not just mine. There were production and printing costs to producing a book, and my job as an indexer was the last task in the long, arduous process of publishing a book. If I missed the deadline, most likely the book wouldn't arrive on bookshelves when it was supposed to, and that in turn would cost the publisher revenue, and most likely me my job.

I gathered myself the best I could, made sure I was correct in what I had heard, then sent Jaeger and Lester on their way. I had a phone call to make before I could do anything else.

The closest telephone, obviously, was inside the funeral home, which meant returning to an empty chapel still filled with sad floral bouquets and lingering hymns that promised salvation and eternal life. I shivered as I imagined Calla's lonely casket sitting in wait to be transported to the crematorium.

My panic about the index suddenly receded as my thoughts turned away from myself and back to Calla. I had to wonder what Calla would have thought about Herbert being arrested for her murder, which prompted me to wonder even more if she had known all along who her killer was. Or was the act a surprise to her? Did she have time to be scared, to be frightened for her life? Or was her death a shock to her as much as it was to everyone else? One minute you're here and the next—well, it's all over. No time to fix things, no time for regrets, no time to say goodbye. It wasn't the first time I'd hoped that Calla's death had been quick and painless, and I was sure it wouldn't be the last.

I shivered again and decided I didn't want to go back inside the funeral home. Ten more minutes, if it took that long to find another phone, wasn't going to calm Richard Rothstein down or change his attitude. But putting off the call any longer than that seemed a bad idea, too. Once I called him, I'd turn right around and call Olga at the hospital and check on Hank, then rush right over there. It was the best plan I could come up with, considering the news Jaeger had brought me. Tea with Nina and Claude Tutweiler was out of the question, as much as I hated to admit it. I wanted to talk to them, Nina, in particular. She was a link to Calla, a way forward, but socializing would sadly have to wait for another day.

I closed my eyes and tried to think where to go. It only took me a second to realize that the next closest telephone was at the library. Even with Delia Finch there, it was the one place in my life that had always given me comfort, and in an odd way it felt fitting, like going to someone's home after a funeral to pay your respects. The library was where I had spent most of my time with Calla Eltmore. It was where she had lived, and, unfortunately, where she had died. It would always be her home as far as I was concerned.

As I got out of the truck, I thought I heard a rumble of thunder in the distance. I looked up at the graying sky and silently hoped for rain. A dry October in North Dakota was a rarity, but it was more than that. I felt the dryness from the inside out. There was nothing more I wanted than to stand in the middle of a storm and allow it to soak me to the bone. Then maybe I could cry again. Tears had left me, drained out of me like a well that had given up its last drink and offered the promise of nothing more.

There was more rumbling swirling around me than just in the sky. The street in front of the library was filled with traffic, gawkers coming and going. I struggled to find a parking place and ended up walking two blocks just to find my way to the entrance.

I stopped before ascending the steps and pressed down Lida's black dress the best I could. I wasn't comfortable in it, which didn't help when it came to facing Delia Finch. She had looked down her nose at me on our first meeting; I could hardly imagine what she would think about my state of dress this time around. But it didn't matter. It couldn't matter what she thought of me. I had every right to come to the library. I just didn't have the right to use the telephone.

The inside of the library sounded like the aftermath of a concert, where the audience lingered, discussing a great performance, reluctant to leave, to give up the experience. But this was no celebration. A crowd had gathered in the expansive main hall. I knew it was a delayed reaction to Calla's death now that the truth of it had come—that she had been murdered and had not killed herself. Herbert's arrest had changed everything. The town could grieve openly, and for that, at the very least, I was glad.

I stopped just inside the vestibule, not by choice but because I had to. The crowd between me and the counter, where I assumed Delia Finch stood, seemed to be at least ten people deep. There weren't anywhere near that amount of people, really, but I was accustomed to the library having only one or two patrons in it at a time, not a hundred.

I made my way to the front counter and immediately found myself under the steely gaze of Delia Finch.

"Mrs. Trumaine," she said. "What a surprise to see you." She didn't mean it, of course. I could almost taste her sarcasm.

"I have a favor to ask," I said.

Delia Finch leaned in close enough to me that I could smell the aftermath of her tuna salad lunch, and said, "I'm sorry?" Then she cupped her hand to her ear, showing me that she couldn't hear me.

"A favor," I said a little louder. "I need a favor." I didn't want to be too loud, draw any undue attention to myself. I was tempted to look over my shoulder to see if I had, but I didn't. I didn't break eye contact with Delia. *Never show an angry dog any fear at all.* It was Hank's voice offering me advice on how to navigate the natural world.

Before she could answer, or decline my request before even hearing it, Delia Finch's attention was drawn away by a man who had suddenly appeared at my right shoulder. It was Nils Olson, a reporter for the *Dickinson Press*.

Nils was a frumpy man who looked and smelled like he had just come from the Wild Pony or one of the other taverns in town, but he was a good writer and, as far as I knew, an honest and hardworking journalist. He had cut his teeth as a reporter during the war, come home and gotten a degree at the local college on the GI Bill, and stayed in the same house he was born in. Not much happened in and around Stark County that Nils didn't know about.

"Excuse me, Miss Finch, could I speak with you a moment?" Nils said, turning his attention to me quickly. "Oh, beg your pardon there, Marjorie. I didn't mean to cut you off."

"That's all right, Nils. It's good to see you." I stepped back from the counter.

"How's Hank?"

"Holding his own." I felt Delia Finch's glare on me. I was stealing her spotlight. Her gaze was so intense and hateful I had to look away. When I did, my eyes fell on the door that led into Calla's office. It was cracked open, like Delia had rushed out of it without pulling it all the way to. I had used the phone on Calla's desk before, and I hoped to use it this time.

I looked back to Delia and smiled. "Never mind," I said to her as I stepped back. "Nils, it's good to see you."

"Same to you, Marjorie. Give Hank my regards."

"I'll be happy to." I stopped and waited for a brief second as Nils turned his attention back to Delia.

"Is there somewhere private we can talk for a moment?" he asked her.

Delia looked over her shoulder to the office. I held my breath. I really needed to call Richard Rothstein. Time was ticking away, but something told me she would deny my request even under the best circumstances.

"Outside, maybe?" she said to Nils.

He nodded and I held my place, trying my best to blend into the crowd until they both exited the library.

CHAPTER 39

I closed the office door behind me as easily and quietly as I could, stepped over to the side, and rested my back against the wall. I tried to blend in, disappear like a sagebrush sheep moth seeking refuge from a hungry blackbird. Big sagebrush (*Artemisia tridentate*), of course, was one of the common plants in North Dakota, a subject that had been, and remained, at the forefront of my mind. The plant was a host to the moth; its larvae fed on it, making it vital for the moth's survival. Once the moth lit on the sagebrush, it was almost invisible and mostly safe from predators. All of its troubles were over—for that moment. Unlike mine, which still hinged on facing a frothing Richard Rothstein over a late index. I would've rather stared down the blackbird.

But it was more than hiding from Delia Finch and the lingering crowd in the library that had brought my back to the wall. My heart raced a mile a minute because I was sneaking around, going into a sacred place without permission; it was a curious, desperately rebellious act that was as uncommon to me as a blooming red rose was on the winter prairie. My world was orderly, dictated by a strict style guide—the seasons—and a dose of old-world morality that constantly butted up against the modern, present world. Stepping outside of my known behavior was uncommon to me, at least to this degree. I was essentially trespassing with the intention of stealing, even though I would pay for the long-distance call one way or another. I would admit to my crime after engaging in it.

The truth was, I'd wanted to see for myself where Calla had died all along, if only to make sense of it all, or to convince myself that it was true, that she was really dead—I constantly needed to be reminded of that fact because I'd always thought that Calla would outlive me. Even now, I expected her to barge through the door at any second, demanding that we go smoke and talk about the latest book I was indexing or that she was reading. Her death was a shock, and I still couldn't resolve my struggle with mortality.

I needed to hide, and I needed to be propped up. Two seconds in the room and I already regretted being there.

There was still a heavy smell of bleach in the room. A odor of a cleaning agent and disinfectant of some kind mixed with the bleach that had washed away the blood and whatever else. It was as if the murder had never existed, like it all had just been another nightmare. But it wasn't. Bleach and pine-scented disinfectant were as much the fragrances of reality as funeral bouquets were. My eyes immediately began to fill, even though I thought I had used up all of my tears.

I bit my lip. *Get ahold of yourself, Marjorie*. I blinked and stiffened my back at the same time.

The office looked normal, all put back together, nothing out of place other than an accoutrement of Delia Finch's; an orange and brown striped, fake leather purse sat in the middle of Calla's desk. It didn't belong there, was as out of place as I was.

I wondered if Herbert had been the one to clean up the aftermath of the deed. A lot had fallen to him, including the specter of guilt. If he *had* murdered Calla, then there was no lack of irony in his duties. But what if he hadn't? I still wasn't convinced of it, and though it seemed as impossible as it was improbable, I wanted to ask him myself. I would know for sure then. When I'd sat with Herbert at the Wild Pony he hadn't seemed nervous or like a man afraid of being caught. He was stunned just like I was, entering the first phase of mourning: Denial.

My speculation had to wait, unfortunately, for the law and the courts to do their jobs. Until then, Herbert was innocent until proven guilty. I knew that as well as I knew much of anything else. Herbert's fate was out of my hands.

The back wall of the office was lined with nothing but bookshelves filled with the forbidden books—*Lady Chatterley's Lover, The Price of Salt, Tropic of Cancer*, and a host of how-to nonfiction books that broached worldly, carnal subjects that I could barely imagine but was sure Calla had read every word of. A patron had to request each of those books before it could be checked out of the library, and only then after a long moment of scrutiny from Calla. I knew exactly what Betty Walsh had meant when I'd asked her what people around town had thought of Calla. "*She could be snobby about the books that you checked out, even though it wasn't any of her business.*" It was, according to Calla, her job, her responsibility and duty to society and the community, to know what was inside every book that came into the library so she would know what was going out of it. She had lived most all of her life inside of books. I was sure of it. And for what?

I listened for a second and then decided that I either had to make the call to Richard Rothstein or sneak back out of the office—flutter my moth wings away from the sagebrush and take my chances.

The disinfectant made my stomach turn. It would have been easy to run straight to the hospital without another thought. Some days it would have been easier to just be a farmer's wife. Not have the worry or pressure of writing a usable, professionally produced index and turning it in on time. But I wasn't just a simple farmer's wife. Not anymore. I was a farmer's wife caregiver. And the farm was collapsing all around me. If I gave up indexing, I would have no way to feed Hank and me. Other than sell the farm. And I wasn't going to do that. Not now. Not ever. Those acres and that house were as much a part of me as my heart and bones.

I heard nothing. I feared the possibility of Delia Finch rushing into the office and catching me there. Instead, there was a low rumble of respectful voices, evidence of a crowd in a quiet place.

I made my way to the desk, focused my mind on the task at hand, not on what once was or what could be, and picked up the phone—Calla's phone—my connection to the wider world. I had to face Richard Rothstein and get past that. Hank was waiting for me. I could feel his loneliness and need for me in every breath I took.

I dialed zero.

"Operator. How may I help you?" It was a voice I didn't recognize, thankfully. Perhaps I had clicked into the Bell switch offices in Bismarck.

"Long distance, please."

"Phone number?"

"212-555-0408." I knew the phone number to H.P. Howard and Sons by heart.

"One moment please."

All I had was a moment. That and a lifetime of worry and sadness. At least that's what it felt like as I ran my hand over the top of Calla's desk. It felt cold, impartial. I couldn't sense her at all there, and I desperately wanted to. I needed her to urge me on, and it was a realization that at first was uncomfortable, then a relief. I had needed Calla in my life for a long time. I hoped she had known how much she meant to me.

The phone clicked, then a second of silence, then a ring. The magic of technology never ceased to amaze me. Somewhere in a New York skyscraper, a harried editor was being summoned to the phone from the middle of the country, from a farmer's wife standing, sweating, in a chilly librarian's office.

"Richard Rothstein's office," a fast-talking receptionist answered.

My spine stiffened, and my voice cracked as it exited my lips. "This is Marjorie Trumaine, returning Mr. Rothstein's call."

"One moment."

Silence. The line hissed distantly as she transferred the call. At least I didn't have to worry about Burlene Standish listening in. This was a dedicated line, not a party line.

"Miss Trumaine," Richard Rothstein snarled.

He always did that. Called me miss. I had corrected him a few times, told him I was a missus, but obviously he had not noticed—or refused to be corrected.

"Yes, I'm sorry . . ."

"There is no excuse for being late." He interrupted me. I was ready for that and pursed my lips together. It didn't matter what I had to say. My job was to listen. I was a subordinate, at his mercy, that had been made clear over and over in our dealings. Hank hated to hear the name Richard Rothstein. I was certain more than once that, if he'd been able, Hank would have stood up, walked out the door, caught the first airplane to New York, and boxed Mr. Rothstein's ears for the way he talked to me. That was not the kind of trouble we needed, so I suppose there was even a reason to be grateful for paralysis.

"We had an agreement, Miss Trumaine. The index for *The Last Tower of Rome* was to be on my desk two days ago. I have to say I am extremely disappointed . . ."

I did not hesitate to interrupt *him*. "I beg your pardon, but what title did you say?"

"*The Last Tower of Rome*."

I said nothing. I had, of course, never heard of that book.

"Miss Trumaine? Are you there? Are you aware of the severity of this situation? This is a very important book for us."

Not so important that you know who the indexer is, I wanted to say, but I didn't. I said nothing. It was the first time he had made such a mistake, but I couldn't imagine that it would be difficult, juggling as many books to be published as he did.

"Are you still there, Miss Trumaine? You have done acceptable work for us in the past. I am amazed at your lack of concern." His New York accent was difficult to decipher, but I'd had some practice. And honestly, I had never had a conversation with anyone who spoke so fast as Richard Rothstein. I could barely keep up.

"I've never heard of that book," I finally said.

I swear I could hear him suck in air like he had been punched in the gut from a thousand miles away. *That one was for you, Hank.*

"Oh. Are you certain?" he said.

"Absolutely."

"Let me look." Silence, though I was tempted to tap my fingers on Calla's desk. "Oh, dear," he said. "That book is assigned to Prudence Wilkins. You're on the *Common Plants of the Western Plains: North Dakota* book and it's due . . ."

"In five days, if my calendar is correct."

"It is. Hum. I suppose I will have to call Miss Wilkins. Good day, Miss Trumaine." Then the phone went dead. No apology, no goodbye, no nothing. Just a click. It was all over. The end, that's it. I'm finished with you. On with the next thing. I suppose that was how publishing worked, but I would never get used to it.

CHAPTER 40

I didn't hesitate, didn't set the receiver down. I tapped the switch posts in the cradle of the telephone and spun the hospital's number as fast as the rotary dial would turn. I knew that number by heart.

Olga Olafson picked up on the second ring. "St. Joseph's Hospital. How may I help you?"

As much as I found Olga irritating, I was glad to hear her voice, encounter a semblance of normalcy. "Hello, Olga, it's . . ."

She cut me off. "Oh, hey there, Marjorie. How are you doing?" She sounded casual.

"I'm fine. I called to check on Hank." I hushed my voice so Delia, or anyone else out in the foyer of the library, wouldn't hear me.

Olga didn't hesitate with her answer. "Oh, he's just fine, other than he's gettin' anxious to go home. Poor man can't fidget a lick."

The word "other" sounded like *udder*, just like my father used to say it. Olga's North Dakotan accent gave me another moment of comfort, and I smiled slightly.

She went on without missing a beat. "Oh, I'm sorry, I didn't mean to be impolite about Hank's condition."

"It's okay, Olga. It's the truth of things, I know what you mean."

I heard an audible sigh, a release of momentary shame. The silence between us only lasted for a brief second. "You all right yourself, then, Marjorie? I can barely hear you," Olga said, restored.

"I'm at the library. There are a lot of people here."

"I'd imagine there are. Who would've thought that poor, simple Herbert Frakes could ever do something like that? I always thought he and Calla were . . ."

I cut in this time. "You're sure Hank's all right?"

Olga let out a slight harrumph. I pictured her nose sailing straight to the ceiling in one swift, offended move. "Yes," she answered. "Doc said he could go home this evening once he makes his last rounds and makes sure Hank himself is fit to make the trip out to your place. I told you that."

"All right, I'll be there shortly. Can you tell him?"

"You betcha, but there's no hurry. Doc's got his hands full with one thing or another. He won't sign the release papers till he sees Hank again. You know how Doc is, slower'n Christmas but just as certain to show up."

I nodded. "Thanks, Olga."

"Sure is a shame about Herbert," she said, wanting to go on about the arrest.

I wasn't interested in discussing Herbert's fate any more than I had to. I'd seen and heard enough. "I have to go, Olga. Goodbye."

I stood next to Calla's desk and tried to gather myself. I was still stunned that Richard Rothstein had made a mistake, and I was relieved that Hank was all right. My emotions were so conflicted that I didn't know if I was coming or going. But Hank was ready to go home. More than anyone, I knew how much he hated being at the hospital. Inside that shell of a body of his, he was tapping his fingers and toes to a ragtime beat, but nobody could see the severity of his discomfort. Nobody but me.

I drew in a deep breath and looked around the office, taking the time to examine everything a little closer than I had when I'd first stowed into it.

This was probably the last time I would ever be in this room. Or at least, while there was still a hint of Calla in it. The next librarian, whomever that would be, would surely make it their own. As it was, all I could see of Delia Finch was her ugly purse—from what I knew she was the temporary librarian, not appointed yet. The rest of the room reeked of Calla. Her long, enduring presence was hard to miss; I could almost smell a hint of her ever reliable Ivory soap lingering in the air, mixed with the wonderful smell of polished walnut bookshelves and books. It would take a concerted effort and a great amount of time to erase the fact that Calla Eltmore had spent her entire professional life at the library, in the office.

I was sad and nervous, but, beyond that, I was driven by my own curiosity and lack of faith in Duke Parsons and the local police. I wasn't convinced that Herbert had killed Calla—that he *could* kill Calla—but then I didn't know what the police knew. I hadn't all along. Duke and Guy had been quite adept at hiding the inner workings of their department. I was more than a little miffed at Guy for allowing me to believe that Calla had committed suicide for one second longer than I actually had to. I wouldn't have told a soul. He knew that. But I understood that he couldn't tell me. I just didn't like it.

I didn't know everything about Calla, either, and that was nearly as unsettling as everything else.

Nina Tutweiler had introduced me to her husband as Calla's local celebrity. I blushed at the thought of such a thing. An indexer as a celebrity. How silly. It wasn't like I was an author, for land's sake. But I appreciated knowing that Calla felt that way, that I was something special to her.

Nina had also said that Calla had kept a list of all of the questions that I had ever asked her. I knew we shared the compulsion to organize things, it was part of our bond—that and our love of books, of reading, of taking our own silent, private adventures that only we could talk about in our own special way—but I hadn't known about *that* list. We both listed things to organize our days, our lives, but I had never considered that Calla had kept a list with my name on the heading. It made perfect sense to me that she would do such a thing now that I thought about it.

I had to wonder, then, what other lists she had kept over the years. Was there one with Herbert's name on it? One that revealed her fears of him, or other things I couldn't imagine? Had Duke or Guy found it, and that was what led them to see Herbert as a suspect in a crime that wasn't initially a crime? There was no way to know. I could only speculate. And my gut told me that Calla wouldn't leave such things lying about. She would hide them, or, at the very least, keep the lists in a safe place that only she knew about. I was certain of that much. I *did* know a few things about Calla and her ways.

If I were Calla, where would I hide my lists? I looked down to the desk, at the three drawers on each side, and contemplated opening them. *You're trespassing . . .* the voice inside my head warned. *Besides, Duke would have already rifled through each drawer.*

I looked at the door for any sign of Delia. The foyer was still loud with the noise of the crowd. So far, so good. She had her hands full.

Instead of relying on what I thought I knew, I grasped the brass handle of the top drawer. The metal was cold, warning me off, but it was too late. I had already committed myself to going somewhere I shouldn't.

CHAPTER 41

I didn't know how much time I had. Calla's reference log was on the very top of a disorganized pile of notebooks, envelopes, and thin stationary boxes. There was no question that someone else had been through the drawer, confirming my earlier suspicions. I couldn't go through everything. Delia would have caught me for sure.

I heard footsteps walking toward the office door and I froze. I was no moth, had nothing to camouflage myself with. I could hear my heart beating, could feel it in my chest. It was going to give me away if it pumped any louder.

Whoever it was passed on by and I relaxed for a second. I had to go, get out of there. Hank needed me. He was fidgeting; I could feel it in the depth of my soul. But just as I started for the door, something caught my eye, something out of place, something that I immediately recognized.

A single book lay on top of a file cabinet next to the forbidden bookshelf. The book was red leather with gold gilt letters. It was *Men and Women* by Robert Browning. The same book that Nina Tutweiler had dropped when she had taken the tumble down the outside steps.

I stopped and wondered why the book hadn't been properly shelved. Surely Delia hadn't been that busy since her arrival—or perhaps, she wasn't as efficient as Calla. I doubted that anyone really was.

I eased my way over to the file cabinet and stared at the book, then glanced down. Letters of the alphabet fronted each of the six drawers. Without thinking any further, I slowly opened the top drawer, which was unlocked, and peered inside.

The drawer was full of books. Old books like the one on top of the file cabinet. The aroma of them was like a whiff of an ancient tree, sweet and slowly rotting. I picked up the first book that I recognized—*Poems* by Elizabeth Barrett Browning, her most famous work. Then I opened it to the plate page and quickly discovered that it was a first edition.

Calla had kept the books in a safe place, off the shelves, out of ordinary circulation. It, and the rest of the books, must have had value of some kind, either financial or otherwise. I didn't know about such things.

The paper of the plate page was yellowed and fragile between my fingers, and I suddenly worried that I was doing damage to it. I closed the book and went to put it back exactly where it had come from, and a piece of paper fell out of it, fluttered into the file cabinet drawer like a leaf falling from a tall, dying tree.

Unlike the Barrett Browning book, the paper that had been dislodged looked pure white, new, recently pulped. I picked it up and slid *Poems* back where it belonged.

Curiosity forced me to open the paper, which looked like a note or letter. Reading it would not have been appropriate under any other circumstance, but this felt different.

Robert and Elizabeth's relationship had been famous because of their correspondence and the love affair that it provoked. Calla had been enamored with the Brownings for as long as I could remember, had tried to engage me with her passion for the subject, but unfortunately her attempts had fallen short. I knew little of either of the poets' work, just the basics—*How do I love thee, let me count the ways . . .* that I learned as a child, picking petals off a daisy. I had been thinking of Hank, of course. I wasn't even sure that I knew who the poet was back then.

I looked over my shoulder before I opened the letter, to make sure that I was still safe. Confident that I wasn't about to be caught and shown to the door—or have the police called on me—I began reading:

~*C.*

We both know there is far more at stake than being disinherited, as our dearest Elizabeth was. My agreement for appearances seems a lasting mistake, and one I regret with the coming of each autumn. I fear the sight of the wedges of snow geese that fly overhead, south to a safer, warmer clime; I wish to travel upon their wings and take you with me. I know we have dreamed of this together before, but it is an impossible dream. The wrong look or touch in the wrong place is certain to bring a push of wind I have no desire to face. I am growing bitter and bereft with each passing day that I am separated from you.

How can it be so wrong? Robert and Elizabeth weighed the price of their love, and love won out. We know that. I wish with all my heart that I could be as confident as you that a life together would meet the same success. It is a storm that neither of us is equipped to handle. We are fated to stand on opposite sides of a deep canyon. I can only watch you from afar and marvel at the human being that you are. I can only imagine what a simple, unworried moment alone with you would feel like.

I must watch carefully now. Time is ticking. This first year seems different. It will pass, too. They all do once the boredom of the season sets in. It is my burden, my penance, my deception to the world, to myself. Let's try *Men and Women* next time. I will look for your response in it.

~~N.

My hand trembled as I finished reading the letter. I looked over my shoulder and wondered if I had time to read it again. More footsteps, more voices. Sooner or later Delia was going to discover my presence. But my feet were glued to the floor. I was shocked by the letter. It seemed so personal, so intimate, so secretive.

I knew right away that it wasn't from Herbert. The initial at the bottom noted an N, not an H. The whole town had thought that Calla and Herbert were involved in a relationship of some kind. I had too, and now it looked like we were all wrong. This was a love letter, or it seemed that way, exchanged secretly through the checking out of books. They hadn't even trusted the post office with their correspondence. Maybe Herbert had discovered something, discovered who the writer of the letter was. Maybe he had killed Calla in a jealous rage. Maybe he had loved her, but she hadn't loved him.

Taking the letter to the police would prove nothing. Most likely they had seen it. On the surface of things, the letter didn't seem to have anything to do with Calla's murder. But my suspicions suggested otherwise.

I drew in a deep breath and looked back at the book on top of the file cabinet. *Men and Women*. Then I looked back to the letter and closed my eyes. In my memory, as clear as a summer day, I saw the book fly out of Nina Tutweiler's hands as she fled the library.

Nina.

N.

Could it be her? Could N. be Nina Tutweiler?

What on earth did that mean if I was right?

CHAPTER 42

The most important task for an indexer was to decide what information went into the index and what was left out of it. There was no possible way to put access points to every concept, idea, name, and place that appeared in the book. There simply wasn't enough room or allowed pages from the publisher. Something valuable was *always* going to get overlooked or left out. And that was exactly how I felt standing there with the letter in my hand. I had missed something all along, but I still had no clue what that something was. The letter created more questions than it answered.

Another vital quality for an indexer to possess was a good memory. If I made an entry on page two and saw it again on page one hundred, then I had to add it to the first. An indexer's mind had to have the ability to track a multitude of things all at once.

I closed my eyes again, doing all I could to remember the index I had written to organize my mind when I'd first started to believe that Calla had been murdered:

D

death, surprise of
depression, no sign of

G

gun, what kind?

F

Frakes, Herbert
    found Calla
    no violent history

M   S

Men and Women   suspects
   by favorite poet—Calla   Herbert, found Calla
   woman dropped   woman at library
motive?
   What don't I know?   W
   What to gain?

   woman at library
   doesn't believe suicide
   dropped *Men and Women*
   need to find

And there it was. I had only been able to come up with two suspects at the time. The police had obviously agreed with me when it came to Herbert.

I'd been reluctant to add Herbert to my index, but now I was wavering on my suspicion. He might've killed Calla; it *was* a possibility, no matter how much I hated the idea of such a thing. It would help to know what the sheriff knew, but I didn't think I was going to find that out anytime soon. Guy Reinhardt had been tight-lipped as a bank vault when it had come to the investigation. I was obviously still miffed at him for being so distant.

I had been just as reluctant to consider the "woman at the library" a suspect. The woman that I now knew to be Nina Tutweiler. Who may or may not have written the letter to Calla. I still couldn't settle my mind to that fact. But I had put her in my personal index because she had been so distraught, so mysterious, so unknown to me. A stranger might be more capable of murder than someone I knew, like Herbert. Could I have been as wrong about her as I had been about him? After all of these years, I'm just now learning of Nina's existence and her importance in Calla's life. That didn't settle well with me. I thought I knew Calla.

There was only one way to find out if something was off about Nina, if she was involved in the murder in any way. As crazy as it seemed, I had to accept the invitation to stop by the Tutweilers' for tea. It was a risky proposition, fraught with far more peril than I needed to put myself into at the moment, at any moment. But what choice did I really have, especially if I was wrong? Nina Tutweiler was grieving just like I was—and I had some questions. Even though I wasn't quite sure how to ask them of her.

I eased out of Calla's office reluctantly. "Goodbye," I whispered. I knew the room would never be the same again, and it was highly possible that I would never have the privilege, or opportunity, to enter the librarian's private domain again.

It was still unsettling that the library was noisier and busier than I had ever experienced it, but that also made it easy to lose myself in the crowd that had assembled to mourn Calla. I was dressed in Lida Knudsen's best funeral dress. Everyone, it seemed, was dressed in black. Now I *was* a sagebrush moth, easily camouflaged and grateful for it.

I caught a glimpse of Delia Finch still holding court at the counter as I stepped out of the double doors. I hoped beyond hope again that she would only be a temporary replacement. Nothing she had done since our first meeting had endeared her to me at all. Just the opposite. I knew though, that no one could ever replace Calla Eltmore. Not even the sweetest, wisest librarian in the world—which Delia Finch was not—would have a chance with me. Had I known Delia before Calla had been killed, I would have put her at the top of my suspect list. As it was, I wasn't sure that Delia and Calla had ever met. She had no reason to kill Calla that I knew of. It was a silly thing to consider. Especially with Herbert in jail.

The weather had changed since I'd been inside the library. The air was cool and moist, the sky gray and growing grayer. A front of distant clouds looked like they could transition into black at any second, so they too would be in in mourning with the rest of us. But I knew better. The clouds were full of rain. I could see the steady sheets dropping to the earth from where I stood, in that crucial spot where Nina Tutweiler had launched her fall from. I should have been happy—the farmer's wife, rejoicing—because the autumn season had been so dry. Worryingly so. Nearly a drought. No amount of index money would ever get me through that catastrophe. Besides, I could only do so many indexes. It wasn't something one could speed through in a day and send out a bill for services rendered. A good index took weeks to create, sometimes months, and ultimately, the publisher never seemed in a hurry to pay the bill. A check could take three or four months to arrive, after the fact.

It looked like the rain was about ten minutes west of town, which gave me plenty of time to hurry the two blocks to where I had parked the Studebaker without getting soaked. The wind was as riled as the sky, pushing hard at my back, hurrying me along as I went.

I ignored the cars and trucks and the people coming and going from the library. Honestly, I was glad that I hadn't run into anyone that I knew. Taking the time to stop by the Tutweilers only put more distance and time between Hank and I. Olga had assured me that I had plenty of time before Doc Huddleston signed the release papers, and I knew if I showed up too early I would only add to Hank's discomfort and fidgeting. He would be upset that he was keeping me from something that I needed to get done. He'd always hated being a burden.

The Tutweilers' house was easy to find. It sat a block and a half from the entrance to the college, just off of 7th Street West. Professor Tutweiler could most likely walk to class on a nice day, or come home for lunch if he so chose. The in-town options of life were foreign to me, of course, but I had to admit that I was envious at times of the ease of access to life and living. Like now. I felt so disconnected and far away from my normal life. It would be nice to have the ability to run home, open the door, breathe my own air, and check on Shep. But that was not to be. I was miles away from the comfort of my own home and the worried dog that waited there for my return.

The Tutweilers lived in a lovely little two-story, clapboard house, a dark maroon instead of the normal white. The front door was arched, as were the windows. The front yard was well-tended—the bushes trimmed and shaped, and all of the leaves carefully raked so not one blade of dormant grass was out of place. A rare single-stall attached garage sat off to the right of the front door, and I assumed there was an entry inside it as well. Most houses had a garage in the back, accessible by the alley, or no garage at all—one of the downsides to town living. Most folks had heaters they plugged into the engine blocks of their cars and trucks in the winter, so they would start in subzero temperatures, but I always felt sorry for those houses that only had the option to park along the street.

The Tutweilers' house looked warm and inviting, even as rain started to pelt the windshield of the Studebaker. More to the point, it looked like the perfect English professor's house—pulled straight out of a fairy tale and placed gingerly on a perfect small-town street.

I could have lived in that house, it was that cute.

I sat in the truck, not anxious in any way to jump out into the rain. I lacked an umbrella, but I was glad to see an overhang above the front door that would help protect me, partially, from the persistence of the coming storm. The wind pushed the rain sideways, but that was nothing out of the ordinary. Gray skies had turned to black, and the rain I had seen from the library had arrived in full force on 7th Street. I had nothing in me that would allow for a celebration of life.

There was a part of me that didn't know what I was doing here. My arrival was less out of politeness, having accepted an invitation, and more out of curiosity. But beyond that, I was afraid. What if Nina Tutweiler had killed Calla? What if I had been right to put her on my suspect list? I had no way to protect myself. The shotgun was in the wardrobe at home where it belonged, and I'd left the .22 with Pastor. There'd been no need to bring the gun to the funeral or ask Jaeger to put it in the truck after he'd repaired the tires.

Could Nina have been the one to have slashed the tires in an attempt to keep me from the funeral? I couldn't make the connection, find a motive. Besides—and this was still a thorn in my side—Shep would have heard her and barked. He hadn't. I still couldn't figure out why that was.

I closed my eyes and listened to the rain pound the top of the truck, waiting for a reprieve from the downpour. Nothing I could think of really led me to believe that Nina had killed Calla. Just the opposite, if she had written the letter. There had been no anger there, no hate. Just longing. I'd understood that as soon as I read it.

It didn't take long for the rain to slow and offer me a chance to hurry to the front door. There was not enough power in the clouds to encourage a day's worth of rain like we needed, but it did promise to come and go for a good while. It was go to the Tutweilers' now, or go to the hospital.

To die, to sleep—To sleep, perchance to dream—ay, there's the rub, For in this sleep of death what dreams may come . . . The line from *Hamlet* that Nina had quoted outside of the funeral home crossed my mind before I could make another move, and I wondered for the first time if she had been trying to tell me something instead of challenging Claude. Or both.

CHAPTER 43

Just as I started to push out of the truck, something brushed my ankle and made me stop. I reached down and touched the musk thistle I had placed there and completely forgotten about. Lightning plant, or thistle in general, had special protection powers gifted by Thor, the Norse God of Thunder, according to the book I was trying to finish the index for. Which was not late to the publisher, thank you very much. But it seemed I couldn't get far from that book, or Norse mythology, for that matter. But since Norwegian is the root population of the majority of folks around here, it shouldn't be a surprise that I'd run into Thor on occasion. I suppose we all could use some protection, but I didn't really need the reminders.

I scooted the plant back under the seat just as a clap of thunder rumbled in the distance. I shivered, opened the truck's door, and hurried to the Tutweilers' stoop, clutching my purse with the purloined letter safely inside of it. I pressed the doorbell right away, then waited as patiently as I could. No one answered the door immediately, nor did I hear anyone coming. Rain pushed at my uncovered hair, and no amount of Aqua Net could have held it in place.

If I stood at the front door too long, I would be soaked to the bone. I pressed the doorbell again, listened to it buzz, and continued to wait. *Perhaps I had misunderstood the invitation.* I tapped my foot to the beat of the rain.

Somewhere inside the house a radio or television set played soft, comfortable music. The tune was instrumental, orchestral. No voices, no singing, much like we had heard earlier at the funeral home, except the music wasn't hymns of praise or salvation, just something that seemed to set the proper mood for company.

There was no other sign of anyone at home. I had expected Nina and Claude, still dressed to the nines, not a hair out of place, like their yard, like their house, sitting in wait to mourn Calla over tea and cookies. But that didn't seem to be the case.

I was tempted to leave, not ring the buzzer again, but I gave it another try, held the button next to the door a little longer than I had before. I had, after all, overcome all of my suspicions to face them both.

With that thought in mind, I peered in the side glass hesitantly, uncomfortably, before I hurried back to the truck. There could have been a million reasons why either of the Tutweilers had failed to come to the door.

What I saw didn't make sense. At least not at first.

A dining room chair was tumbled over on its side. My mind immediately recognized the sight of something that shouldn't be there, a broken pattern. Everything with the Tutweilers had been in place. Everything except what I was seeing as I peered inside. That *and* the damage to their Cadillac. It was a mar on something perfect in every other way. I had misplaced the memory if it or deemed it unimportant, I wasn't sure which. The windshield had been shattered, and the driver's side fender had been dented in. I'd assumed the damage had been caused by a normal everyday fender bender. But maybe I had been wrong. A new pattern was starting to take form, precipitated by a chair on its side.

I opened the screen door and knocked on the front door a little more heavily than I normally would have. "Is everything all right? Hello, is anyone home?"

I was answered by a gust of wind and a clap of thunder that sounded like it erupted over the library. Close, but not overhead. Still, my whole body vibrated and my purse slipped down my arm and fell to the ground. I reached down to grab it and stood up slowly, eyeing the inside of the house from a lower perspective. There, just above the chair, barely in view, was a pair of shoes dangling motionless in midair. There was no doubt in my mind that they were a woman's shoes. I had admired them earlier in the day.

I couldn't process what I was seeing or what I was thinking. My entire body felt like it had been shocked. I bolted straight up, yanked on the screen door again, and pounded on the door. This time it eased open, like it had been unlocked all along.

I knew enough not to touch Nina Tutweiler any more than I had to determine that she was dead. Her hand was cool, not cold, and her finger still had flexibility in it. Rigor hadn't set in yet, so her death seemed recent.

Nina Tutweiler hung from a rafter in the dining room by a make-shift noose that was nothing more than a double-wound orange, heavy-duty extension cord. It must have come from the garage. She was still dressed in her funeral clothes. Her head was cocked to the side, her neck snapped, and her tongue, fading pink, hung out of the corner of her mouth.

There was nothing that I could do to save Nina. I rushed to the phone to call the police, to call for an ambulance, without giving a single thought to Claude Tutweiler's presence or my own state of being or welfare. Why would I?

Words burbled out of my mouth once a human being came on the line. I was relieved not to be alone.

I gave the address to the operator and told her what I saw: "The lady of the house has hanged herself."

It was so easy to think that was true when you were looking right at it.

CHAPTER 44

Tornado sirens were a common sound in the spring but reasonably rare in the autumn. When the wind was just right we could hear them moan and wail all the way out to the farm. I'd stop and listen, then look at the sky in wonder and sudden fear, especially if the sky was threatening and angry. I hated spending time in the storm cellar. It was like a grave you could walk into and never leave. But the shelter was a necessity out on the plains, and now, in modern times, it was the first place to run to when the Russians dropped the A-bomb. That was a different siren.

I'd seen my fair share of twisters drop to the ground in my life. They danced about willy-nilly like they had a mind of their own, hopping about like they'd just been stung by a bee. The siren had served its purpose, even for us, more than once. Other times, the siren was nothing more than a test, just to make sure it would work when the time came. What I heard, distantly, was like that, like a tornado siren on an unexpected day. A warble heading my way.

I could barely breathe, standing in the Tutweilers' perfect house, staring at Nina hanging there. I was overcome with a deep sadness that I could hardly explain. I didn't know the woman. Not really. But she had meant something to Calla, and she had been kind enough to invite me to her house for tea after a funeral. It felt like I had lost a friend. Her death was sudden, unexpected, too real not to acknowledge, and I stood there with my hands glued to my sides, wishing like heck that I could step outside and smoke a cigarette.

I was fine until I heard a thump overhead. My heart stopped.

The thump was followed by a pitter-patter of little sounds, and

I quickly realized that the sound was tiny footsteps, that most likely belonging to a four-legged creature. I assumed that the Tutweilers' owned a cat, and it sounded like it had jumped down from a bed, roused from its afternoon nap. I breathed a sigh of relief.

The siren drew closer and I waited, stood in place right next to the phone, which sat on a wonderfully ornate and highly polished writing desk. I would have liked to admire the interior of the house, with its rich, textured, Bing-cherry-red wallpaper in the formal dining room, the squishy, ornate rugs that most likely had been imported from some far off place like Afghanistan, and the hundreds of books that seemed to have a place in every room of the house, not just the small library past the front door. But it was difficult to be in awe of a highly refined decorating taste when there was a dead woman hanging from the rafters.

In the blink of an eye, a knock came at the door, followed by a familiar, "Hello."

"In here," I called out. I still didn't want to move, to leave Nina for a second, even though I was relieved to hear Guy Reinhardt's voice. I had hoped it would be him that answered my call.

The front door creaked open and then slammed behind him as Guy made his way to me. "What have you gone and got yourself into this time, Marjorie?" he said, as he appeared under the arched door that led into the room. "Oh, that's it, then isn't it?"

"Sadly so," I said.

Guy froze to assess the situation, not taking his eyes off of Nina. I knew he'd seen a dead body before, so it wasn't a matter of being stunned, but he did look surprised.

"I touched her to make sure she was dead," I said. "Then called the police. I'm glad it's you that's here."

"Duke's got his hands full with the newspapers and such."

"I'd imagine he does." Guy was dressed in his brown and tan uniform, his shirt was heavily starched, with military creases, the one on the left cutting behind his badge—a silver star that looked like it had been hung there with perfect care. He looked put together, not a hair out of place, just like the Tutweilers. Any resentment that he might have held against Duke Parsons for getting the acting-sheriff appointment was nowhere to be seen. Guy wore a police uniform well. It seemed appropriate for him, like it was a comfortable place for him in the world. I was glad of that. I needed some calmness at that moment.

"You shouldn't have touched her, Marjorie," he said.

"What else was I supposed to do?"

He shrugged, then turned his attention back to Nina. "Nobody else around, I suppose?"

"A cat upstairs, I think. I didn't wander off and go look. No sign of her husband, though, which is a little odd."

"What're you doin' here, Marjorie?" Guy said, walking to the opposite side of Nina, looking her up and down.

I followed his every movement. "She was a friend of Calla's. I met her at the library, and after the funeral she and her husband asked me to stop by for tea."

Guy stopped and looked me straight in the eye. "That's a long stretch away from Hank."

"Doc's gonna release him this evening. I had some time to mourn Calla. He wanted me to." I was sure my tone narrowed.

"I wasn't pryin', Marjorie. Probably a good thing you stopped by, but I suppose her husband woulda found her when he got home."

"I assumed he'd be here," I said.

Guy didn't react, just ran his eyes up from Nina's feet to her head. "Pete'll be here any time. We called for the ambulance. Looks like this time it'll be a real suicide. Still can't believe Herbert Frakes could have done such a thing to Miss Eltmore."

My eyes had stayed on Nina's feet. Or, more specifically, on her shoes. I was trying to make sense out of something I saw. "I wish you would have told me," I said.

"Couldn't, Marjorie; you know that."

"I do." Everything about Nina was perfect. Everything except her shoes. The heels of her shoes, really. Everything else—the toes, the soles—looked like they'd just come straight out of the box. But the heels were scuffed and marred. "But you had to have a reason to arrest him," I continued.

Guy stopped his inspection, looked at me over his shoulder. "I suppose I can tell you now, since it's no secret, or isn't gonna be. We found Herbert's watch in his room in the basement. It had blood on it. Same type of blood as Miss Eltmore's, and there was no one that could vouch for his whereabouts. Said he'd been to the Wild Pony and was sleeping one off, if ya know what I mean."

"He didn't have an alibi? Maybe he got blood on the watch when he found Calla," I said.

Guy shook his head. "No. He didn't have any blood on him when we got there, and he wasn't wearing the watch. He had no explanation for why there was blood on it. He said he'd misplaced it."

I nodded. "That's what he told me at Calla's showing. He said he took it off every evening and put it in the same place, but it wasn't there. He was befuddled."

"He said that to you?"

"Why would I tell you otherwise?" I broke my gaze away from Nina's shoes to glare at Guy. He was starting to annoy me. Or something was. I looked back at Nina's shoes. "Why do you suppose her shoes are scuffed on the heels?"

"I don't know." Guy said. He looked at Nina, then at her shoes, then back at me. "Why would you ask that, Marjorie?"

"Seems out of place to me. I've been trying to think of a way I could scuff up the heels of my brand new shoes if I had them. I suppose if I rubbed them up against something long enough that would make a mark. Maybe even a mark on both shoes. But those shoes have no wear on them, just like everything else on . . ." I paused, connected her shoes to another piece of Nina's pattern: The broken windshield and dent on the Cadillac. Something had happened there, and it hadn't looked like it had been something Nina or Claude had done, but something someone had done to them. Like run into them—or smashed up their car on purpose.

Guy looked at me curiously. "What?"

"What if she was dragged here from somewhere, Guy? What if someone moved her?"

"You mean to make this look like a suicide just like Herbert made Miss Eltmore's death look like?"

"That's exactly what I'm saying, Guy. Maybe this isn't a suicide any more than Calla's was. Maybe we just think we know what we're looking at, just like that's what you were supposed to think with Calla."

"Then that might mean that Herbert didn't do it."

"Could be," I said, "but this time, someone was in a hurry and they overlooked her shoes." I took a deep breath and didn't take another second to consider the implication of the idea that Herbert could be innocent. That wouldn't have surprised me in the least. "I think you better talk to Claude Tutweiler as soon as you can, Guy," I said, moving my doubt from one man to another. "He might know more about the deaths of both of these women than he should..."

CHAPTER 45

I think we both expected the next person to walk through the front door to be Pete McClandon, the coroner, but it wasn't. Claude Tutweiler burst through the front door in a rush, a panicked look on his face, his overcoat soaked to the seams, and his once perfect hair an unexpected mess. He was pale, almost gaunt with fear, a far cry from the man I had sized up at the funeral.

"Where is she?" Claude demanded, coming to a stop as soon as he saw her, answering his own question. "Oh, dear God. It's come to this." He collapsed to his knees like he had been hit in the back of the head with an invisible baseball bat. A wail of grief so deep, so hurt, emitted from his mouth. The heartbreaking sound was distorted. His face was pressed hard against the Afghani carpet as he beat it with his fists. Thunder clapped overhead at the same time, so that it was difficult to tell the two sounds apart.

I was taken aback by Claude's entrance and show of emotion. I felt bad for questioning whether it was all an act. My mind had already created a suspect index for Nina's death, and there was only one entry on it: Claude Tutweiler. It was no index, and, witnessing Claude's obvious pain, I felt guilty for even thinking such a thing.

"Sir," Guy said, making his way to Claude. He put his hand on his shoulder. "Maybe you should come in and sit down. Get ahold of yourself. The ambulance is on the way."

"She's dead?" Claude said, looking up at Guy with tear-filled eyes.

Guy nodded. "Yes, I'm sorry to say."

"Damn it." Claude pounded his fists again. "It didn't have to be this way." He looked at me then, and said, "I'm sorry you had to see this.

I was only going to be gone an hour or so. I should never have left." He did nothing to stop the tears from dripping onto the ground.

I was speechless, which was a rarity. I didn't know what to say. Instead, I shrugged, opened my purse, pulled out my handkerchief, and offered it to Claude.

"Dear God." He took the white cotton square and dabbed his eyes, then sighed heavily.

I was about to close my purse, when I saw the letter I had taken from Calla's desk. There hadn't been time to tell Guy about it, nor had there been any time to consider what all of it meant, if anything. Now wasn't the time, so I closed my purse.

We sat in the parlor, just out of view of Nina's body. Pete McClandon had arrived and was doing his coroner's job, whatever that entailed. He was waiting on Duke Parsons to show up before making any changes to the dining room or removing Nina from the house. Guy had told Pete about the marks on the shoes, about our suspicions.

"I dropped Nina off after we left the funeral home," Claude said. "I had some papers at the office that needed some urgent attention. I was in a hurry. I didn't even come in the house." He was sitting in a double-arched settee that looked like it had been made in the last century. Probably French. The upholstery was yellow, and it looked like it had never been sat in.

I sat opposite Claude in a smoking chair. A clean ashtray sat next to it on a glass stand, with a calabash pipe and leather pouch of tobacco waiting to be enjoyed. Claude didn't look interested in pleasure at the moment. He was distraught. Exactly as he should have been.

Guy stood at the door, a few feet from Claude, blocking the view into the rest of the house, with an occasional glance over his shoulder.

"Did anyone see you drop Nina off?" Guy said, ignoring my presence in the room.

"I beg your pardon," Claude answered. He suddenly looked like the college professor that I knew him to be. "Why would I be concerned about such a thing?"

"It's just a question. I'm just curious if you can account for your time after you left the funeral home until you came home."

Claude's jaw tightened, and he shifted uncomfortably on the settee. "My wife just committed suicide, Officer. Don't you have a sense of decency? Is there a note? Did she leave anything behind? I have questions. I shouldn't be answering questions."

He looked at me, and I tried not to show any emotion at all. There had been no note that I had seen. But I hadn't looked for one, either. Honestly, I hoped there was one, that it would explain everything. I really hoped Nina Tutweiler had killed herself. What an awful thing to think.

"The investigators still have their work to do," Guy said.

"The investigators?"

"Yes, Pete and Duke, once he gets here. It's been eventful, as you can figure it would be. I don't mean any disrespect, Mr. Tutweiler. Just asking questions, that's all."

"Professor. It's Professor Tutweiler."

I shifted uncomfortably in my chair. The division between academia and the rest of the world always felt like a splinter that was stuck too deep to pull out with your fingers.

"Sorry about that, Professor," Guy said. "I didn't mean nothin' by it."

"I know you didn't." Claude stared at Guy for a long second, then nodded. "I suppose Mrs. Henrikson across the street might've seen me drop off Nina. She's the one that called my office and said there was someone at the house and that the police were here. We've had some trouble recently. Everybody on the street is looking out for each other."

"What kind of trouble?"

"First, someone slashed the tires on Nina's car. Once we got that fixed, they broke the windshield and dented the fender, either with a baseball bat or a sledgehammer. We have two cats, and one of them has run off, but Nina was convinced that someone did something to it. It's been one thing after another."

"Did you report this to the local police?" Guy was completely focused on Claude now.

I had seen the damage done to Nina's Cadillac, used it to give me confidence about the patterns I was seeing, so I knew he was telling the truth, at least about the damage—although maybe not how it had happened. I was surprised when Claude buried his face in his palms and shook his head.

"You had all of these things happen and you didn't report them?" Guy demanded. He was confused and perplexed.

"No, we didn't call the police."

"Why? Did you know who was doing them?"

"I don't know," Claude Tutweiler looked up. "Maybe. I think so. Yes, I think so."

CHAPTER 46

More sirens. More footsteps into the house. But Guy had not changed his position guarding the entrance—or exit, depending on how you looked at it—to the parlor. I felt trapped, like a grasshopper stuck inside a Mason jar. I wanted to leave, to jump away from the Tutweilers' as quick as I could. I'd had enough death in my life, and I wanted no more. And Hank was waiting for me. But I couldn't excuse myself, or find it in myself to flee. Not yet.

"You have to understand, officer, our lives are different. Were different," Claude said.

"You can call me Guy." He shifted his weight as he spoke. As he did, his unsnapped holster rubbed up against the door jamb. Guy was calm, unflappable. His height and uniform gave him all the authority he needed.

Claude looked at him, sizing him up like they were playing a game. It was obvious to us all that this was more than just a little afternoon chat.

"Nina was raised out East," Claude continued. "Her childhood was lonely. Lonelier than I suppose any of us can image. Her parents were well-off, had an apartment in New York City and a summer house in Maine. She rarely saw either one of them. Nina spent most of her time at one all-girls boarding school or another, here and abroad. Literature, and more specifically, Shakespeare, became her great escape, her great passion. It was our bond."

Claude Tutweiler had a mesmerizing voice, skilled after so many years of lecturing college students, I assumed. Before I knew it, I was hanging on every word, and I easily understood how a young Nina could have become smitten with him. He oozed charm, polish, and a worldly knowledge that I could only begin to comprehend.

Claude reached inside his blazer and took out a narrow pack of cigarettes from the breast pocket of his blue-striped Oxford shirt, which was unbuttoned at the top and without a tie. "Do you mind, Officer?" he asked Guy.

Guy flinched and shook his head. "Go ahead."

Claude proceeded to light the cigarette, a Dunhill, a sophisticated Canadian brand that I rarely saw anyone in my own circles smoke. He took a deep draw and exhaled before he began to talk again, all the while ignoring what was happening in the dining room. There were murmurs of voices, scuffling of feet, the occasional flash from a camera, all mixed with the unrelenting rainstorm that was pounding down outside.

"We had a whirlwind romance. Met and married within a month. My parents were upset at first, until Nina won them over, of course. But her parents were glad to be rid of her, it seemed. Cold fish if I ever met any. I wondered how they ever produced a child, and I wasn't the least bit surprised when Nina told me she didn't want any children of her own. I was fine with that, since I was focused on my career, had high aspirations of my own that wouldn't allow for the normal sense of domesticity, but I suppose it would have changed things if we had had a child. Or it may have made our life worse. Who knows?" Claude shrugged and drew on the Dunhill again, looking wistfully at the ceiling, like it held all of the answers he had ever sought. "We were vagabonds, bouncing from one college to another, with me searching for the ever-elusive tenured position and the opportunity to publish. Which is how we ended up here, in this loneliest of the lonely places. Sorry," he said, looking directly at me.

I didn't know what to say. I understood what he meant, but I was accustomed to the emptiness of the prairie. Craved it, actually. But I was raised in it, and I supposed that made things different for me. I couldn't imagine what North Dakota must be like for two world travelers.

Guy broke the brief moment of silence. "How does this have anything to do with the troubles you've had recently, Mr. Tutweiler?" He wasn't pushing, just interjecting, reminding the man that he was a policeman and this was an unusual circumstance. There had been no inference from Guy that he thought the suicide might have been staged, just like Calla's had been, or that he, Claude, was a possible suspect. We both knew more than Claude did—or we assumed so. Hoped so, really.

"Our lives are complicated, Officer," Claude answered with a heavy sigh. "I'm not sure you would understand."

"Try me," Guy said.

A thunderclap erupted overhead, and it startled both Claude and I. Guy didn't move. He was staring straight at Claude, certain, I am sure, that he would miss something. A tell of some kind, a clue that he was lying, or that he was telling the truth; I wasn't sure which.

"I suppose it was all bound to come out sooner or later," Claude said. He looked at me with a concerned look on his face. "This may be uncomfortable for you."

I looked past him, at the door, feeling even more trapped, even more of a pull to return to Hank. "I don't want *you* to be uncomfortable," I said.

Claude forced a smile and tapped the ash off his cigarette. I was afraid he had forgotten about it. "Too late for that. This nightmare refuses to end," he said. "Nina and I have been married a long, long time and been through our ups and downs like any married couple, but her sense of isolation grew, especially after we moved here. But before that, really, almost from the start, she had an untouchable place in her heart that I couldn't access. We drank, we socialized, did all of the expected things that came with the academic life. She grew restless and disappeared into her books. I thought, mostly, that's where she went. I had my own path to navigate. And I grew restless, too, got bored, needed some excitement. The weight of her loneliness was oppressive. I had a couple of affairs. Flings, really. I don't expect you to understand, and certainly I am fair game for judgment, but after a while Nina found out, or I told her, and it just became an accepted, if unmentioned, way of our life. She was loath to get a divorce. She had nowhere to go, you see." Claude looked up at Guy, who was hanging on every word just like

I was. "It won't take much digging, even by the worst detective, to find out that I was cheating on my wife, Officer, and that I had just recently ended another sordid relationship. I can assure you that's not why she killed herself. I was open with her about my life, and she was open with me about hers. Well, as open as Nina could be."

Guy didn't react in any way at all. His face was flat of emotion. He had always been a good listener. I liked that about him.

It was like a light went off in Guy's head at about the same time it did mine.

"Oh, so you think it was this person who smashed the windshield and took the cat?" Guy said. "They were angry because you ended things with 'em?"

"I have thought so all along," Claude said. "But I couldn't prove anything, and neither could Nina. She had the same suspicions. It wasn't the first time a gal had taken the breakup poorly. The younger girls don't have the experience to handle such things. Heartbreak is hard for them, even though I try my best to let them down easy. If Nina ever had any complaint that she voiced openly, it was that my taste ran toward the doe-eyed first years who always thought I was more than I was. Desire is a powerful drug, Officer." Claude took a final draw on the Dunhill and ground it out in the ashtray.

I shifted uncomfortably on the settee. Something Claude said sounded familiar. My hand reached over to my purse, grazed the top of it, and came to a stop. I was after the letter. I wanted to check it for a reference, a pattern: *First year.*

I pulled my hand back, as my mind raced through its collection of self-made indexes and lists, searching for more connections to what Claude was saying.

Claude's hypnotic voice broke my train of thought. "Nina was upset after the breakup, then afraid after Calla died. More afraid than I'd ever seen her. She was convinced that the librarian had been murdered from the start."

I nodded my head.

"Marjorie?" Guy said. "You knew this?"

"Yes," I said. "You know I thought the same thing. I ran into Nina as she was exiting the courthouse after talking with a deputy. I'm guessing that was you. You didn't believe her any more than you believed me."

Guy stiffened, stood even taller. It was easy to see how he had been naturally built for the sport of basketball. I imagined him touching the clouds when he jumped for the ball. "It was an ongoing investigation, Marjorie. We couldn't tell everyone what we knew. Duke was afraid Herbert'd run off and that would be that. He was our main suspect from the very beginning. The watch was a big giveaway. We just needed time to get the details right. I couldn't go blabbin' everything I knew to you."

I stared at Guy, annoyed all over again, then turned my attention back to Claude. "She saw the same thing I had, that the bullet was in the wrong place, but I sensed she wanted to tell me more than that but couldn't find it in herself to do so."

"Nina was incredibly private," Claude said.

"I didn't even know of her or of her friendship with Calla until after Calla was dead. I talked to Calla, or saw her, a couple of times a week, and she never mentioned Nina. All she ever said was that I shouldn't avoid the college types, there were some nice ones there that would welcome me. She'd see to it."

"They wanted it that way. What they had together belonged only to them. I think they had a secret way of communicating that even I didn't know about." Claude lowered his face into the palms of his hands and began to weep.

Guy and I said nothing. Work continued in the dining room and the storm pushed past outside, but I was so focused on Claude that I barely noticed.

After a long moment, Claude looked up at Guy. "I'm sorry; I can't believe she's dead. She was always so afraid someone would find out. Not for her sake, but for Calla's. There's twice as many churches in this town as there are taverns, for Christ's sake. It would have been a scandal that none us of could have weathered, and I'm as close to tenure as I've ever been. She didn't want to damage that, we'd both worked hard for it, but she was so lonely she couldn't help herself. It wasn't the same for

Nina as it was for me. Her love was forbidden, mine was just insatiable. I had no trouble coming to terms with my appetites, but Nina did."

A blank look crossed Guy's face. He didn't understand what Claude had said, but I thought I did, if only because I had read a private letter between the two women. Deep inside, I was sure I was shocked. I had always believed that Herbert and Calla had a secret romance. Everybody had. But Herbert hadn't been the secret. Nina had been.

We both know there is far more at stake than being disinherited, as our dearest Elizabeth was, the opening line of the letter had said. Claude had validated it. And this, for me, tied it all together—*I must watch carefully now. Time is ticking. This first year seems different. It will pass, too.* Like Claude said, Nina feared being discovered, felt the pressure of it, that it was close.

I wanted nothing more than to read the letter again to make sure I remembered everything in it correctly, but I couldn't share it. Not now, if ever.

I looked at Claude closer. He had been a mess when he'd walked in the front door. His hair and clothes were all out of kilter. He'd looked hurried, thrown together, not his buttoned-up, proper self. It was like the phone call had interrupted him . . . I had assumed he'd been telling the truth about the papers he'd needed to take care of, but that was most likely not the case. He had been with someone.

"Will it be embarrassing for you to have someone vouch for your time after you left Nina here?" I couldn't keep myself from asking. I didn't think Guy knew what question to ask next.

Guy shot me a hard look that indicated I had crossed a line, but he didn't say anything. He let me have my way.

"Yes, actually. How did you know?" Claude said.

"The same first year?"

"No. Oh, God, no. I avoid her as much as I can, but she's there at every turn, it seems, with that daft smile on her face, like she's waiting for just the right opportunity to tell the world what she knows."

I knew the answer to this question before I asked it, even though I didn't want to believe it. "She was at the funeral, wasn't she?"

"Yes," Claude said. "She had the audacity to march right up to us and speak like nothing had ever happened. She's brazen that way."

Guy's face had gone from puzzled to frustrated. "Who are you two talking about?" he demanded.

"The person who killed Calla and Nina," I said to Guy, standing up as everything came together in my invisible mental index. I stopped, as fear struck my heart, overtaking any satisfaction that I might have found the revelation. "You said she slashed Nina's tires?" I said to Claude.

He didn't reply, just nodded.

My tires had been slashed, too. "I have to go. We have to go, Guy. I'm worried about Hank."

CHAPTER 47

We were halfway to the hospital before Guy said a word to me. "You shouldn't have said that to him, Marjorie."

To his credit, Guy let the siren of his police car remain silent. He had the bubble on top flashing, and he blew the horn when he came up on another car. His foot was pressed hard on the pedal, and the engine revved loudly, pushing every horse to its limit.

"Said what?" I asked.

"That his wife had been killed. You don't know that for sure, Marjorie, and you can't go sayin' such things to anyone if you don't have the answers from someone who knows about those things and says so."

I stared at Guy and didn't say a word. I wanted to ask him what had happened to him, why he had become so hesitant and cautious. But the truth was, I knew the answer to my own question. He had taken a blow to the head and to his pride when he'd confronted a killer and ended up on the wrong side of a two-by-four. If he'd come out a hero instead of a victim, it would have been him that was in the running for sheriff, not Duke Parsons. His second marriage had failed at about the same time, and I supposed if there was one place that was consistent in his life, it was his job as a deputy sheriff. It was all he had, and the last thing he needed to do was risk losing it.

"You're right, Guy. I shouldn't have said that. I say a lot of things I shouldn't say."

He glanced over at me, looked me in the eye, then returned his attention back to the road. "You're sure about this?"

"As sure as it's raining cats and dogs."

"If you're wrong..."

"I'm not." I followed his gaze as St. Joseph's came into view. It looked like Frankenstein's castle on the night the villagers gathered to burn it down. "But if I am, it won't hurt to have questioned her."

"Duke'll be mad about that. That I didn't get his approval before doing this."

"I can handle Duke. He can't fire me, and I doubt he can fire you until he's the real sheriff instead of an acting one."

Guy tapped his fingers on the steering wheel, then laid on the horn to push a milk truck out of the way.

"How come you're worried about Hank?" Guy asked, as the truck pulled over and he easily maneuvered around it.

I had to recompile all of the index entries in my mind in their right places all over again. I didn't have time to tell Guy everything—I wasn't sure he would connect the dots about Calla and Nina—but I thought he would understand my basic fear once I told him the root source of my suspicion. "My tires were slashed this morning, just like Nina's were. All of them. And the phone line was cut. I was isolated, on my own. Luckily, Pastor John Mark stopped by and drove me over to the Knudsens' place. But the odd thing was that Shep didn't alert me that something was wrong. Normally, he'd bark his fool head off if a stranger set foot on our land, but he didn't even let out a single growl."

"He must've known the person," Guy said.

I nodded. "Yes. He must have known her."

"You think she'd really hurt Hank? There's no cause for that."

"I don't know what to think. I just know she said she had a shift at the hospital today, and Hank's there, too. I want to make sure he's all right. You need to talk to her, Guy. For Herbert's sake, if nothing else. If someone else did this terrible thing, murdered two people and tried to make them both look like suicides, then you owe it to him to make sure she didn't have anything to do with this."

"You're right. I would want to check on Hank, too, if I was you," Guy said, as he wheeled the police car into the hospital parking lot.

We rushed by Olga Olafson without saying a word. Her face was full of questions and her tongue full of rules, but none of that mattered now. All I wanted was to see Hank as healthy as he could be, sitting up in his bed, his bag packed, ready to go home.

But that's not what I saw as I entered his hospital room.

I stopped just inside the door. Guy was on my heels and nearly knocked me over as soon as he saw what I saw. I suppose he should have been in the lead, but my first concern was seeing to Hank. I was going to leave the police work to Guy.

Betty Walsh stood over Hank with a pillow in her hands.

I didn't know if she was pulling it up, or putting it down. She'd frozen in place when she heard us enter the room. At first glance, she looked like a perfect statue of a candy striper doing her duty, caring for a patient unable to care for himself. But what I saw was more than that.

I was already convinced that Betty had killed Calla and Nina, and it wasn't a far stretch to imagine that she could be capable of killing Hank, too.

I'd known all along that the only reason Hank hadn't taken his own life was that he hadn't been able to. He'd begged me in his deepest, darkest moments to put a pillow over his face and walk away. *"No one would know,"* he'd whispered. But I couldn't, wouldn't do such a thing. He knew that. But maybe Betty Walsh would. She'd made him laugh, flirted with him. I'd been jealous of her with him. They'd been alone together. Had time to talk about things I couldn't know about. I knew what Hank Trumaine was capable of, how desperate he was to end the suffering his accident had brought to us both. And I was starting to see the same thing about Betty. If she had killed twice, she could do it a third time.

What I saw in Betty Walsh's hand wasn't a dutiful, caring act, but a weapon. A weapon that would finally answer Hank's prayers.

"Put the pillow down, Betty," I demanded.

Guy had eased to my side. He looked at me oddly, but said nothing.

"Oh, hey, there, Mrs. Trumaine. I was just gettin' Hank some comfort," Betty said, without missing a beat.

Hank snapped his head toward me. The skin on his face was as tight as an overripe tomato and just as red. He started to say something, but I was too far away from him to hear the words.

Just like she was dropping a feather, Betty released the pillow from her grip, and it landed directly on Hank's face. He couldn't bat it away, move it with anything other than the turn of his neck, but he didn't make a move.

Instinct demanded that I rush to Hank, rescue him, but I didn't move.

In the blink of an eye, Betty Walsh had pulled a gun from somewhere inside her uniform and was pointing it directly at me.

CHAPTER 48

Time has a way of stopping when you're staring down the barrel of a gun.

"Don't move. Neither of you," Betty ordered. Both of her hands were clasped on the grip of the handgun. They were as steady as her voice. She meant business.

I'd never doubted that about Betty Walsh. But I meant business, too. I would have moved heaven and earth to keep Hank safe, and it looked like I was going to have to.

"You're makin' a big mistake, there, miss," Guy said.

I didn't give Betty time to respond. "Shut up, Guy. She knows what she's doing," I said, without looking him in the eye. If he didn't know he'd just been put in his place then he didn't know anything about women at all—which was entirely possible, considering his previous record.

I think my tone threw Betty off. She looked at me curiously, then smiled slightly with an upturn of her bright red lips. Our eyes locked.

Guy sucked in a breath. I didn't need to glance at him to know the look on his face. He had interrupted my bark correctly and was upset with me. But if he was smart, he'd pay attention and let me talk to the girl.

"I do know what I'm doing," Betty finally said. Rain pounded on the window behind her. The blinds were pulled tight, and it was impossible to see outside. An overhead fluorescent light bathed the small hospital room in false sunlight. It could have been any time of the day, anywhere in the world, but all that mattered to me was happening right in front of me. Nothing else existed.

I tried to slow my heart rate down. *Never show an angry dog fear.* I had done that before; faced down a mad dog and a crazed human being. I needed to draw on that experience more than anything else. My wits were all I had. Indexing couldn't save me now.

"You know there's no way out, Betty," I said. "Not this time. Why don't you tell me what this is all about?"

A bead of perspiration had formed on Betty's forehead and started to drop down her face, cutting a rivulet in her foundation as it went. Freshening up was out of the question.

The mar in her makeup was the only thing out of place. I had to give it to her. She had cleaned up well after hanging Nina from the rafters. I was sure of that now. Sure that Betty had killed both women.

She shook her head. "There's always a way out, Mrs. Trumaine."

"There's more police coming, Betty."

Guy shifted his weight next to me. I knew he was calculating his odds, looking for a way to detain her without somebody getting hurt, without ending up at the wrong end of the stick himself.

Betty's hand wavered for the first time. Her trigger finger twitched, came off the gun for just a second. "I'll shoot him. I swear I will. I'll spin around and put him out of his misery."

"Hank has nothing to do with this, Betty," I said, as calmly as I could. I thought I could see a slight rise and fall of the pillow; Hank was breathing, but it must have been difficult for him, not being able to move. He had to know what was going on, that I was in danger and he couldn't do anything about it. I was sure that was more difficult for him than anything else. He couldn't rescue me any more than I could rescue him.

I focused on Betty. "It hurt when the professor broke it off, didn't it?"

"What do you know?"

"I know how hard it is to end something with someone you don't want to. My heart's been broken before." That was a lie, but she didn't need to know that. I had only loved one man in my entire life, and that man was Hank.

An impatient look crossed Betty's eyes. *Please, Guy, just let me handle this.*

"That's what you think this is?" Betty sneered. "That I'm acting like a jilted brat just because the professor tossed me aside? Do you know why?"

I shook my head.

"He lied, that's why. He lied to me every day. They all do. Walking around acting all high and mighty, all the while they're sneakin' around doin' ugly, despicable things. Nobody is what they say they are. Nobody. It's all lies."

"Life can be disappointing sometimes," I said. "But that doesn't mean you go around hurting folks, Betty, just because they hurt you."

"Don't lecture me. I get enough of that at home. That I'm not good enough, not tryin' hard enough, not pretty enough. You don't know anything about my disappointments, so don't try to tell me anything about what hurts and what doesn't."

"I'm not here to take sides, Betty. I just want to take Hank home. That's all. I just want to make sure he's all right and go home where we both belong. You understand that don't you?"

Nothing changed in Betty's expression. It was like she hadn't heard a word I'd said. "He wasn't ever going to leave her, no matter what. Even though she didn't love him. She loved someone else. The librarian. Did you know that, Mrs. Trumaine? The professor's wife and the librarian loved each other. I found their letters in a book. It was awful, and he knew. He knew!"

I felt Guy stiffen next to me. "We don't get to choose who we fall in love with, do we, Betty?" I said.

She looked at me curiously, then narrowed her eyes as they filled up with more hate. I needed to calm her down again. The beads of perspiration had multiplied on her forehead. Her skin was pale white underneath the thin coating of makeup.

"I thought about it for a long time," Betty said. "And then I realized, I just needed to practice. It was like playing piano. I had to devote time to it, and then I figured it all out by going hunting with Jaeger, that killing wasn't as hard as I thought it was. It's kind of like sex, Mrs. Trumaine. It hurts a little at first, you get all sweaty, and then it's over quick. But it gets easier. You learn to not feel a thing about it. I practiced for it just like I would for a piano recital. I practiced until I got every note just right."

"Calla was more than a piano recital, Betty." I blurted out the words and regretted them as soon as I said them. "She was my friend."

At that moment, I heard distant footsteps clomping down the hall toward us. Guy rubbed his elbow against mine. I didn't know what Betty would do if someone else came along, pushed into the room and saw her with a gun.

"You don't know what she was," Betty snapped. "I wanted Claude's wife to suffer like I was suffering. I wanted her to hurt and long for something forever because that's what I was going to do. My heart is broken forever, and so was hers once the librarian was dead. I watched her crumble just like I did. I watched her hurt.

"I could have told on them, could have told about us, but who would listen to me? A scrawny first year? The professor would have wiggled out of it just like he had all of the other girls' claims about him. He didn't know that I knew that. He thought I was stupid, too. I told him he was good at lying. You have to believe me."

I did. I believed Claude Tutweiler was really good at lying. Nina, too. If only to themselves. But my immediate concern was that somewhere in Betty's young mind love, hate, and judgment had got all twisted up and exploded into a rage that knew no boundaries. I didn't know what had set her off, what had entered her mind that had suggested that killing another human being would solve all of her problems, but something had. It was something that I would never be able to understand or comprehend, even if it was just a simple breakup, a simple goodbye from Claude. That might have just been the final straw that snapped her mind. Honestly, I had no words to place on her behavior. I only knew what *I* felt at that moment, and I wanted to get her out of the way. I had to get to Hank before something else happened, before another life was taken, before she killed again.

"Someone is coming, Betty," I said. "I just want you to know that."

I waited a half beat. Hoped that she would flinch, look for a way out, take her eyes off mine, but she didn't move, didn't act like it mattered. Maybe she knew she had been caught and it was all over, but I didn't think so. She'd planned her way out of everything this far, and she had nearly gotten away with murder. I figured she had to have something else up her sleeve.

Hank was fifteen feet from me, and she stood in between us, fully capable and willing to pull the trigger of the gun she was holding. But there was no way out of the room other than the door.

Betty gripped the gun tighter. "I should have killed you when I had the chance, Mrs. Trumaine. But you know what? You have Pastor John Mark to thank for that. He came along and saved you. He saved you. Think about that. I knew if anybody'd come close to figurin' me out, it'd be you."

"You've ruined Herbert's life, too, Betty. You've hurt a lot of people. Did you steal his watch and plant it to be found after you killed Calla?"

"It was easy. Everybody knows he's a drunk. I snuck in after he'd had one too many at the Wild Pony. I knew they'd go after him, but I wanted to make sure. I made sure it had blood on it and left it behind so they'd find it."

"And Jaeger? He'll be heartbroken," I said with a sigh.

"He's an empty old sad sack who's only good for one thing," Betty said. "Makin' sure no one suspected that me and Claude had anything going on. That's all. I could never love someone like him. I'm not gonna be a farmer's wife. Not ever. Not me. I got bigger things planned for my life."

"You used him."

"He used me," she said. "He got me into bed every chance he had. Good thing I got the pill from the Rexall. I didn't have to worry about bringin' his kids into the world."

The footsteps got closer. They were heavier than I'd originally thought. A single pair. I was sure it was Doc Huddleston.

Betty heard them, then looked past Guy and me for just a brief second. Long enough for Guy to see an opening.

He dove toward her, stretching out with every inch of his six-foot, five-inch basketball player's body and tackled her mid-waist before she knew what hit her. Any sign of a limp, of the old injury that had halted Guy's chance at a professional career as an athlete, was not to be seen. He looked like a lion leaping after a young gazelle. A thing of beauty and horror all at once.

The gun flipped out of Betty's hand, flew upward, and nearly tapped the ceiling with the barrel before it crashed to the floor. The clatter of metal against linoleum mixed with rain hitting the window, the grunts and groans as Guy subdued and pinned Betty to the floor, all melded into a crescendo of music that I had never heard before and hoped to never hear again.

"What the hell?" a voice from behind me said.

I turned and came face-to-face with Duke Parsons, his face twisted in confusion and recognition at the same time.

I took a short breath, cast a glance at Guy pinning Betty to the floor, and said, "Looks to me like Guy just caught your killer, Duke. I think Herbert Frakes might have something to say to you about that."

CHAPTER 49

Nothing in my life had prepared me for this. I sat in a worn, brown, vinyl chair watching my husband breathe, unable to communicate in any way, flat on his back, hooked up to machines that seemed to talk to everyone but me. After a long, lingering sickness, you thought you were ready for the moment when everything changed for the worst, but you weren't. You really weren't.

Outside the hospital, the storm had passed and the blinds remained drawn tight. The larger world—the price of grain, the Soviet threat, the coming winter, completing the index for the *Common Plants* book— was the least of my concerns. I couldn't even begin to confront the guilt I felt for having left Hank's side for one second. That had been the risk of my obsession with Calla's proclaimed suicide—that I would be away from Hank in his hour of need. I'd been naïve, convinced that all of the monsters in the world had been rounded up and the key thrown away. I had been wrong. The responsibility for Hank's safety was all mine, and I had failed. Failed greatly. Honestly, I didn't know how I was going to live with myself.

Inside, the storm had passed, too. Betty Walsh had been carted off in handcuffs, finally subdued, finally stopped. She could hurt no one else. What she did to herself, locked inside a jail cell, was no more important to me than the color of the sky beyond the window. I had no idea whether it was day or night, no idea what her fate would be, though I had a suspicion our paths would cross again. The law of the land dictated such a confrontation, no matter whether it was healthy, sane, or necessary. I had no desire to see Betty's beauty and youth turn on her.

Doctors and nurses had swarmed around us once the room had become safe, the gun unloaded, the monster chained. Somewhere in all of that fury, a nun floated into the room dressed in a full black habit. She leaned down to me and offered me her rosary for comfort. She smelled of starch and freshly waxed floors. I had refused the nun's gift and asked Olga to make sure that Hank and I were left alone from then on out.

I wasn't sure whether Hank was aware of my presence or not. He was comatose, unresponsive, still alive, stuck somewhere between life and death. In my own way, I was in exactly the same place.

There was no such place as purgatory for Lutherans, but I was on Catholic soil, and it seemed to exist in some touchable theory that I had never considered before. The open prairie of the plains had always been desolate, lonely, but where I sat now was lonelier, filled with more fear than I had felt in my entire life. I felt small and helpless. It was a terrible feeling.

There was nothing to do now but wait. Wait for answers. Did Betty Walsh do this? Did Hank ask her to? And more. More questions about Calla, Nina, and Claude that would surely be answered in the days to come, splayed open for the entire town to see on the front page of the *Press*. I shuddered at the thought. Calla would have been mortified to have had her private life exposed to the world in such a way. I was sure of it. Anybody would be.

I laid my hand on Hank's chest, felt the warmth of his body, and, finally, it all became too much for me. Tears and sobs came at the end of my storm, once I knew no one could see me, hear me.

After a good cry, I drifted off to sleep, even though I fought against it with all of my might. I didn't want to leave Hank, but I was only human. I was exhausted.

The sun was starting to tilt toward the western horizon. Late afternoon, the end of a long July day, was starting to show its certain promise of the coming night, but there was still plenty of light left. The sky was a radiant blue, reflecting a perfect day below it. A cool breeze kept the temperature in the low seventies and pushed any humidity that the air held far to the east. Swallows and martins swarmed the freshly mowed hay field in squadrons, zipping and turning, then arching upward at the very last moment to avoid a collision with other ravenous, insect-eating birds. It was a feast of plenty, a perfect confluence of luck, hard work, and bounty. The kind of day that was rare anywhere but especially in July in North Dakota. On this day, it was a blessing that the nights were short and the days were long. The sun would finally set an hour before midnight, and a hearty man could fit two days' worth of work into one.

I looked up and saw Hank walking toward me, and I smiled at what I saw. He'd been up since dawn, out with the Knudsens cutting hay. Baling would come next. Two hundred acres of backbreaking work that was a summer ritual for all of us who lived off the land.

Hank had his hat off. His hair glowed sweet yellowish-brown and looked like it had been dyed by the grain he worshiped, like he had become a stalk of promise himself. He had a sweat-soaked short-sleeve shirt on, and I could see the ripple of his muscles through the thin cotton. His shoulders were straight, and he wore a calm, satisfied smile on his face. Most of the day's work had been completed; it was time for a break.

I had laid out a blanket on the ground in one of our favorite, private spots. A thin copse of cottonwoods that sat up on a slight ridge and protected us from the direct sun but gave us a wide view of our rolling, simple land. We owned everything in every direction for as far as the eye could see. Our world seemed to go on forever, and it was a comfortable feeling knowing that we were alone, that we could see or hear anyone coming from miles away. We lived in our own little world and didn't worry about our privacy or prying eyes. Not there in that special spot.

I had a picnic basket full of Hank's favorite things—ham salad made from Mills Standish's best bologna, fried potatoes, sweet lemonade, and a chiffon cake that I learned from Peg Graham and her

Women's Club of the Air radio program. It wasn't much of a late afternoon snack, but it was what Hank had asked for as he'd walked out the door to work.

I had been preoccupied with the correspondence course that I'd been taking to learn back-of-the-book indexing. I could hardly contain my excitement as I closed in on the finish of it. Just the thought of contributing to the farm, making some extra money in the winter by reading books, made me as giddy as a school girl.

I stood up and pressed the front of my sleeveless summer dress down. I was barefoot, comfortable in the white linen that was hardly more than a smock. The fabric caressed my skin, along with the breeze, and it felt like a luxurious massage.

"You're a sight for sore eyes," I whispered to him as he drew near. "I was starting to worry you weren't coming."

Hank said nothing, just grinned that silly little grin of his, walked right up to me, took me in his arms, and kissed me like he hadn't seen me in a month. I felt every ounce of his being in that moment, and I knew he had been pushing himself, that every cell in his body was alive, engaged, grateful. He was stone hard from head to toe.

He pulled his head away, but kept ahold of me. "I've been thinkin' about you all day."

"I missed you, too," I said, a little flushed. The temperature had suddenly risen to August extremes. A month had flown by in a matter of seconds. I didn't mind the aroma of Hank's body. It was sweet, not pungent. He smelled like he had been rolling on the ground for hours and enjoying himself the entire time.

"I'm famished." Hank looked away from me, to the picnic basket, then back to me with warm and wanting eyes. "But that can wait."

In one swift, practiced, knowing move, he reached his hand down and pulled my dress up over my head and tossed it behind him. I had nothing else on underneath—I had hoped he would want me as much as I wanted him.

The white linen fluttered away like an errant kite wafting to the ground. No one was going to chase after it, and I didn't protest, didn't stumble, didn't worry that we would be seen. Nothing existed but Hank and I in our moment of paradise.

I returned the favor and unsnapped his belt and began to undress him as we became a tangle of tongues, arms, legs, and desire.

If I could have lain in the crook of Hank's arm forever that day, I would have been the happiest woman in the world. Forever seemed like a possibility then. Everything did. We had so much hope, so much optimism that we could almost taste it. A happy life, a happy future had been so real. But sadly, those moments disappeared all too quickly and the realization that nothing lasted forever was the hardest lesson.

After making love, Hank dozed briefly, woke up, and smiled when he saw me staring at him, watching every little muscle in his face twitch to life. His cornflower blue eyes looked like jewels dug from heaven's soil as he returned my gaze with satisfaction and the kind of love I had never felt in my life before him. I knew he had been the man for me when I'd first seen him in grade school, and that smile of his had proven me right time and time again.

"You make a fine snack, Mrs. Trumaine," he said, sitting up, still naked as the day he was born. We were comfortable with each other that way. Always had been. There was no shame or worry about our bodies between us.

"Why thank you." I sat up so that our legs touched, so we remained as one for as long as possible. I wasn't ready to give him up.

"And the ham salad wasn't half bad, either." He laughed as I swatted at him. He pulled away just in time.

"I don't know what I'm going to do with you," I said.

He laughed again, but this time his joyfulness was shorter, and he stared out over the empty plain toward our house. "Jaeger's turnin' out to have a head about him. Ran the outer field on his own today," Hank said with certain pride in his voice.

"The boy's only twelve," I said.

"Not gonna be a boy much longer, not that Jaeger. Erik has a tougher time with Peter. I don't know if that one has any interest in the land."

"You can tell, can you?"

"I can. He's not interested in the work. Peter would rather be throwin' rocks at the ducks in the pond than ridin' on a tractor and takin' a lesson in it."

"He'll grow to love it, you wait and see."

"Maybe." Hank reached over to the edge of the blanket and picked a blade of grass and stuck it in his mouth. He didn't like to smoke—that was my sneaky habit—but I knew when he chewed on something that there was a problem brewing somewhere deep in his mind or heart.

"What's the matter?" I said, scooting even closer to him.

"Nothin', really. I just worry about us, sometimes, that's all. The Knudsens are good people, the best neighbors a man could hope for . . ."

I knew what the problem was before he went any further. I put my finger to his lips and stopped him. "You worry too much."

He shook his head. "What if the problem is me, Marjorie? What if I'm the one that's keepin' us from havin' a child?"

It was my turn to shake my head. "Doc says we're both fine. You know that. And you know it took my mother and father seven years to have me. Maybe we're just like them."

"I just want us to be like Erik and Lida, to know that all of this isn't for nothin', that it'll go on, ya know?"

"I know." I sighed, stared at him, drank in his earnestness and love for us, for our land, our life, then slid my hand across his leg. "Maybe we should try again."

Hank stood up to get dressed. The sun reflected golden off his naked body, shimmering with the sweat of making love, of reaching into the future the only way he knew how. It was one of the best days of our lives. Sadly, the child never came, and what followed a few years later, when Hank stepped in the gopher hole, changed everything.

I started awake with that image of Hank in my mind, of him dressing, kissing me like he would never see me again, then walking away as the sun set behind him. He walked off toward more work, more of what made him the happiest, and I tried to hang onto that feeling too. Remember every second of it. But I couldn't. It was a dream, and the sight of a happy, healthy, walking, talking Hank faded away with the scream of seven machines bringing me back to the world in which I truly existed.

There was nothing I could do to save him, to stop him from leaving me. Somewhere deep in the recesses of my mind, I heard Nina Tutweiler's voice again as I stirred awake—*For in this sleep of death what dreams may come . . .*

Hank never woke up again. But I was sure he knew I was there with him. I had to believe that. It was all I had left. He slipped away gently two hours later.

CHAPTER 50

Shep, of course, was beside himself with all of the cars parked in the yard. It wasn't the first time that it seemed like the whole town had gathered at our house, but I sure hoped it would be the last time.

Olga Olafson and her family were there, along with Pastor John Mark, always in my periphery, always keeping a close eye on me. I had kept a stiff upper lip in public, at the funeral, and I wasn't going to break down now, not in front of everyone.

Jaeger was as distraught as Shep, but for different reasons. I worried about him, but he'd assured me that he was fine, that the farm would keep him busy just like it had when he'd lost his parents. Time would tell if that were true. But I'd keep an eye on him, just like Pastor kept an eye on me. I guess that's what we all did. It was nice to know someone would be there if you fell.

The house was full of people and funeral food, more kinds of hamburger hot dishes and fried chicken than I could ever eat. Something told me that the winter pig was about to put on some quick weight, since I hated to think I was wasting the kindness of folks. One thing fed another, I supposed.

The only person missing from the house and the funeral was Herbert Frakes. I'd heard he was holed up in his room in the basement of the library, and I couldn't say that I blamed him for not wanting to come out in public just yet. To my surprise, Delia Finch had told him he could stay there as long as he wanted.

The house was too full for me, honestly, so I'd sneaked out to the back side of the garage to take a quick puff off a Salem. Luckily, it'd been a fine October day when we'd buried Hank, one day's worth of

Indian summer. It had been the first moment I'd been able to steal for myself since I'd landed at the house.

"I thought I saw you head back here." The voice startled me but didn't surprise me. I had seen the police car pull into the drive shortly after I'd arrived at home. "You mind if I join you?" Guy said.

"Not at all." I exhaled smoke as I spoke.

Guy dug into his breast pocket, just opposite his badge, and pulled out a cigarette of his own. He lit it and stared at me for a long moment. "You all right?"

"As all right as I can be."

"I suppose so."

More silence. At least between us. Voices filled the air, rode the wind, and convinced me that I was alive and not in another nightmare, even though it felt like it. I kept looking at the house worrying after Hank, even though he wasn't there. I wondered how long I would do that.

"Well, I suppose you heard that I'm gonna run against Duke in the election."

"I think that's a fine thing, Guy. I really do. People will make the right choice. I'm sure of it."

"I hope so," he said, taking a long draw off his cigarette. "Duke'll fire me first thing if *he* wins."

"I suppose he will. Jaeger could probably use another good hand come spring."

Guy smiled, then kicked the ground with his boot. "I probably shouldn't tell you this, Marjorie, but Betty Walsh claims she didn't do nothin' to Hank. Claims she's innocent of it all."

I really hadn't wanted to hear that, but I was glad it had come from Guy. "Thanks. There'll be more of that to deal with in the coming days. I don't see how she can be innocent of killing Calla and Nina, but I hope she's telling the truth about Hank. I sure do hope that's true."

"I wish it wasn't that way for ya, Marjorie."

I shrugged, took the last puff off the Salem, and dropped it on the ground. "You see that weed over there?" I said, pointing to a tall, withering thistle growing at the corner of the garage.

"Yeah, sure." He looked at me curiously.

"It's called musk thistle. *Carduus nutans*. It's not supposed to be here. Isn't native to this land, but it looks just like all of the other weeds. I wish there was a guide book for evil people, but there isn't. They blend in with the rest of us, just like that weed."

"A book like that sure would make things easier, Marjorie."

I tried to smile, but I couldn't find it in myself. "I better get back. People will be wondering where I am and come looking for me."

Guy flashed a smile. "I suppose they will."

I turned to walk away.

"Marjorie," Guy said.

I stopped. "Yes?"

"You call me if you need anything, you hear. I'll come as soon as I can."

"That's nice, Guy; I appreciate it. Jaeger's close. We'll be just fine. No need to worry about me," I said, then walked away.

The day after a funeral was even lonelier than the day of one. I woke in the middle of the night and found my way to my desk. I had a lot of work to do, and the morning passed even quicker than I hoped it would.

It was just before noon, and I was putting the finishing touches on the *Common Plants* index, when the phone rang. I was tempted to let it ring, but it kept on going insistently, leaving me little choice.

"Trumaines," I said, like I always did when I answered the phone.

"Ah, good, Miss Trumaine."

My heart sank. It was Richard Rothstein.

"I know I was wrong the last time," he went on, not bothering, of course, to say hello. "But there is no mistake this time. Your index *is* late."

I knew that. In all of the turmoil and necessity of things after Hank had died, the last thing on my mind, that I had had time for, was working on the index. "I'm sorry," I said. "But my husband passed away, and his funeral was just yesterday."

"That's no . . ." And then he stopped. "Oh, I'm sorry."

Silence between a thousand miles. The wires crackled, the wind whipped the lines, but business still churned on. Five seconds passed as a condolence.

"I'm finishing it now," I said. "I will take it to the post office by the end of the day."

"That is unacceptable. I need the index today."

"I'm sorry. That's just not possible."

"Well, then, I suppose I will have to adjust the schedule."

"You will."

"This does not bode well, Miss Trumaine."

"Missus," I said. "It's Mrs. Trumaine."

"Yes, I suppose it is." He paused. "I'll expect the index by the end of the week, then."

"That should be enough time for it to get there. I'll start on the *Zhanzheng: Five Hundred Years of Chinese War Strategy* book right away. It won't be late; I promise you that."

"I'm sorry for your loss, Mrs. Trumaine. Goodbye." And he hung up. It was the first time Richard Rothstein had ever said goodbye to me.

AUTHOR'S NOTE

Although the suicides portrayed in this book were staged, suicide is a topic that I take very seriously. If you find yourself in need of someone to talk to (24/7/365), please contact the National Suicide Prevention Lifeline at 1-800-273-8255.

Also, the town of Dickinson, North Dakota, portrayed in this book is real. Streets, names, history, and specific locations have been changed to serve the narrative of the story. Any mistakes are my own.

Information about indexing as a profession may be found on the American Society for Indexing (ASI) website (asindexing.org).

ACKNOWLEDGMENTS

Indexing, like writing, is a job best done in isolation. The strict deadlines portrayed in this book are not an exaggeration and, in reality, most professional indexers juggle multiple projects at one time. That said, I've had to miss a lot of activities with friends and family, pleasurable and otherwise, since taking up indexing and writing as a profession. Apologies for my absences are probably past due.

A special thank you goes to Cheryl Lenser, who has always been there with a quick answer for the most difficult indexing question. You've been there every step of the way, and you've been a great mentor as well as a great friend. Thank you.

Thanks also goes to Dan Mayer and the entire Seventh Street Books staff for the passion that they all put into every book. You've given Marjorie a great home. And, as always, thanks to my agent, Cherry Weiner. You believed in Marjorie from the start.

Again, thanks to Rose for riding along and working harder than you ever get credit for. I couldn't do what I do without you.

ABOUT THE AUTHOR

Larry D. Sweazy (www.larrydsweazy.com) has been a freelance indexer for eighteen years. In that time, he has written over 825 back-of-the-book indexes for major trade publishers and university presses such as Addison-Wesley, Cengage, American University at Cairo Press, Cisco Press, Pearson Education, Pearson Technology, University of Nebraska Press, Weldon Owen, and many more. He continues to work in the indexing field on a daily basis.

As a writer, Larry is a two-time WWA (Western Writers of America) Spur Award winner, a two-time, back-to-back, winner of the Will Rogers Medallion Award, a Best Books of Indiana award winner, and the inaugural winner of the 2013 Elmer Kelton Book Award. He was also nominated for a Short Mystery Fiction Society (SMFS) Derringer Award in 2007 (for the short story, "See Also Murder"). Larry has published over sixty nonfiction articles and short stories and is the author of ten novels, including books in the Josiah Wolfe, Texas Ranger western series (Berkley); the Lucas Fume western series (Berkley); a thriller set in Indiana, *The Devil's Bones* (Five Star); a mystery novel set in the dust bowl of Texas, *A Thousand Falling Crows* (Seventh Street Books); and the Marjorie Trumaine Mystery series (Seventh Street Books). He currently lives in Indiana with his wife, Rose.